MR. WILSON'S WIVES

Mr. Wilson's Wives

KAITLYN BOLYARD

Blind Goose Publishing

Contents

Timeline

1953 - Charlotte Tremblay
1955 - Elenor Martin
1957 - Hazel Adams
1970 - Katya Petrov
1973 - Stella DeVries
1974 - Natalie Bernard
1976 - Miriam Cohen
1980 - Ruby Harris
1981 - Eva Hoffman
1983 - Clara Santos
1984 - Rose Schmidt
1985 - Valerie Thomas
1990 - Laura Bianchi
1995 - Daisy Stevens
1996 - Isabel Lopez
1998 - Millie Walker

2000 - Leila Ahmadi
2001 - Joanna Adamo
2002 - Thea Sarris
2004 - Celeste Lewis
2007 - Daphne Hamidou
2010 - Helen Aung
2015 – Melanie Angelos

Chapter 1

I drove for hours and hours and slowly felt the stress slip away. With it, all vestiges of civilized society dropped out as well. With each mile, I moved further and further away from the manic movement of Chicago and closer to the land we so often forget. Eventually, I turned off the radio and opened the windows to feel the breeze blowing through my newly shorn hair. At least until I smelled the sweet "dairy air," my agent had warned me about. I said a silent prayer that there wouldn't be any fresh farms next door to the cabin I had rented and set my intentions. This summer would be a personal discovery, and I would mine my thoughts, ideas, and memories to write my next best seller.

One thing they never tell you about writing for a living is that the first book is easy. You've spent years dreaming and fantasizing about that one story that you must tell, the story that is yours through and through. Everyone has at least one story to tell. For me, it was my family. I won't say I'm not creative, but real life has always been much more interesting to me. Even as a child in the library, I gravitated more toward non-fiction, especially history books. I just couldn't believe what people used to do, the things they got away with. So, when it came to writing my story, it was true. Maybe too true for some.

With the speed limit at 55 mph, I cruised above 70 as the road dipped and curved. I allowed my mind to wander, which was especially easy because there were no cars. I once thought

Wisconsin was flat, like the plains states here smack dab in the middle of the country, but there are a surprising number of hills, many of them plowed for planting. The tallest are on the west side of the state, carved out by glaciers eons ago. My destination drew me more northward than that, a straight bee-line to what many affectionately refer to as "up nort," leaving the "h" off like a silent afterthought. As a child of The City, I had never been, and what better time than now when I needed to rediscover myself and my passion?

I hadn't written in months. As the residual income from royalties, the great success of my first book, started to wane, I shuttered myself into my cramped studio apartment in Chicago. I avoided all contact with my immediate family, for which they were, for the most part, grateful. After all, it hadn't been just my story I told, but their story as well. With my fascination with true stories also came an unscrupulous disregard for who those stories belonged to. You may know me from the swath of radio and daytime talk shows I featured on before and during my great book tour. I'm Elizabeth Rodriguez, author of *The Women of My Family*, which was accepted to great acclaim by everyone but my family. Although I wrote about myself, I also wrote about my mother and older sister, neither of whom will talk to me now. Who knew writing about strong, independent women would scare them away? My mother was shocked and ashamed of the stories I told about them (all of them true, I swear to God), but the truth didn't matter much regarding family matters. I think the only one who wasn't bothered by my oversharing is my little brother Luis, but of course, the book wasn't about him, was it?

But I drove all day trying to put all this nonsense behind me and even further as the road deteriorated from fresh asphalt to broken potholes, gravel, and finally to a thin dirt pathway. "No Trespassing" signs heralded the actual end of civilization, and my no-longer clean and shiny car pulled up to the cabin I had rented for the next few months. I parked, shook my head at the dust-covered state of my windshield, and took a good look at my lodging. I'd be lucky if any technology worked out here, but that was also part of the appeal: no distractions. There was a Boy Scout camp on the far side of the lake, but my cabin sat in a more secluded area, with a few other cabins several miles out. I could sit and stew in my thoughts and eventually come up with that great eureka moment to pull me out of these doldrums. I imagined myself as a Walt Whitman of sorts, in every way but social status, because I could never be a middle-class white man.

I hadn't packed much, and what I had I left in the trunk in favor of airing out the place. No doubt it had been empty since the past summer and would require some cleaning. The front door was sealed shut solidly, and I had to jam my shoulder against it like a linebacker to get it to even budge an inch. When it finally creaked open, I stumbled into a room covered in dust and cobwebs. What furniture there was in the living room looked old and dilapidated. With any luck, I wouldn't be spending much time lounging around anyway, but if I did take a break, none of the assorted chairs looked exceptionally comfortable. There also was no television, just a vast stone fireplace stretching up two stories to the ceiling. That I would be more likely to use if there were a few cooler nights. I pushed my way through the living room to the kitchenette, which held avocado appliances that looked like they had been picked straight out of a 1960s catalog. It has always amazed me how colors once deemed attractive are now looked down on as the exact opposite now, but everything is cyclical. Wait a few more decades, and they'll be back in fashion again.

Trying to ignore the obvious signs of mice, scratches across the floors, and hard black pellets on the countertops, I climbed to the loft above the living room. There were no stairs, just an angled ladder, which would be easy but get a few glasses of wine in me and forget it. I could wind up sleeping in the living room on occasion. At the top were two small bedrooms, one with a full-size bed several inches smaller than my queen at home and the other with bunk beds clearly intended for children. I spread my sleeping bag out on the small bed. On the website, they had described this cabin as a "perfect family get-away." They meant your typical husband, wife, and two kids combo, but how many places would advertise a cabin as a "writer's retreat for one." Only those of us crazy enough to spend days at a time staring at a pen and pad, trying to make something out of nothing, could understand the need to escape sometimes. This time, I wasn't trying to escape from the drudgery of writing, though I was trying to find it.

After easing myself down the ladder, I checked the closets on the ground floor and found what I needed: a broom, a handful of rags, and some Pledge. I would need to find and turn the water on as well because, no doubt, it had been turned off for the winter season. Despite the daunting cleaning ahead of me, it felt like a relief. I have always heard that cleaning your space helps clean your mind, and I believe that, too. There is something ritualistic about it that is so relaxing once it's done. In the process of cleaning, expect to hear me swearing up a storm. This was usually why you could find my apartment in various stages of disarray. I vaguely recalled an extra service I could have purchased as I wiped down the counters, demolished cobwebs, and swept up the fallen mess from the floor. I could have paid someone else to get the cabin "guest ready" for me, but I did prefer it this way. It helped me feel more connected to the space like it was mine. I opened the windows to the sunshine, hoping it wouldn't heat the space too quickly. Surely, I would keep them closed during most of my stay as the days grew warmer and the heat permeated everything, but for now, the fresh air helped override the stale stench of dust and mothballs.

When I was finally satisfied with the place's state, I returned to the car and grabbed my things from the trunk. My duffel bag mainly held clothes, a swimsuit if I needed to cool off, and my writing supplies. For a first draft, I usually started old-school with my handwritten chicken scratch before putting anything into a typed document. For this purpose, I purchased several black-and-white composition notebooks and some fresh gel pens. Although the pens tended to smear, they wrote so much better than rollerball options, so I could stand to have my hand constantly stained with black ink. When I was younger, I considered that the mark of a true writer, that constant ink stain. Maybe it's just an indicator of what a fool I am to try to make a living this way. I also brought my cell phone so that I could communicate regularly with my agent, but most likely it would only work in the nearby town, not out here in the boonies. I also brought the prerequisite toiletries: toothbrush, comb, etc. but if anyone was expecting me to wear makeup during this excursion, they had another thing coming. After hefting the duffel bag strap across my shoulder, I nestled my sleeping back in the crook of my other arm and struggled unsuccessfully to shut the trunk with my chin. Instead, I left it gaping open as I dropped my things by the front door. I struggled to pick them all up again once I had successfully opened it.

What I really needed was a nap. Feeling too lazy to climb the stupid ladder, I hefted the sleeping bag over my head to toss it up, failed the first time, and tried again. On second thought, I should have stayed at a hotel or something, but I wouldn't have been able to afford a whole summer, even at a roadside motel that charges by the week. After climbing up after the bedroll, I spread it out over the twin bed. At least this would be easier to deal with than sheets. I quickly realized, however, that I didn't think to bring a pillow. Regardless, as soon as my head hit the bed, I was out. The warm sun shining on my face, the calm of the woods, and the smell of cedar surrounding me were all I needed to descend into a deep, deep slumber.

I woke up what must have been several hours later, groggy, and the cool wind blew on my face from the open window. It was dark already and my stomach growled in protest. I hadn't eaten since earlier in the afternoon – a greasy burger, fries, and a milkshake from a roadside greasy spoon. I hadn't thought to stock up on food immediately, figured that would be something I could attend to once I had settled in. With the nap out of the way, however, I was already regretting this decision. I glanced out the window and saw nothing but the dark, heavy blackness of night in the country. I groaned, rolled over, stretched out again, and pushed myself up from the bed. There wasn't much else I'd be able to do tonight, at least.

I made my way down gingerly to the living room and propped open the front door. Night had surely descended already, like a heavy blanket over the world. Out here, without the light pollution of the city, it felt so much darker, and you could see the stars, so many little pinpricks, like looking up into a planetarium. That was probably as close as I had gotten to stars in Chicago. I stood on the porch, letting the cool air embrace me, running up and down my bare arms and legs. As I looked out across the lake and examined the reflection of the moon across the still water, I suddenly realized that in my haste, I had left the trunk of my car wide open. I returned to the living room to slide back into my sneakers and struck out onto the grass to close it. Thankfully, there was no one for miles around to steal anything from me, but that didn't mean I wanted to leave it open to the elements either.

When I got to the car, I gave my surroundings one last good look. No one could deny that this was a different world entirely, out here away from the city. It felt simultaneously comforting and terrifying. I moved to slam the trunk shut, this time with both hands free, and something dark and furry leaped at me. I jumped back, letting forth a high screech. The creature scurried away, bumbling into the reeds. I looked after it, realizing it was only a raccoon, investigating my trunk.

"No food for you, trash panda!" I said aloud, reasserting my dominance. It had given me such a scare, I had to say something, but now I felt silly, talking to woodland creatures like they could understand me. Never mind that, I needed to get back inside. Although my stomach was still protesting, there would also be no food for me, at least not until the morning. Nothing in town would be open at this hour.

Chapter 2

At dawn, I woke, not to an alarm, but to a chorus of birds. So many things I would need to get used to in the next few weeks: being out here alone, surrounded by nature and away from the sights and sounds I had grown so used to. I had always lived in the city, and everyone referred to it as "the city" – that city being Chicago, of course. When you live there, the place becomes a part of you, just as much as the cloudy skyline and Lake Michigan marking the horizon to the East. You become accustomed to the constant sound of cars, buses, and people passing by. Although it may not live up to the New York adage of "the city that never sleeps," sometimes it feels like a runner-up.

Today, I would spend some time getting a feel for Orchard Square, the nearest town, if you could call it that. At the very least, I'd grab some grub there. Then I would most likely drive further into the next populated area for supplies, and food I could make myself at the cabin, and then get down to the business of writing. Maybe I'd even contact my agent to reassure him that yes, I was alive, had made it to the cabin, and would be working straight away. I just needed to get my feet settled under me.

I debated if I needed a jacket in the cool morning air and settled for a cardigan instead. Who knew what kind of air conditioning, if any, they would have in the restaurant in Orchard Square? Worst case I could tie it around my waist the way I used to wear sweatshirts so often as a kid. I wasn't trying to impress anyone. When I did my research about this place, I quickly saw that Orchard Square was barely a two-horse town with a population set at only a few hundred. The unincorporated village contained the bare necessities: a church across the street from a bar, a few dozen houses, a gas station, a diner, and acres and acres of surrounding farms. On a road trip once, I remember my sister Maria telling me how people would spend all Saturday night drinking and then show up bright and early at the church to confess their sins. She also regaled me with stories of Rumspringa, the Amish version of a coming out party where young men and women were allowed to engage in all kinds of things they weren't normally allowed to. She read a lot, which gave her some of this random knowledge, but mostly she pretended confidence in everything she said whether it was the god-honest truth or not.

The diner in Orchard Square was called The Deep Dish, which was weird to me because it was clear they didn't serve pizza, or anything close to the deep-dish delicacies of Giordano's. I doubted there were many Italians around here anyway, mostly just the whitest white folk around, a lot of Swedes and Germans. I suppose I looked a little out of place, too, with my toasted marshmallow hue. I also wouldn't find any palatable tacos or Mexican food around here, either, but you just work with what you can find. The Deep Dish was a bit dilapidated but brought back the vibes of a 1950's diner with its black-and-white tile, gold-rimmed countertops, and red vinyl stools.

As I took my seat, the woman who greeted me looked old enough to have been middle-aged several decades ago. Her cheeks sagged into deep jowls and wrinkles creased her forehead. She wore a stained apron knotted at the back and clutched a yellowed notepad. Despite this, her blue eyes sparked with the vivacity of a much younger woman.

"Never seen you around," she remarked before taking my order. "Just passing through?"

I looked up from the menu, trying to decide between pancakes and eggs. "Actually, I've got a cabin up at Oatmeal Lake."

She smirked. "You know why they call it oatmeal, don't cha?"

"Actually, no."

"Well, I wouldn't try swimming in that. One foot in and the mud'll pull ya in." She laughed, mostly to herself. "Like oatmeal, that whole damn lake."

I frowned. So much for cooling off.

Seeing my reaction, she backpedaled. "It's fine for other things – fishing, canoeing, you know. But I wouldn't recommend swimming. Maybe just dipping your toes in, if that's your thing. Anyway, listen to me just blatherin' on. What'll it be, Missy?"

I pushed my menu toward her, still unsure what I wanted to eat. "Anything you'd recommend?"

"Well..." she tapped her pen against the yellowed pad. "We've got yer basics – toast, eggs, hash browns, that sort of stuff, nothin' too fancy." She paused, then smiled. "Tony's got some eggs benedict he's been workin' on, homemade biscuits and all that."

"Sounds good."

She scribbled my order down. "Alright, I'll get that in for ya. Toast or pancakes?"

"Toast would be fine."

"Anything to drink besides water?" she asked.

"Coffee would be great."

"Cream? Sugar?"

"No, I drink mine black."

She smiled again, revealing a few gaps where she was missing teeth on the bottom. "Good girl! Don't need all that crap anyway, right?"

I nodded, not sure how to respond. Most people drank theirs with so many additives you could hardly call it coffee anymore, but I had learned sugar and cream weren't always available and I drank it more for the caffeine than the taste, really. "I suppose not," I finally mustered before she hurried away. I glanced around the diner, trying to get a better feel of the place but it was pretty empty on a Tuesday morning.

I glanced at a newspaper sitting on the edge of the counter and moved to grab it. I was surprised to see Orchard Square even had a paper, but I quickly noticed it was not a daily, but a weekly. It was dated for Sunday, so the news I found there wasn't even new anymore. How a weekly paper could even survive in the age of instantaneous news on the web eluded me, but nevertheless, it might spark something in my sponge-like brain. Now that I have already told "my" story, maybe inspiration from someone else's story might suffice. The front page of the Crawford County Gazette featured a handful of smiling youngsters presenting their award-winning cattle at a fair. The next page listed several recipes, including one for "Grandma's Blue-Ribbon Cranberry Cobbler." Oh, yes, this made for some very exciting reading, I thought. Best-seller material right here.

I sighed a little too loudly, apparently, because the waitress, who was already at my elbow, gave me a disapproving glare.

"You city folk..." she muttered to herself, but before she could get another word out, a man's voice boomed from the kitchen.

"Darlene..." he said, drawing her name out to at least three syllables. Then the chef's head popped up in the open window between the kitchen and the dining area. He looked a little darker skinned than I was expecting, but still on the lighter side. Probably white mixed with something else – not black but maybe Hispanic. He wore his beard in a neatly trimmed goatee with a thin mustache.

"Fine, fine, Tony," she hollered back, not even turning to look at him. "I know."

Not even acknowledging me, she placed my steaming food before me. With dismay, I realized the poached eggs had been jostled enough to break the yolk already. Slicing eggs open to release the yellowy goodness is one of the few things I like about runny eggs, and she had deprived it of me with her abrupt movements. I reached for my fork, and she quickly admonished me.

"Plate's hot," she muttered before turning to leave.

Not sure what had caused her sudden change of heart – she seemed friendly enough when I first sat down – I began the business of slicing my eggs Benedict into smaller and smaller pieces while I waited for the food to cool. After the first few bites, I returned to the newspaper. There couldn't be much there, seeing as it was only about six pages, but maybe something would catch my eye – some strange country flair I would find mildly interesting.

After the recipes, there was a trite and cutesy poem written by an elderly woman. It rhymed and ran the full length of a column alongside a photograph of her sitting placidly in a garden of pink and purple flowers. Alongside that were a few ads, mostly old furniture people didn't want anymore, Rick Richardson had a litter of border collie puppies – free to a good home, then the obituaries. I skimmed over the obits until I got to the last, which seemed extraordinarily long. I quickly realized the length was due to a long list of surviving relatives, including no less than a dozen wives. Now, this might be worth digging into, I thought to myself.

"Wilson, Erwin passed away suddenly at 2:15 p.m. on June 26 at the age of 87 years old. Predeceased by his sons Richard and Delmar, both of whom were killed in action during the Vietnam War. Survived by his loving wife of seven years, Melanie. Lovingly remembered by his many children, and ex-wives

Charlotte, Eleanor, Hazel, Lucy, Stella, Natalie, Ruby, Eva, Clara, Rose, Valerie, Daisy, Isabel, Millie, Leila, Joanna, Miriam, Thea, Celeste, Laura, Daphne, and Helen, as well as several grandchildren and great-grandchildren. Services will be held on July 1 at 10 a.m. at Saint John's Church."

I shook my head, amazed at the sheer number of wives this man had throughout his life as well as the fact that they were all listed in his obituary. Then I read the obituary again. I took a dreg from my coffee and read it again. It almost seemed like a joke, and I couldn't wrap my head around it. Who in his right mind would have 23 wives?! I hadn't touched my plate in the past ten minutes or so and Darlene came back to remove it.

"Anything interesting in there, darlin'?" she asked, suddenly congenial again, my supposed transgressions forgiven in the brief space between her deciding I was an outsider and just someone staying outside of town momentarily.

"Did you know Mr. Erwin Wilson?" I asked.

She leaned over me, grabbing the corner of the paper with one hand. She glanced at the photograph included with the obituary. It was a much younger photo of the man, looking dapper with a strong chin, suit jacket, and wide scarf. He had one hand in his pocket while the other held a cigar.

"Of course, I know him!" she remarked. "Been a while since he looked like that though." She leaned back and shouted to the kitchen. "Hey, Tony!" she called.

The chef's head appeared in the service window again. "You're lucky we're not busy, Dar. What do you want?"

"Remember Mr. Wilson? Paper says he died last Thursday."

"Really? Poor bastard. When's the funeral?"

"The first."

"You going?"

"I don't know," she replied. "But I'll let you know." She turned back to me. "Can I get you some more coffee, ma'am?"

"No, just the check. Unless you can tell me anything about Mr. Wilson."

"What do you want to know?"

She tore a sheet from her notepad, totaling out my breakfast. I dug in my purse for some bills and loose change to pay. I could tell she was thinking of what to say.

"I think the last time I saw him was a few months ago with a much, much younger wife." She took up my money and stashed it in her apron. "Actually, I'm sure of it. They had a little boy and she looked about to burst with another on the way."

"Really?" I asked, leaning into the conversation. "Wasn't he in his eighties?"

"You know what they say," Darlene motioned, winking at me. "A woman's got a quick biological clock, but a man's just keeps ticking. While most women are done with children by the time they're forty, a man can just keep cranking 'em out, like about until he dies, or can't find a woman willing."

"Now, Darlene, what a horrible thing to say," remarked Tony, clearly listening in.

"But it's the God-honest truth." She smirked and walked behind the counter to grab a wet cloth. "What else are you doing today, Honey?" she asked me.

"Going over to Weston for supplies," I replied. "I guess they have a Walmart Supercenter out there."

"Sure do," said Darlene, as she started wiping down my table. "You know, I didn't catch your name, Hon."

"Sorry, I'm horrible about introductions," I apologized. "Elizabeth Rodriguez."

"You mean the writer?"

"Have you heard of me?"

"I mean, they had you on Wake Up America and everything."

"Ugh, I forgot about that. Yes, the writer."

She dropped the rag, wiped her hand on her apron and shook hands with me. "Darlene."

"I know."

"Yeah, I guess you heard me and Tony yelling at each other. It's a real love / hate relationship we got going."

After leaving the diner, I resolved to eat at least a few of my meals there, maybe try to run into a few more locals who might know more about this mysterious Mr. Wilson. It might prove an interesting story, or maybe the man was a constant philanderer who didn't have the sense to stay single. Regardless, I couldn't quite put my finger on it, but there seemed to be more at play. I drove nearly half an hour to Weston, a larger town with more amenities, and hit up the Walmart. My haul of eggs, sandwich fixings, and TV dinners would last me at least the next few days. I also purchased a cheap pillow that should suffice for the duration of my working vacation.

Chapter 3

By the time I returned to the cabin, the sun had already risen high in the sky and the heat beat down upon me. I lugged everything into the kitchen, put it all away, and slapped together a peanut butter and jelly sandwich. I eyed the six-pack of beer but decided that would be more of a reward once I had done some work. To keep the heat out, I shuttered all the windows and then settled into one of the chairs in the living room, reaching for the first of what would eventually be several notebooks.

I wrote the date in neat cursive and began to fill the page with my thoughts. Years ago, I had learned the value of brain dumping, just writing everything down as it came to mind, without considering whether any of it was any good, or was going anywhere in particular. I could usually fill up to three pages, front and back this way, before pausing to think. Then I could focus on the real writing, once my brain had been cleared of all the busy thoughts clogging up the space. This time, my words ended abruptly, though. So far, I had just journaled the goings on of the past few days, but I still had no idea what my next topic would be, or where my next book would lead. Maybe I needed to do something else to get the juices flowing. I started to write a list of what I knew, what interested me, and then my phone rang, jerking me from my reverie.

It was my agent, Michael.

"Hey, sweet thing, what've you got cooking?" he asked.

We had a strangely flirtatious, but entirely business relationship. No doubt, he wanted news of my plans, and where I planned to go from here.

"I think I might be a one-hit wonder," I replied.

"Oh, don't say that. You're not the type."

"You think?" I was inviting him to rally me up, but I needed the encouragement badly.

"Besides, I need to make more money off you."

"I see, so I'm just your show pony. You want to know what's in it for you."

"I'm just joshing you, Liz. You know you got this."

"No, I don't." I sighed loudly into the phone. "Actually kinda surprised I've got any signal out here."

"So you made it to the cabin alright? Think you can survive away from the city?"

"I'll be fine, but I did fight with a raccoon already."

"Oh, do tell." He chuckled, and I wished we were chatting over coffee rather than hours apart.

"I'm exaggerating, but there are woodland creatures to contend with here. Mice, for instance." I suddenly remembered I had forgotten traps.

"Can't be as bad as rats."

"True. I'm sure they're small and cute, but they still want to steal my food." I would also need to remember to put the bread in the fridge, rather than leaving it sitting out on the counter. "At least I've got a generator and electricity out here. I'd die without microwave dinners."

"So, any ideas yet."

"Actually, you are currently interrupting me from my writing."

"Am I? I'm the worst, aren't I?"

"A pleasant distraction." I glanced at my too-small list and doodled alongside it. "I'm going nowhere and fast."

"You just have to let the seeds germinate. You'll be crafting something clever in no time."

"It's just...." I punctuated my speech with another heavy sigh. "I feel like I've already told my story. There's no other story to tell."

"Dig a little deeper, Liz. I wouldn't have signed you on if I didn't think you were worth it."

"Right."

"Maybe get outside. Go for a walk. Go to an art museum."

"An art museum?"

"Right, sorry. But there's got to be something in podunk nowhere that you find interesting. Talk to any locals?"

"Went to a diner."

"Good, start with that."

"Start with what? It was just me, this ancient waitress, and a fat chef."

"And? Anything can be a story if you find the right angle."

"I forgot you used to work in news."

"I did! Speaking of, have they got a newspaper? Maybe there's something there."

"Hah! What a paper it was, only a handful of pages and maybe one real story."

"Sad day. But you took a look?"

"Yeah."

"A good look?"

"What is this, an interrogation?"

"Just making sure. Nothing there?"

Finally, it clicked. The obituary for Mr. Wilson. "Yeah, there might have been something, but I have to do a little digging."

"Keeping secrets now, are we? That's not fair."

I walked over to the couch and dug into my purse. Before leaving the diner, I had folded up the obituary page and crammed it in. I glanced at it again, and murmured under my breath, "Twenty-three wives. That crazy bastard."

"Who're you calling crazy?" retorted Michael.

"Sorry, just thinking out loud. I might have something." I checked the time and date of the funeral. "Is it illegal to crash a funeral?" I asked.

"Not illegal, but likely frowned upon. What are you planning?"

"I'll let you know when I know."

"I'll be waiting with bated breath."

Another thing I needed to buy was a modest black dress.

For the rest of the evening, I sat out on the porch swing, working my way through the six-pack, scribbling my ideas down, and brainstorming possible reasons why a man would marry so many women. I didn't get far. Not having been married, I could barely grasp why people marry in the first place, even when they claim to be in love. Who is willing to make that kind of commitment? My mother didn't. She had a houseful of children with no known father to speak of. That was one of the many things we didn't talk about, after all, but it was one of the things I wrote about. The women of my family are so strong they haven't needed men. They have survived just fine on their own. Struggled sometimes to keep everything together, but survived, nonetheless.

What right did this Mr. Wilson have to marry all these women? Was it some sort of sister wives thing, like the Mormons? But in that case, usually, they didn't legally marry all of them – being married to multiple people at the same time was bigamy, and illegal. This man must have married and divorced these women in quick succession to have married so many of them. And then there were all the children – what a mess that must have been. The only way I could get a foot in the door would be to dig in deeper – go to the funeral. But what then? I didn't have a solid plan and the beers were starting to kick in. There was always tomorrow, and the funeral wasn't until

Friday. I'd have something solid figured out by then, or at least some idea of what the hell I was doing.

I gathered up the empty beer cans, as best I could and kicked the rest in a messy parade to the kitchen. Wouldn't have to worry about recycling out here, I reasoned. After smashing each, I dumped them into the trash and glanced at the ladder leading to the loft. I didn't want to chance it and thankfully I had thrown the pillow on the couch anyway. It would suffice for the night. I collapsed back onto the cushions and fell into a deep doze.

In the middle of the night, I heard a frantic scratching and bolted upright. No burglars out here, for certain, but I turned on the flashlight on my phone regardless. My heart leaped into my throat. In my drunken haze, had I left the door open? I checked it was closed tight, then returned to the living room. I heard it again, a scratching, scrambling noise from the kitchen. I swung the light across the countertops and saw it: a small mouse nibbling at the loaf of bread I had left sitting out.

Hesitantly, I went back for my notebook and returned to swat the mouse away, but it had already scurried off. I glanced at the loaf to see a large hole chewed through the side of it. After tossing the remainder and closing the garbage can away in a closet, I made a mental list of the things I needed to buy the next day: bread, mouse traps, black dress. What else? Surely there was something else, but I couldn't remember it now. Feeling sobered, I threw my pillow into the loft, climbed the ladder, and settled into the bed for some better rest. I shivered, then drew the sleeping bag around me, not eager to meet any more rodents, fuzzy creatures, or creepy crawlies. Who knew that out here, all alone, I would wind up feeling so surrounded?

Over the next few days, I bought more supplies at the Wal-mart in Weston, cleaned the cabin more thoroughly, and spent my afternoons attempting to write. For the most part, my agent left me alone, except for a few encouraging texts. Other than that, I was alone with my thoughts, which can often be a scary place. The last thing I wanted to think about right now was myself, much less what I would do if I couldn't get suddenly inspired by something momentous. The back of my mind swarmed with all these questions and conjectures about Mr. Erwin Wilson, but none of it made any sense. Most likely, it would end up being a wild goose chase. After all, if I couldn't get anyone to talk to me about the man's life, I wouldn't get very far. I figured, if I went to the funeral, and expressed my sympathies, I might be able to have a conversation with his widow, or at the very least overhear some gossip that might lead somewhere. For now, I was only in the "discovery" stage, as Michael reminded me, and it was perfectly fine to not have a clear direction yet.

Chapter 4

18 MONTHS AGO

I stood a stack of books on end, straightening them with the heel of my hand and examining the spines for knicks and scratches. The glossy covers shone back at me, pristine and perfect. I couldn't stop myself from looking for imperfections, though. It was like looking at my own reflection – I always managed to find something to criticize. Even worse, these were copies of *my* book, so I was bound to find fault with them.

So absorbed with my set-up, I didn't notice the bookseller standing just feet behind me. He tapped me on the shoulder, making me jump, then handed me a frothy beer. I accepted it gratefully, taking a tentative sip.

"You have no idea how much I need this right now," I said.

"Well, I'm glad my niche little bookstore fits the bill," he replied, smiling.

He had a beer of his own, a darker stout to my golden IPA, and wore his hair in a messy man bun. We clinked our glasses together. My agent was right; holding my first signing at Books & Brews was the best marketing plan he had come up with yet. I definitely needed the liquid courage.

"Don't overdo it, though," the bookseller warned. "We had a guy here last month who could barely read his poetry. He was so drunk. I think he had a few before he came in, though."

"You don't need to worry about me. Just one should do the trick." I set my pint down on the table's edge and examined my display one last time. "Do you usually get a good turnout for these things?" I asked.

"Have you been reaching out to your fan base?" he countered.

"My what?"

"Fan base, loyal readers, whatever you want to call them?"

"I don't have that, yet."

"Friends and family?"

I shook my head. This was a primarily secret project. My first book wound up being a memoir of all things. I had always been told to "write what you know," and I had done just that.

"Well, I guess we'll see then." He returned to his place behind the register, setting his beer on a coaster. I wondered how much employees here were allowed to drink on the job and then supposed it couldn't be any worse than bartenders doing shots with the regulars. They were probably limited in their intake.

People started to trickle in, one or two at a time, and then in small groups as the start time quickly approached. Again, I thanked my lucky stars that I had gone with a traditional publisher and that my agent Michael was more outgoing and resourceful than mo. Without him, this whole event would have been a flop, and I would have been taking an armload of books back home, my tail between my legs in defeat.

Most of the attendees were women, which wasn't surprising given the focus of my memoir. I had written primarily about my mother and older sister, how they had served as role models throughout my formative years, and how they had inspired me to become a strong, independent woman. Well, strong-ish. I was still clearly working on the confidence part.

A few women gravitated toward the small bar at the back of the shop, snapping up glasses of white wine. Others milled around the shop, running their fingers over cozy mystery titles and gold-embossed classics. There were a few older men, but they were few and far between. Maybe husbands who were coerced into coming. I stood awkwardly in the corner, circling my table like a mother bird, afraid to stray too far from her nest. Thankfully, no one approached me just yet.

The bookseller directed people toward the folding chairs set up for the event and introduced me. I heard my name, and the title of my book, The Women of My Family, but it all felt surreal like it was happening to someone else. I struggled to speak when he handed me the microphone and managed a soft "hello."

Everyone was staring at me now, judging me, no doubt. "Welcome to my first book signing." The room erupted with genuine applause that sounded more than just polite pity. I opened my copy of the book and started reading. I imagined I was still sitting at my computer at home, reading the rough draft aloud, again and again, looking for every little error. The words were warm and familiar to me, comforting even. I began to forget about the crowd gathered around me and delved back into my writing. They surrounded me with applause when I finished, their faces breaking into delighted smiles. And then they had questions.

"What inspired you to write about your family?" one woman asked.

"I love my mother and my sister. I have always looked up to them, been in awe of them."

"But not everything you've written is flattering," she added.

"True, but I wanted to show that despite everything, they are still real people with faults. I wanted to be as honest as possible in how I portrayed them."

Another woman raised her hand cautiously.

I called on her. "Yes, in the red?"

"What is your process like?"

Just then, the door flew open, and a woman came rushing in. Half her hair was in hot rollers, and the rest hung limp around her shoulders. Just before she started shouting, I realized that this was my sister, Maria, and she did not look happy.

"Here you are!" she yelled. "Telling more lies!"

I froze, unable to move, unable to speak. What was happening? My entire audience shifted, ready to witness the unfolding drama. The bookseller swept in to intercept Maria before she could get to me. He placed one hand on her shoulder, and she shook him off. She stared furiously in my direction.

"Ma'am," he tried. "Can you please step outside for a moment? You're interrupting an event."

"Don't you ma'am me!" she replied, pushing him away. She stormed up to me and stood about two inches away from my face, raining down a tirade of insults. "You ungrateful little brat! Do you have any idea what I went through this afternoon?"

I managed a single word. "No..."

"I was at the salon, trying to get my hair done, trying to relax for once, and these other women, once they realized who I was, started laughing at me. Laughing, Elizabeth! They all think I'm some kind of joke."

I cringed, pulling into myself. This was not the reaction I was looking for. Not from my readers and definitely not from my sister. The audience looked on, their faces eager.

"The things you said about me in that book of yours... why would you say those things?"

One of the male audience members posed a question. "So, would you say you're not happy with how you were portrayed in the book?"

Maria turned to him, suddenly aware that all these people were now staring at us. Her face flushed with embarrassment. "I'm mad as hell," she said. "If you can't tell."

With her focus off of me for a moment, I was finally able to react sensibly. "Maria, can we step outside for a moment?"

She turned back to me, gave me a curt nod, and then walked back out the door. I looked at my fans, who were all on the edge of their seats. I muttered a brief apology and then followed Maria out the door. I heard it slam shut behind me and took a deep breath before sitting on a bench in front of the store. Maria hovered over me, pacing back and forth.

"Ma told me you'd be here," she said, by way of explanation.

"You called Ma?"

"I did, and she's got my back, by the way. How could you? I mean, I knew you were writing a book, but the things you said in there. Why would you want to drag our family through the mud?"

"I didn't. I was just being honest."

"Honest?" She scoffed. "Brutally honest, for sure." She sighed and then finally stopped pacing and sat down next to me. "I just don't understand, Liz."

We sat in silence for a moment.

"So you just left in the middle of your hair appointment?" I asked, trying to lighten the mood.

Maria ran her hands over her face, then briefly touched the curlers still hanging in her hair. "I must look a right mess."

I didn't dare agree with her.

"I mean, the world doesn't need to know how I got pregnant at thirteen. You make me sound like a slut."

"But nothing I wrote is a lie, and not once did I use the word 'slut'."

"And never mind me, what horrible things did you write about Ma? I know she hasn't read it yet, but I'm sure when she does...."

I didn't even want to consider it for a moment. If Maria was furious about her part in the story, Ma might be enraged. Our mother had three children, Maria, myself, and our younger brother Luis. None of us knew our fathers. As far as we were concerned, we could have been born through immaculate conception because there were never any male figures in our lives. On top of that, we all had the surname Rodriguez, our mother's maiden name. I saw this as a point of strength that our mother had raised us and kept the family together, all on her own. Others might see it as a scandal.

"I mean," continued Maria after a moment. "Why couldn't you have at least consulted us, asked for permission, something? Instead, you just went ahead and wrote this book. It's just out in the world now."

I didn't have a response. My agent had encouraged and prodded me along when I first conceived of this idea, but I couldn't blame him. Instead, I chose to shift gears. "I need to get back inside, Maria. Those people are waiting on me."

"Of course they are," she replied.

I left her sitting outside on the bench. The rest of the event went smoothly, for the most part. I pretended nothing had happened and moved straight from the Q & A session to signing books. I got a few anxious questions from the fans, but they stopped trying once they realized I wouldn't answer them. By the time everything wrapped up, Maria had left. The book-seller offered me a second beer, and I accepted, gratefully.

"Can't say I've ever seen that happen at a reading," he mused.

"It definitely wasn't planned," I countered. I felt I could use a few tequila shots on top of the beer. "I hope you'd be willing to have me back again if I ever write another book. I enjoy the space." I took another gulp. "And the beer."

"Are you kidding? Next to the drunk poet, this was amazing."

"Glad I could offer some entertainment."

* * *

I dreaded going home. I thought of calling Michael but decided to jump right in. Rip off the bandaid, so to speak. After all, I couldn't avoid the inevitable confrontation forever.

Thankfully, when I entered the front door, Maria was nowhere to be found. She must have had other errands to run. My brother Luis sat in front of the living room TV, playing video games. He wore a headset to talk to other players online and was completely unaware of the real world. I walked right past without him noticing. My niece Cecelia must be at soccer practice. The question was whether Ma was home and whether or not Maria had told her anything.

I went room by room through the house looking for her. It didn't take long because our house is tiny, and I knew the only bedroom I might find her in would be hers. She wasn't in the kitchen making dinner yet. She wasn't in the bathroom with its peeling flowered wallpaper. She wasn't in her own bedroom, which always smelled faintly of lavender. Could she be in the attic? There was nothing up there but lost and forgotten storage - things that had been placed up there never to be brought back down. It was possible she wasn't home at all, but I didn't bother asking Luis - it would take at least ten minutes just to get him to pause his game.

I went down the last hallway, where Maria and I had our rooms, and saw the ladder to the attic had been pulled down. I climbed halfway up and called up to the attic.

"Ma? Are you up there?"

She didn't respond, so I climbed the rest of the way up, clinging gingerly to the ladder's sides. She shouldn't be going up and down these steps at her age, but she was stubborn and wouldn't admit that she had slowed down physically. As I neared the top, I crawled into the attic and glanced around the space.

Our attic is little more than a crawl space, and you wouldn't be able to stand up without bumping your head. There were boxes and boxes of forgotten memories up here, mostly things from our childhoods that Ma couldn't bear to part with. It had been a few years since I had been up here. Cobwebs and dust coated almost everything. My mother was sitting cross-legged in the corner, bent over a box of photographs. She took the pictures out, one at a time, from the box, spending a few moments looking at each one before placing it in a small pile by her feet.

I called to her, but it seemed as if she were in a trance. She didn't respond, she just kept carefully going through the photos.

"Ma, what are you doing?" I asked as I crawled toward her.

She still didn't acknowledge me.

As I came upon her, I could see what she was looking at. They were photographs of my siblings and me from when we were younger. Then I realized she was making two piles as she went through them. Every photo that had me in it wound up the pile to her right, and the photos without me went to the left. Why was she separating me from Maria and Luis?

"Did Maria talk to you?" I asked.

She finally acknowledged me, raising her head. Her eyes were dark and glistening like she had been crying, her cheeks streaked with faint red lines.

"She must have talked to you," I realized out loud. "What are you doing up here, with these photographs?"

Usually, my mother was a force to be reckoned with, a woman who spoke her mind and didn't sit quietly by while the world happened around her. She was always in the middle of the action. Now she looked like a shadow of herself, a mere sliver of the strong woman I knew her to be. She still didn't respond to me, she just returned to sorting the pictures.

I leaned in, getting right up into her face. "Ma, why are you pulling out my photos from the others?" I asked.

She picked up the pile on her left, the one with only Maria and Luis, and began pushing it back into the box. Then she turned to the pile of my photographs and found one of only me. It was a photo of me at age 6, smiling awkwardly at the camera. I didn't remember the occasion, but I remembered the awful haircut, long in the front, short in the back, and too curly and frizzy to manage. She held the photograph in both hands, looked at it for a moment, and then began to tear it, right down the middle.

I gasped and lunged at her. "What are you doing?" I yelled at her.

Despite my protests, she tore the photo in half and then reached for another. I slapped her hands away from the pile. "You can't do this!" I screamed. "Those are my photos!" In a mad scramble, we fought for possession of the pile. I scooped some of them up and shoved them back into the box. She squirreled others away, sliding them into the pockets of her cardigan. In moments, we were sweaty and breathing heavily, wrestling as if we were competing. She rolled away from me, a momentary grin on her face, but she said nothing.

Just then, Maria yelled up the stairs. "Who's up there?" she demanded. "What's going on?"
I made one last grab for a few of the remaining photographs. I held them in my hands, fuming. "This is my childhood," I explained. "Why would you want to destroy it?"

Sitting up again, the fire returned to my mother's words. "You are no child of mine," she said. "No child of mine would spread such lies."

"But none of it was lies!" I shouted back.

By now, Maria had climbed into the attic and looked on. "What are you two doing up here? Ma, you shouldn't be crawling around with your knees!"

We all grew silent, looking from one to the other. In happier times, we might have broken out into laughter. The whole situation just felt strange. I heard another set of footsteps on the stairs, behind Maria. Luis had apparently torn himself away from his games.

"What's up?" he asked, popping his head up into the attic. "You having a party up here I wasn't invited to?"

This should have broken the tension and let us all let go of the anger and frustration we were holding, but it didn't.

Instead, Maria told him to go back down, that everything was fine. We'd be down in a minute. She looked back at our mother and me, shook her head silently, and climbed back down. I looked back to the piles of photographs, the memories we had so carefully sealed away, which now my mother was willing to part with. Not just part with but actively destroy. Her cardigan pockets still bulged with several of them.

"Are you really going to rip up my memories?" I asked.

She paused, looking at me with her dark eyes as if she didn't recognize me or know me as her daughter. "You shat all over my memories," she said. "You took something beautiful and made it ugly. Made it a joke for everyone to see."

"That wasn't my intention," I said. "I never meant to hurt you or Maria."

"There are just some things that should be kept in the family," she said. Slowly, she emptied her pockets, laying each photo carefully in the box. "I won't destroy these, but I can't have you in my house."

My face grew hot, but I didn't know how to respond.

"It hurts just to look at you," she added.

Chapter 5

PRESENT DAY

The day of the funeral arrived, and I donned my new dress, double-checking that it wasn't too short. I paced anxiously back and forth through the cabin, rehearsing my condolences and what I would say as my heels clacked against the wood floor. I would need to keep my mind sharp, had already downed two cups of coffee but hadn't eaten much. There would be no tape recorders, but I would need to gather my intel covertly, without being too obvious about what I was doing. I checked my makeup in the mirror again and made sure my mascara hadn't been smudged. Despite my best efforts to put little effort into my appearance this summer, I was already holstered into a push-up bra and life-sucking stockings. If it were up to me, I'd wear sweatpants and an oversized t-shirt every day, but unfortunately, society has other expectations of me. The last thing I wanted was to stand out like the outsider I was.

As I arrived at the church, I had to hunt for a space to park. The small lot was already packed and most of the mourners seemed to be inside already. I pulled my car into a space, fought with my purse, which had gotten wedged between the passenger seat and the console somehow, and finally shut the door behind me. I snuck into the back of the church and settled into one of the pews, taking a good look around me. The place was packed, the way it would be for any minor-town celebrity. A pastor stood at the front, straightening his robes, alongside a choir of mostly elderly ladies who fidgeted while reviewing their songbooks. Each pew had been decorated with white ribbons and calla lilies, more like a wedding than a funeral.

I quickly noticed there seemed to be many more women in attendance than men. I wondered if Mr. Wilson had just been particularly popular with the ladies, or if any of them might be among the many ex-wives. Several of them were older, and moved about with walkers or canes, which leaned against the outside aisles or next to them in their seats, but there was also a handful of them who were younger. In the front pew, I spotted the woman who must be Melanie, based on her elaborate black dress and veil, as well as the two children she carried in tow. One was a young boy, no older than five, and the other a mere toddler who sat in her lap. It seemed Darlene had been right about one thing, the old man was still able to procreate, right until the end. As I tried not to stare, I started calculating how old Mrs. Melanie Wilson must be, because she looked younger than me, and must have been even younger when her first child was born. Everyone settled into their seats and the pastor began the ceremony.

As we bowed our heads in prayer, a latecomer snuck in the back. She wore a wide brimmed hat covered in a dark veil and walked hunched over a cane. Looking around, she seemed to settle on the pew I sat in, and I moved over to make room for her. I could barely see her face behind the veil, but she smelled strongly of patchouli with a hint of sour milk. "Thank you," she murmured in my direction. "Wouldn't miss this for the world."

Completing his prayer, the pastor raised his head, looking over the crowd as if to appraise the number of us in attendance. "We meet here today to honor the life of Erwin Wilson," he began. "To bless these, his ashes, and transfer his spirit to

God's keeping. We give thanks for his life and ask God to bless him now that his time in this world has come to an end."

A large urn stood on the altar, undoubtedly containing the late Erwin Wilson. It was ornately decorated with an intricate floral pattern that shone under the natural light streaming from the oculus above. If I still believed in God, I might think He favored Mr. Wilson in his death.

The pastor continued. "For Erwin Wilson, the journey is now beginning. But for us, there is loss, grief, and pain. Every one of us here has been affected – perhaps in small ways, or perhaps in transformative ones – by Erwin. His life mattered to us all."

The patchouli-smelling woman coughed loudly. "What a load of crock," she muttered under her breath. I tried not to react when she swore. "Fucking shit stain, good riddance."

The ceremony continued with a rendition of "Nearer My God to Thee" and "Amazing Grace." One of the few men in attendance approached the podium for the eulogy. Before he began to speak, the woman next to me started talking again.

"How'd you know the deceased?" she asked. "Did he try to get in your panties, too?"

I gasped, not sure how to respond.

She lifted her veil, revealing a liver-spotted chin, and smiled wryly. "You don't have to be shy about it. Everyone knows he couldn't keep it in his pants."

I gulped, trying to think of a plausible excuse for my being there.

"Doesn't matter, really. I wouldn't judge you. Just him." She directed her eyes forward again, pretending to listen to the eulogy, which seemed to be enumerating the many contributions Mr. Wilson had made to society, even if that only included fathering a ridiculous number of children, all of whom were "well taken care of" according to the orator.

"Anyway, God will be the one to judge him now," she added. "And I hope he judges harshly."

By the time the receiving line was starting to form, she stood unceremoniously and left the same way she had come in, largely unnoticed by anyone but me. I should have said something, I thought, trying to figure out who she was and who Erwin was to her. I could feel part of my story slipping away from me before I had even started writing it. After a minute's hesitation, I followed her. She was limping across the lot, using her cane to support her weight.

"Excuse me, ma'am?" I tried.

She looked back, folding the veil up over her hat this time. The wind attempted to blow it back over her face. "What do you want?" she demanded.

I ran to catch up. "How do you know...um...the deceased?"

She sneered. "That's another story for another day."

"I've got time," I offered. "How's about some coffee?"

She hesitated, assessing me with her cold, gray eyes. "Why do you want to know?"

"Curiosity," I replied honestly.

"Killed the cat," she replied. "You've got to be careful around here. Everything has ears." She sighed. "But I've got nothing better to do and it's a bit of a trek back home. Care to give me a ride?"

"Sure thing."

I helped her into my car and drove to the Deep Dish. It seemed everyone in town was down at the church and even Darlene was out for the morning. A young boy who looked barely old enough to drive poured us coffee and asked if we wanted anything to eat. The older woman declined but I ordered apple pie a la mode. My stomach growled for something more substantial, but I didn't want to talk through a mouthful of cheeseburger.

"Cream? Sugar?" the boy asked. We both declined.

"I see you like it black as death," she commented.

"Something like that," I said.

"So, spill, child," she began. "How did you know Erwin?" She had removed her hat altogether and gave me a sly smile. I knew what she expected me to say, and I felt half-inclined to confirm it. After all, I didn't want to reveal what I was really doing there. Maybe a partial truth would satisfy her.

"Nothing else to do," I tried.

"Strange reason to go to a funeral, if you ask me." She sipped the steaming coffee.

"I saw it in the Gazette a few days ago. Decided to check it out." I tasted my coffee in turn.

"Not as entertaining as a movie, I bet, not that you can catch one of those around here, anyway."

"True."

"Alright let's start from the beginning again," she said. "I'm Freya Pedersen, and you are?"

"Elizabeth Rodriguez."

"Like the writer?" she asked.

"Yes," I admitted.

"Have I got a story for you."

Chapter 6

FREYA PEDERSEN, 1952

Freya Pedersen blossomed into womanhood when she was barely through the third grade. One day she was flat-chested and knobby-kneed and the next she was wearing a C-cup bra and stowing Kotex in her school bag. She caught the eyes of all the boys in her class with tight sweaters and short skirts. By the age of twelve, she was known to have bragged that she could pass for an eighteen-year-old, but she had never kissed a boy, everyone just assumed she had due to all the attention she garnered. The sad reality was that Freya had no friends to speak of because the other girls seethed with jealousy as they counted down the days until they would finally reach puberty. She was like a porcelain doll, fun to look at, but always out of reach. That was, until the summer of 1952 when Erwin Wilson came to work on the farm of a family friend, Henry Hudson.

At seventeen, Erwin was lean but muscular. He rode into Orchard Square on a dusty bus all the way from Indiana in the hopes of earning some extra money over the summer. Erwin's father had been good friends with Henry decades prior and had negotiated for the boy to work as a farmhand for a few months. As a city boy, Erwin knew little about the daily work of keeping up a farm but learned quickly. Each morning he woke at the rooster's crow to feed the animals, muck out stalls and collect fresh eggs. In the heat of the day, about midafternoon, he would get a little free time to himself and often found a bit of mischief with one of the day workers, Frederick. On a hot day in early June, the boys walked down Lawson Field, the big stretch of land that doubled as both a town square and an occasional baseball diamond, for carnival rides that had been set up for a summer festival.

By chance, Freya worked at one of the ticket booths. At fifteen, she wore scant clothing, her hair in braided pigtails, and leaned over the counter, giving the boys a nice look down her shirt at her ample bosom. They appreciated the view, Frederick blushing so much that, with the splash of freckles across his face, he looked like a ripe tomato. Erwin managed a suave approach. He asked for her name, when her shift ended, which was in a mere 20 minutes. They walked around for a minute and then he returned with a giant tuft of pink cotton candy and an invitation to ride the Tilt-o-Whirl.

Frederick insisted on tagging along so she rode smack dab between the two of them on the ride. Once they pulled the metal bar over their laps, the ride started moving and the boys took turns pushing her from side to side in the car, trying to get as much momentum going as possible. The car spun round, and round, and she screeched, feeling giddy and dizzy and a little nauseous all at the same time. It was not lost on the boys that they were squeezing up against her boobs with each spin, but she seemed not to notice. When the ride finally slowed to a halt, Erwin dragged her away to the Ferris wheel. This time they left Frederick behind.

As their gondola rose high up into the air, Freya confessed to a mild fear of heights. Erwin reassured her and clasped her hand in his. He had a strong, sure grip that felt oddly comforting. Yet, her stomach still did flip flops, from both the excitement and uneasiness. The wind blew over them and she shivered. He pulled her closer to him.

"You're not from around here, are you?" she asked.

"No, just here for the summer."

"Where are you from?"

"Indianapolis."

"All the way down in Indiana? What're you doing here, then?"

"Working for the summer. My pops thought it would keep me out of trouble."

"What kind of trouble?" she asked. She smiled, knowing exactly what kind of trouble, and praying some of it would finally come her way.

From that moment on, they spent nearly every afternoon together. They would walk along the creek together and sit for hours on the farm's porch swing, sneaking kisses when they thought no one was looking. One Saturday, Erwin borrowed the truck and they drove to Weston for a nice dinner. Henry Hudson and his wife argued for a full night over that one. She worried the young couple was getting a little too friendly, but Henry reasoned it was just one summer and what harm could it do? The answer was plenty.

After dinner, Erwin drove the truck out to an abandoned field, through tall grass and weeds that whipped against the sides of the vehicle. Freya squealed with delight as the truck bumped along, asking him where they were going. It was late, near curfew, and they would both be in deep trouble if he got her home late. He promised there was something beautiful for them to see, out here in the middle of nowhere. She would take any chance she could get to be alone with him, as it felt like someone was always watching them.

Finally, he parked in a dirt clearing, helped her down from the cab, and opened the tailgate. He hoisted her up.

"What are we doing?" she finally asked. She looked around at the overgrown field, the truck bed cool against her legs. It had grown dark already.

He returned with a few blankets and joined her in the truck bed. He laid down on his back and pulled her down beside him. "Look," he said.

For a few minutes, they stared up at the stars, which shone brightly without a cloud in the sky.

"It's beautiful, isn't it?" she asked.

"Sure is." He hugged her. "Almost as beautiful as you." His lips met hers with a passionate kiss. It was a long kiss, one that she didn't want to let him out of, no matter the fact that she would eventually need to breathe. Reluctantly, they separated.

"What are the stars like in Indianapolis?" she asked.

"Nothing like these. There's too much light pollution from the city."

Then, she finally asked the question she really didn't want to ask. "When do you go back?"

"End of the summer."

"That's in only a few weeks." She tried not to start crying.

"I know."

"Oh, what will we do?" She kissed him again and again, desperately. "You can't leave me."

A sly grin crossed his face. "Maybe I won't."

"You mean you'll stay?" It seemed like a miraculous impossibility.

"Maybe I'll take you with me."

"What do you mean?" She sat up now and stared down into his face as he continued to gaze at the stars. "How would you take me with you?"

"What if I asked you to marry me?"

"Wait, what?" She pounced on him now, wrapping her arms around him and drawing him closer. "You want to marry me? I'm only fifteen!"

He kissed her again, slow and deep. His tongue found hers and their lips moved in sync. If he wanted to have her now, all of her, she couldn't resist. She would give him everything. She felt so lightheaded already. Then reality started to return.

"I need to get back," she whispered, remembering her curfew. "We need to go."

"Not until you promise to marry me, Freya."

"I promise. I promise," she whispered, between frantic kisses. "Never ever leave me."

But in the next few weeks, Erwin grew distant. Whenever she came by the farm, he was busy, or even refused to see her. She didn't know what she had done wrong. Before she knew it, he headed home and she was left with a broken heart. She returned to school and tried, unsuccessfully, to forget about all they had shared over the summer.

By Christmas, she heard a rumor that he and his parents had come back to visit the Hudsons and wanted to see if it was true. She strapped on her snowshoes and made the trek out to Henry Hudson's property. When she knocked at the front door, no one answered. Instead of knocking again, she peered through the front curtains and saw them all there, Mr. and Mrs. Hudson dressed all in red for the holiday, another older couple who must be Erwin's parents, and even Frederick, wearing flannels and smoking a pipe. Before she could get up the courage to knock again, she finally spied Erwin, wearing nice slacks and a tie. He had even grown out his beard and looked so much older now, more like a man than the teenage boy she knew. A young red-haired woman stood next to him, and she watched as they moved together and apart, touching lightly. The woman turned, revealing the slight swell of her pregnant belly. He touched her stomach and smiled. They kissed.

Freya's cheeks burned with embarrassment. She shouldn't be here. She didn't know who the woman was but clearly, Erwin was no longer hers. Maybe he had never been. She felt like such an idiot. Why would someone want to marry her, the foolish girl that she was? How could he do this to her? She strapped her feet back into the snowshoes and started to leave when she fell into a deep snowbank. She sank deeper and deeper until she felt like she was drowning in a sea of white. She looked up and could see nothing but snow. She screamed.

Eventually, a pair of strong arms pulled her from the snow and set her back on her feet. Frederick worked quickly to brush the snow from her head and shoulders. The rest of the family rushed to the front door to see what was happening.

"Are you alright?" asked Frederick. "What are you doing out here?"

Freya couldn't muster any words.

"Get inside now, the both of you," tutted Mrs. Hudson, motioning from the door. "You don't want to catch a chill." She herded them inside, set Freya by the fire with a heavy blanket, and served her up some hot chocolate.

Freya shivered, drawing the blanket tight around her as she sipped at the cocoa. She tried not to look at Erwin and his new lover.

"Whatever were you doing out there, my dear?" Mrs. Hudson asked.

"Going for a walk," Freya managed, but she refused to elaborate.

The others made introductions and she learned the red-headed woman was Frederick's sister, as well as Erwin's fiancé. In an awkward moment, Erwin expressed that he had wanted the two women to meet, maybe not like this, but eventually.

"I always thought you two would get along," he explained. "Freya, this is my fiancé Charlotte. Charlotte, this is Freya. We were good friends over the summer."

Thankfully, Mrs. Wilson, Erwin's mother, butted in before the conversation could get any more awkward. "We need to get you home, Freya," she said. "Make sure you're home safe and sound. You shouldn't be out walking around in the snow like that. Do you think you can take her, dear?" She motioned toward her husband who quickly went outside to start up his car. After a few minutes, he beckoned Freya.

She hoped she could ride home in silence, but Erwin's father had questions.

"So, Erwin says you were friends over the summer?" he asked. "He hadn't told us about you until this moment."

"Well, I suppose you could call us that." She wanted to scream. Friends, apparently, that's all she was to him. Why had he asked her to marry him then? Was it all just some cruel joke to play on a gullible little girl? She wished she could just disappear.

"Well, if you weren't friends, then, what were you?" he tried.

"We were friends."

"Nothing more?" he asked.

Despite her best efforts, she started crying.

"Oh, honey, I didn't mean anything by it. I just know how boys can be. They spend a summer away from home and start making promises they can't keep."

"What do you mean?"

"I mean, they say things and don't think about how they might hurt someone."

"How do you know?"

"Because I was a boy once."

By the time Easter arrived, Erwin and Charlotte were married, but thankfully for Freya, they had moved to Weston by then. Although they were out of sight, they were far from out of mind, though. She would never forget the first summer she was loved, and she would never forget the one who got away.

Chapter 7

PRESENT DAY

When Freya had finished her story, I understood why she still held such a grudge against Erwin Wilson, even after his death. I exchanged contact information with her in case I really did choose to pursue this and write about Mr. Wilson's wives (and almost-wives, apparently).

The ideas were finally brewing. If I could get just a fraction of the women to talk to me, this might be a story worth telling. I just needed the green light from Michael. On the trek back to the cabin, I gave him a call.

"Was that funeral today?" he asked.

"Yes, and I think I've got a what-do-you-call-it? A lead? Yes, a lead."

"Spill it."

"There is this local man who just passed away. Had no less than twenty-three wives."

Michael let out a low whistle.

"You're telling me! Just spoke with a woman who, although she wasn't one of the wives, had some strong opinions about his proclivities."

"A gay man had twenty-three wives?"

"No." I laughed. "Nothing like that. He seemed to be a ladies' man, but instead of love-em-and-leave-em, he just kept marrying them."

"What an idiot," remarked Michael.

"That's what I thought! Anyway, it's gonna take a lot more digging but I think there might be a story here."

"Something book-worthy? Think anyone will go on-the-record?"

"I've got one already."

"Great! Let me know when you have something solid."

"I will."

"And Elizabeth?"

"Yes?"

"Don't work too hard."

I could picture his sarcastic grin and found myself wishing he were here with me. I could use the company. Instead, I hung up and drove up to Oatmeal Lake, my head buzzing with ideas.

I pulled the obituary from my purse again, reread it, and started jotting notes. I wrote some thoughts on what Freya had told me, every detail I could remember, and then wrote a few notes on wife number one, Charlotte. She was sister to Frederick, already pregnant when she got engaged to Erwin, which would mean that they must have met over the same summer Freya knew him so intimately. Either they had met shortly after Erwin had mentioned marriage to Freya, or he had been seeing both women at the same time. If Charlotte was Frederick's sister it would make sense for her to be from Orchard Square, not Indianapolis. I had no idea how to find Frederick or Charlotte to corroborate any of this, only Freya's word.

I doubted Erwin's newest wife would know much about his first wife, but she might be a place to start. After all, it seemed like Erwin was good at one thing at least, making babies. Melanie seemed to be a resident of Orchard Square or at least a nearby town, one of the few reasons it would make sense for the funeral to be held at St. John's. Along with switching wives frequently, Mr. Wilson also seemed to hop back and forth between Orchard Square and Weston. I could see this would take more digging and in general more research. After all, the story I was trying to tell hadn't been fully revealed to me, yet. I would at the very least need to get my hands on a phonebook to reach out to Melanie. It was too bad Freya had distracted me at the funeral because that would have been a great opportunity to speak with her. Now, I had to come up with some sort of backstory without revealing the true reason for my curiosity. All of this would mean driving back into Orchard Square, and I simply didn't have the energy now.

I let myself doze on the couch and woke with no concept of how long I had been out, what time of day it was, or even where I was. I still hadn't gotten used to the cabin and every little creak and moan of the building sounded like an intruder. It didn't help that I'd already made friends with a raccoon and a mouse. Who knew what else lurked in the surrounding woods? Bears? I didn't really want to find out. In fact, I was already regretting my decision to use a cabin in the woods as a writing retreat. But I could start my hunt again tomorrow now that I had a direction. I no longer felt lost and hopeless.

Chapter 8

18 MONTHS AGO

After arguing with both my sister and my mother, I needed some air. I stormed out the door and started walking. For a brief moment, I wished I was a runner. You always hear about the "runner's high" - that they feel exhilarated when they get going, but I've never been much of an athlete, and I wasn't about to start now. Instead, I walked quickly, trying to put as much distance between myself and my family as possible. I had run away a few times as a teen, but I always wound up returning when I realized I had nowhere to run to. I always imagined hitchhiking across the country or hopping on a plane to some foreign country, but I never got that far. Usually, I'd spend a few days on a friend's couch until their parents caught on and sent me back. In the end, I always came back.

I had made it to the end of the block when I decided to call Michael. He, at least, would be willing to listen.

"What's up, superstar?" he answered.

I tried not to break down in tears. "Nothing, just my world falling apart."

"Why so dramatic? Save that stuff for your next book."

"Ha, I don't think I will survive this one."

I found a bench to sit on and settled in. How could I explain what had just happened? The whole thing felt surreal like it had happened to someone else, and I was just observing.

"Liz. What's got you all doom and gloom?"

"I think I'm about to be disowned."

"Oh no! What about your inheritance!"

I know he was just trying to cheer me up, but his humor hit me the wrong way at this moment. "I'm serious, Michael. I think I'm getting kicked out."

"What, really? If you need a place to crash, I've got a couch for you."

While the prospect of couch surfing didn't appeal to me, I would take the chance to get away for a night or two. "I might take you up on that."

He texted me his address in River North, an expensive neighborhood bordered on two sides by the Chicago River. Somehow I hadn't realized that Michael was so successful. Or maybe he was the one with family money. Either way, crashing on his couch might be more luxurious than sleeping in my own bed.

I continued walking with no particular destination in mind. While I was working on the memoir, walking served as a way to work through my thoughts whenever I got stuck. Sometimes, my greatest insights came after I had gone just a few blocks from home, and then they would solidify on the trek back. Today, I kept going until I reached the Gulliver mural.

As kids, we had all kinds of alternative names for him because Gulliver never seemed to fit. What Mexican man would be named Gulliver anyway? He was Jose and Alejandro, and Manuel. He was all of our grandfathers and fathers and uncles; a symbol stretched out in brilliant-colored paints, red and orange and blue. Later, I read an artist's statement saying the figure represented the immigrant experience, which was at least a few generations removed for most of us. But there he was, reaching desperately across the front and side of the building, making his way through painted barbed wire, struggling for freedom in America.

Although I had seen the mural about a million times, I paused and contemplated it once more. Right now, I felt trapped, unable to move forward, caught up in the barbed wire of my family. I resolved not to go back today, not even to grab a change of clothes. Let them worry about me if they cared at all.

I took the stairs up to the platform where I could catch the L, Chicago's elevated train system. Unlike New Yorkers, who take the subway below ground, we like our bird's eye view of the city as we ride. I checked the schedule and determined which line would take me from Pilsner to Michael's side of town. After climbing aboard and finding a seat, I texted him that I was on my way.

Chapter 9

PRESENT DAY

I treated myself to breakfast at The Deep Dish, ordering French toast with strawberries and whipped cream along with my usual coffee. I didn't bother with the week's newspaper but asked Darlene if she had a phonebook handy.

She lugged over the yellow pages, which were much thicker and heavier than I expected. "Now, this is for all of Crawford County," she explained.

I pushed my plate aside and started paging through. Sure enough, under Wilson, there were a few names, most notably Melanie, whom I was looking for, as well as Laura and Miriam. I checked the names against the obituary – they were likely two of his former wives. I wrote all three numbers and addresses down. Two were in Orchard Square and one in Weston. I wouldn't be showing up on doorsteps unannounced, but it was good to know I wouldn't be driving all over the county either. Now I felt like I was finally getting somewhere.

Darlene couldn't seem to mind her own business. I caught her looking over my shoulder again. "Any relations?" she asked. "I heard you were in here with Freya Pedersen the other day. I was out for my granddaughter's birthday."

"No, no relation," I assured her. "Just people I want to talk to."

"Just don't go sticking your nose where it doesn't belong," she warned. "Not everybody is as talkative as me. Or as Freya, that witch."

"Does she actually practice Pagan witchcraft?" I asked.

Darlene laughed. "No dear, it's an expression. Old unmarried women have too much time on their hands. Freya always seems to be meddling in something."

"I see."

"Mr. Wilson's funeral must have been the highlight of her year," she mused.

"It sure seemed that way." I closed the phone book and slid it back to her across the table. "Thank you for your help, Darlene."

"Anytime, sweetheart."

I called Melanie's number and she agreed to meet me early that afternoon. I told her I was interested in writing a feature about her late husband. It wasn't an entire lie, but definitely a stretching of the truth. One could consider a book (which was what I really hoped to write if I could find enough content) a "feature" of sorts, just a much longer one.

At half-past one, I drove up a dirt driveway to the large, rambling estate which covered several acres of land. A beautiful garden full of flowering bushes and apple trees stretched the full length of the house, which looked to be at least a half-dozen bedrooms with enough chimneys for at least three wood-burning fireplaces.

A servant answered the door and escorted me to the study, where Melanie sat demurely in an overstuffed armchair, sipping a steaming cup of tea. Even up close, she looked so incredibly young, her long black hair swept up and pinned in place with jeweled barrettes. I felt like I had stepped back into time. This woman looked like she had never worked a day in her entire life. The floor-length skirt she wore boasted intricate embroidery along the hem, a series of dainty daisies and roses. She looked up at me and then beckoned me to sit.

"Who are you again??" she said, making the statement a question.

"Elizabeth Rodriguez. I am a writer hoping to do a feature on your late husband."

"Why??" she asked.

"I saw his obituary in the gazette and... well, frankly, he had many wives, and it piqued my curiosity. What type of man was he?"

"Before we get started, I want you to know that I couldn't care less about Erwin's life before me. You won't find some sort of scandal here. In fact, we never talked about it. As far as I'm concerned, he was my husband, no one else's."

Feeling rebuffed, I paused and carefully phrased my next words.

"What can you tell me about him?"

She set the teacup down and looked me right in the eye. "He was my knight in shining armor."

Chapter 10

MELANIE ANGELOS, 2015

Even as a young girl, Melanie Angelos attended church at least once a week, sometimes more than that. She loved the way the congregation sang together, raising their voices to the heavens, and praising the Lord. In those moments, caught up in the melody, she would lose herself and become just a small piece of the Heavenly Body. She could feel Spirit coursing through her until her heart felt so full, like it couldn't contain a single ounce more of love. The people there were also always so welcoming, much more so even than the family in her own home.

For many years, it had been just her father and two older brothers who often treated her poorly. As a girl, she wasn't expected to work on the farm, but for the same reason her father saw her as a worthless burden, just another mouth to feed in a poor household. Her brothers, however, were the primary source of her troubles. She would do anything just to get away from them. When they drank too much, came in late, sometimes they would touch her in ways that made her uncomfortable, saying it was "practice for the real thing." Despite her efforts to fend them off, there was little she could do when one held her down and the other did as he pleased.

Church became her escape, the one place where she felt truly loved, not only by the congregation, but also by God. Sometimes she worried that her brothers' sins would become her own. After all, if she couldn't stop them, was it not also her sin as well? She knew she should be able to confess, but also knew that if anything happened to her brothers when she told, her father would get involved and often his wrath proved worse. He would get violent in ways that left black and blue bruises and then she would have to explain those, too, not just the sadness behind her eyes.

She joined the choir and soon she sang solos in most services, her voice reaching to the heavens like an angel. Some of the congregation even joked that was why her surname was "Angelos", meaning "messenger" or "angel". The family name had once been "Angelopoulos," but was shortened after arriving in America from the Greek island of Crete. Unfortunately, she still returned home each night, trying to protect herself from her father and brothers. That home was a type of Hell she couldn't seem to break free from.

Over Thanksgiving, the church often served a banquet for those less fortunate who couldn't afford a turkey with all the trimmings. Melanie begged permission to attend and was granted some respite. She stood in line, serving mashed potatoes to the needy, as well as some of the older congregation who no longer had families of their own in the area. An older man, in his late seventies, approached her with his plate ready. She built a mound of potatoes for him, creating a little pond and filling it with gravy. When he smiled at her, his whole face lit up. She had never seen anyone so glad for such a simple thing. His blue eyes twinkled at her as he whispered his thanks.

When they were done serving the food, Melanie grabbed a carafe of coffee and began pouring out cups to the guests while someone else followed behind with a cart full of home-made pies. The older man beckoned her to join him, and they sat, cozy in that moment, and introduced themselves. Erwin Wilson was not poor by any means, only lonely. It had been a few years since his wife had left him, and he just wanted some company, someone to talk to when his house felt too large for one person. At first, Melanie became his dear friend and a reason to return to church.

When she sang, Melanie sang not just to the Lord, but to Erwin. Just seeing him smile filled her with a sudden warmth, knowing she had caused the change in his countenance. In rare moments, he let his face fall and betrayed the depths of his loneliness. He would stare off into empty space, as if someone had just taken away his purpose. Then, he would hear her sing, and his eyes would light up again. He would stay for hospitality afterward, often opting for decaffeinated coffee or herbal tea. Melanie made sure his tea was brewed just so, with lemon and honey, and a small spoon to stir it, and he gave her all the smiles she could ever need.

Eventually, he invited her to join him for afternoon tea at his home. She accepted gladly but it was becoming harder and harder to get away from these stolen moments, as her father grew older and increasingly agressive. Her brothers still terrorized her regularly. She kept these things secret from Erwin, until she arrived one day, broken, and bruised, holding back tears. She brewed the tea, set it before Erwin and despite herself, began sobbing.

"Whatever is the matter, my dear?" he asked. "Surely, I'm not that ugly of a man!"

This made her laugh, but only a little. "No, no, you could never make me cry," she replied.

"Then who has?" There was an urgency in his voice, which suddenly grew rougher. "If someone has hurt you, I hope you would trust me enough to tell me."

"There's nothing either of us can do." She tried unsuccessfully to put on a brave smile.

"Now, now," he chided. He pulled a folded handkerchief from his pocket and wiped her tears.

She put a hand over her face, stifling her sobs. He looked up at her with those brilliant blue eyes, searching for some reason she would cry in such a way. "Tell me what happened," he urged. Then made her a promise. "Your secrets are safe with me, my darling."

Eventually she calmed down enough to speak more clearly. "It's my family. They – they..."

"What about them? Do I need to beat someone up?"

She chuckled, despite herself. "Oh, Erwin, look at you. You're going to fight my father and my brothers?"

"If they're the ones who hurt you!"

"That would only make things worse. They'd take it out on me for telling you."

"What have they done to you?"

Melanie broke down and explained in detail just what had been happening at the Angelos home. She felt so incredibly hopeless and had nowhere to turn at this point, but she also knew she could not live there much longer without ending up a broken soul, which she almost was already. She didn't even fear her own death any longer, just the injustice of the way her own family treated her.

Erwin took both her hands in his and listened intently, not saying a word until she had finished listing their sins. He ached for her, felt each abuse as if he himself had been the victim. When she grew silent again, he drew her to him, embracing this perfect vessel of God who had been so horrifically violated. He held her that way for a long time, letting her cry on his shoulder until she had lost all her strength and the tears ran dry. He wiped her eyes again with the handkerchief.

"You are never going back there again," he promised.

She looked at him in disbelief. Her eyes searched for the lie. It sounded too easy.

"I couldn't expect you to put me up," she replied. "Besides, they would break in and steal me back. I know them too well. They wouldn't let me just leave."

"They would if you were my wife."

It took Melanie a while to get used to the idea, but his proposal made the most sense of any scheme she could devise. If they were married, it would be a legally binding bond that her family would respect. If questioned, she could reason with them by letting them know she would no longer be their responsibility, that she would be in good hands, and they wouldn't need to bother themselves with her well-being. Not that they really cared in the first place, but that would be how she could put it to them.

She gave Erwin a small kiss, sighing as she drew back from him. "You really want to be my husband?" she asked.

"Oh, look at you," he replied. "You're my beautiful angel. You act like no one would want you. Has no one ever told you how incredible you are?"

"No, no one has." She kissed him again. This time she lingered, feeling the warmth of his lips. Despite his age, they were soft and welcoming.

The two were soon married and Melanie came to live with him in his huge, empty house. She brightened his days, and he offered her the love and support she had always craved. She gave birth to a young son who soon ran through the hallways, bringing light to the old man's eyes, keeping him feeling so incredibly alive. A second son was born shortly after, but Erwin had begun to fade by then. As the children seemed to grow wilder and more rambunctious, he began to lose his energy and spent more and more time in bed, the covers pulled all the way up to his chin. She joined him for tea every afternoon, until one day he didn't open his eyes, and she discovered that he had passed away. She feared she would never know such love and acceptance ever again. She continued to live in the large house, closing the West wing, which had once been his favorite part of the house, and where they had shared a marriage bed. Nothing could tarnish her memory of him.

Chapter 11

I struggled to reconcile the criticism and negative viewpoint Freya held with the undying devotion Melanie had for her late husband. Looking at the same man at two different points in his life was difficult. Had he changed over time or were the two women describing him from two entirely different perspectives, that of the jilted lover and the loving wife? There was still the great age difference between Melanie and Erwin to consider, but nothing she had shared sounded particularly salacious or untoward. In many ways, he had rescued her from a horrible fate and served as her savior even more than she had served as his.

I was still running these ideas through my head as I pulled up to the cabin. I still needed to call the other numbers I had found in the phonebook but likely wouldn't go to talk to anyone until the next day at this point. I needed to take down more notes. It wasn't until I drove up the last crest that I saw a figure sitting on my porch swing, a baseball cap pulled low over his eyes. I saw no evidence of another vehicle. Whoever it was must have walked all the way up the dirt drive, or maybe he was a drifter? I felt my muscles tense as I parked and then walked toward him.

"Hello?" I said, hesitating. He raised his head and I saw a face I hadn't seen in a long time. "Luis!" I nearly squealed and ran toward him, arms wide open. He rebuffed my hug, and remained despondent as I whooped, hollered, and asked a million questions. "How are you? Why are you here? *How* are you here?"

"I don't want to talk about it," he grumbled. He still hadn't moved from his spot on the swing.

"I mean, how did you even know I was here?"

"Dumb luck, I guess."

I grabbed him by the shoulders, shaking him. "Why are you here, little bro?"

He stood, walked slowly across the porch, and tried the front door knob. The door swung slowly inward, and he collapsed onto the couch. "I'm tired." He sighed, closing his eyes, and pulling his cap down to cover his face.

I hurried behind him. "Let me make us some sandwiches and then we'll talk, alright?"

"Yeah. Whatever."

A few minutes later, he hadn't moved an inch, but I descended upon him. I set the sandwiches on the coffee table in front of him and settled into the armchair. I had also poured two glasses of milk. He eventually sat up to start stuffing a cheese and salami sandwich in his face, washing down the first few mouthfuls with a gulp of milk.

"Whoa there, buddy, there's more where that came from. You don't have to choke it down."

I nibbled at the crust of my sandwich while he finished his. Then he leaned back on the couch without a word. Eventually, I tried to suss out what was going on. "How is it going at home?"

"Not sure. I've been at camp. They made me a counselor."

I stifled a small laugh. "You? A counselor? What kind of camp."

"Scouts. But you'd know that if you had been around. I haven't seen you since Christmas."

"They know I'm busy."

"Doing what? Camping in the middle of bum-fuck nowhere?"

"How did you know where to find me?"

"I didn't. Like I said, dumb luck. Took a canoe across the lake and here you are. Seems like I can't get away from you dumb broads."

"Who're you calling dumb?"

"Okay maybe not dumb, but I just wish I could do my own thing once in a while, ya know?"

"I mean…" I took a few bites of my sandwich, swallowing hard. "So you just went AWOL from the camp? You need a place to stay for a few?"

"Why do you think I'm here? Thought I'd be alone, but no such luck."

I made a face at him, then motioned to the loft above. "I've got an extra bed just for you. Let me get you set up and you can take a load off."

While Luis stared blankly at the ceiling, I collected some blankets and an extra cushion so he could sleep on the bottom bunk of the bunk bed. Eventually, he climbed up the ladder and passed out. As a teenage boy, he would likely sleep the rest of the day away. Then, I would have to figure out what to do with him. The last thing I needed right now was another distraction.

Christmas had been the last time I'd seen Luis, or any of my family for that matter, and it hadn't gone well. Ma and Maria were still busting my chops for writing that memoir about them, and Luis and my niece Cecilia tried their best to stay out of it. The least I could do was help my brother out for a few days before I grilled him on why he was ditching the Boy Scout camp. Of course, they'd be looking for him, but I'd allow the boy a bit of respite. It felt like the least I could do.

Trying to refocus my efforts, I sat down to write what I could remember from my conversation with Melanie. Next time, I'd have to record it like a reporter or something, although I wasn't sure when or what "next time" would necessarily entail.

* * *

At some point later in the evening, Luis nudged me awake. I had fallen asleep on the couch again, notebook in hand, having made very little progress. He read over my shoulder, took a sip of a beer and asked, "Who's Mr. Wilson?"

I jerked awake. "Who's only sixteen?" I asked, snatching the beer from him. I took a swig as he sat across from me.

"It was worth a try," he said, smiling.

"Mr. Wilson is a dead man who had twenty-three wives." I set the beer bottle on the coffee table as Luis whistled.

"Jesus. Who wants that many wives?" he reached for the bottle again and I swatted him away.

"I know who. I'm trying to figure out why," I explained.

"So you're a detective now?"

"Not really, but if I find anything juicy, I might write about it."

"Sweet. What do you know so far?"

"Well, I've learned that he had a childhood sweetheart who he abandoned for a pregnant fiance just a few months later. I don't know if he was seeing them both at the same time, or just knocked the second one up shortly after abandoning the first."

"Sounds sketch."

"A bit. I've also got a number for some of the other ex-wives, a possible friend of the family."

"Have you checked out ye olde watering hole yet?"

"What, the bar? Is this just about you wanting some beer?" I asked. I reached over and rubbed the top of his head until his hair stood up on end and he playfully slapped me.

"No, I'm serious. Have you checked out the local bar yet? That's where you go to hear all the dirt on everybody."

"Where did you get that idea?" I asked.

"Only every MMORPG I've ever played."

"Every what?"

"Every video game."

"So video games are real life now? Where'd you get that nonsense?"

"It's worth a try. Looks like all you're doing now is scribbling and napping."

"Alright, fine. Get your shoes on. But no beer for you, alright?"

"Yeah, whatever.

We loaded into the car. As I flipped the headlights on, Luis searched the radio dial for anything but Christian talk radio and country, with little success. Eventually he turned it off altogether. He questioned what I was wearing and I repeated to him the motto I had been saying to myself for the past week - nobody cares what I look like. He reminded me that you catch more bees with honey than vinegar. We argued back and forth the rest of the way to Earl's Pub right on the main road of Orchard Square. The sun had recently gone down and there were only a few select street signs lit up downtown.

The window of Earl's advertised Miller High Life, Old Style and Spotted Cow, each with its own neon lights. As we walked in, I could hear an audible gasp, as if they hadn't had an out-of-town visitor in the last few decades. Or maybe it was that I had a kid in tow. I took a quick look around the dimly lit space, the stained carpet that looked like an odd mixture of green and a faded brown, the vinyl on the bar stools ripped and a few regulars ponied up to the bar.

The bartender looked up briefly from a game of dice, holding the wooden cup mid-shake. "Just a minute, dear," he promised, giving me a wink. He smelled strongly of whiskey and cigarettes. I motioned for Luis to take a stool and we both sat at the opposite end of the bar. Luis glanced up at a baseball game on a TV bolted to the wall. Once the two patrons at the bar finished their shakes, the bartender turned to me and asked what I wanted to drink.

"Let's try a Spotted Cow, and a Coke for the kid," I managed.

"You're not from around here, are ya?" he asked.

"That obvious?"

The bartender just nodded as he opened my bottle and poured a soda for Luis. "Most folks would ask for a beer for the kid."

"Is that legal?" I nearly whispered.

"Sure is in Wisconsin." The bartender grinned, as did the two men at the bar. One of them was missing several of his teeth. "As long as you're the guardian, it doesn't matter what age, either."

Luis looked at me with pleading puppy dog eyes.

"Don't bet on it," I chided. "I don't care if it's legal or not, you're not drinking."

"You heard the lady," said the bartender. "She don't want this one growing up too quick, I think."

One of the men at the bar who wore his trucker hat backwards laughed heartily, his large belly shaking. "Man, I've been drinking since I was old enough to swallow. My mama was putting brandy on my gums when I was an infant and I was pouring my daddy old-fashioneds by the time I was five."

"Yeah, we train 'em young around here," his companion agreed. "Where are you guys from?"

"Chicago," I answered.

"Ah, city folk. I'm Dale and this here's Earl," said the man in the hat, motioning to his friend.

"The Earl?" I asked.

"Actually, that's my father, rest his soul, but the joint is mine now. Bartender here is Brandon."

I introduced myself and my little brother, ordered up a frozen pizza for us to share, and exchanged shots with the men. We played a few rounds of dice. After a few rounds, they became incredibly talkative and willing to answer any question I posed to them. Then they started volunteering stories of their own.

"What do you know about Erwin Wilson?" I asked.

"That the guy who died about a week ago?" asked Dale.

"Yes, the one with twenty-three wives."

"I've got a few stories on that guy," said Earl. "Wound up with his first wife because of a bet."

Chapter 12

CHARLOTTE TREMBLAY, 1953

When Erwin Wilson first arrived in Orchard Square, he was a privileged brat who couldn't even ride a horse. The first few weeks at Henry Hudson's farm the men worked hard at breaking him in. For Erwin, this proved a painful process, not only physically but also for his pride. He had to learn what it meant to no longer be top dog at everything. He had to earn his respect, rather than buy it.

Frederick Tremblay, who had worked the farm the past few summers, proved to be an almost immediate friend. With his carrot-top hair and freckles, Frederick was still a low man on the totem pole, despite his experience. The others pushed him around, teasing about his tooth-pick thin legs and ginger coloring. He welcomed Erwin in, partially because he had few true friends.

When Erwin took up with a young local girl named Freya, Frederick tried to steer him in another direction. His older sister couldn't seem to find a match among the local gentlemen, at least none that were considered desirable. Erwin wanted nothing to do with it.

"Why are you so keen on me dating your sister?" he asked. "Seems like you're trying to get rid of her."

"No, nothing like that," Frederick promised. "I just think you should meet her. Give her a chance."

"You know me and Freya have something going."

"Freya is only fifteen. A little young don't you think?"

"Your sister is twenty. A little old don't you think? I don't want to be with a woman who's older than me. Besides, she's looking for marriage, I bet." Erwin took another swig of his beer before setting it up on a fence post for target practice. "I'm just here for the summer, not to make any attachments." He walked several paces back and hoisted a shotgun to his shoulder. The recoil sent him stumbling backward.

Frederick showed him the proper way to hold the gun again, nestled up in the crook of his arm, the butt of the gun pressed firmly against his shoulder. "Try this."

Erwin tried again, this time holding his ground, but still missing his mark.

"Better, at least," said Frederick. "Me and a few of the guys are going to the track in Weston tomorrow. You in?" He knew Erwin would be good for the money at least.

"Are you betting on horses again?" Erwin asked.

"Why not? Not much else to do around here in the late afternoon. Besides drink, that is."

"Sure. Freya won't like it any, but she's been getting too clingy lately anyway."

The next night the boys joined up with a few other farm-hands, borrowed a truck and piled in for a trip to the next town. They were already well soused by the time they got there and started placing bets based on horse names, rather than odds of winning. Frederick set his sights on a tawny one named Peachy Keen and Erwin put a heavy bet on Bambi-Eyed Surprise. As the jockeys started lining up for the race, Frederick upped the ante with a personal bet between them.

"When I win, Erwin, you've got to go on a date with my sister, Charlotte," he demanded. "And I mean really give it go, take her someplace and be a gentleman, all that. Not just making out in the field like you do with Freya."

"And if my horse wins, what do I get out of this?" asked Erwin.

"I'll keep my mouth shut and never mention her again."

They shook on it, then leaned over the railing for a better view of the race.

Thirteen horses waited at the line, each in their individual starting gate. The jockeys leaned forward, ready to begin and as the gun went off, one horse struggled and bucked straight out of the gate, and then again, throwing the jockey to the dirt, and then continued running behind the other horses.

"Is that your horse?" asked Frederick, nudging Erwin with a grin.

"Sure is," Erwin grumped. "But the horse is still running, you never said he had to have a jockey on him."

"It wouldn't be a legal win," quipped Frederick.

Bambi-Eyed Surprise kept running, but brought up the rear, not even close to the front line. The other horses bolted, their great flanks heaving, the short little jockeys hanging on, some as if for dear life. Peachy Keen's jockey kept his crop flying, beating the horse to a faster speed. He maintained a pace at least three or four horses behind as they ran around the first turn.

"Doesn't look like your horse is winning either," breathed Erwin, caught up in the excitement of the race.

"But he's beating yours by a mile!" replied Frederick.

Peachy Keen edged forward, struggling past the third, then the second horse, then neck-to-neck for first as they rounded the second turn. In the final stretch, he gained speed and galloped ahead, crossing the finish line first. Frederick whooped and hollered in Erwin's ear. The other horses followed close behind, including Bambi-Eyed Surprise, still without a rider. The horse kept running as the jockeys slowed their mounts, taking another lap around the track until the owner, on another horse, rounded him up.

"I call for a rematch," said Erwin, as Frederick slapped him on the back.

"No can do, brother. You're taking Charlotte on a date."

Erwin grimaced. Great. How would he explain this one to Freya?

In the end, he opted not to tell her. When she asked where he was going that following Saturday night, he claimed he was going out with the boys. What she didn't know couldn't hurt her. He had let slip some nonsense about wanting to marry Freya the other night, but it seemed to be what she needed to hear to shut up about the end of the summer quickly approaching. After the past few months of working, he was ready to return home to his life of luxury. There was just this one last thing, which he viewed more as a promise to a friend than anything. The last thing he needed was another girl hanging onto his every word.

He arrived at the Tremblay homestead just as the sun was setting to pick up Charlotte. She waited anxiously by the front window for him, repeatedly smoothing her skirts and carefully watching each passing car. They lived just outside of the town proper, so cars regularly passed their doorstep and she didn't know what type of vehicle to expect. Erwin arrived in a beat-up Ford and stared at his feet while he walked to the door.

Charlotte stepped away from the window, trying not to look too eager, but as soon as Erwin entered, a broad smile crossed her face and she giggled. She had never been on a real date before. Most of the boys she had known were local farmer's sons, who were more eager to drag her into the hayloft than take her anywhere. She wore her orange-red hair in two braided pigtails, which made her look at least a few years younger, and freckles covered the bridge of her nose. She had managed to avoid getting entirely burned over the summer, but her cheeks and forearms still bore a light pinkish hue.

She bounded to Erwin and greeted him eagerly, first shaking hands and then embracing him with an exuberant hug. She didn't even notice him cringe away from her, just grabbed his hand and skipped out the door with him. He seemed so tall, so dark, so serious, like the men she read about in romance novels she had squirreled away under her bed.

As soon as they settled into the truck, she began chattering. "Where are you taking me?"

"Where would you like to go?" asked Erwin.

"You mean you don't have a plan? You're supposed to have dates planned out, to surprise your lady. You should hold doors open, too, and pay, and kiss me goodnight." She immediately blushed. "I mean, kiss me if you want to, if you had a good time."

Erwin tried not to groan aloud. Charlotte was acting like a child, but maybe she was just nervous. He hadn't been nervous on a date since, actually he didn't think he had ever been nervous on a date.

"If you could go anywhere, where would you go?" he tried.

"Can we go to the bowling alley? They have pizza and soda and bowling is fun. I bet I can even beat you."

"I'm fine on betting for now, thank you," he said.

As it turned out, Charlotte was surprisingly good at bowling. She had excellent form and Erwin didn't mind the view when she bent to pick up her ball. She had worn a red polka-dot skirt and a tight white sweater that fit her form perfectly. She continued chattering, but eventually he learned to tune out the insignificant things she prattled on about and just pay attention to any questions she might ask. She had the most brilliant green eyes he had ever seen and she looked at him eagerly as she spoke.

"How much longer will you be in Orchard Square?" she asked.

"Only a few weeks. Then I go back home," he replied.

She was pulling the cheese off a slice of pizza, wrapping it around her fingers and then nibbling at it. Her hands were covered in tomato sauce. "It's too bad I didn't meet you until now," she said. "Frederick has told me great things about you. Are you sure you can't stay any longer?"

"I have to help my dad with the business," he said. "I'm just here for the summer."

She wiped her hands on a napkin and then fixed him in her gaze. "Then I'll just have to give you a reason to stay," she said. She looked to make sure no one was looking and then moved to sit on his lap.

A jolt of excitement went through him like he was being suddenly electrified. He felt the heat and shape of her on his thighs. He shouldn't be doing this, he knew, but he also couldn't resist her. She kissed him lightly on the lips, like she was taste-testing a new sweet. Then she pressed herself against his chest, allowing her curves to envelop him. They stayed like that, pressed together for a few minutes, until she got distracted again, and jumped up for a drink of her soda.

This girl was dangerous.

Despite his desire to see Charlotte again after that night, Erwin managed to resist. The last thing he needed was a girl who would cling to him like that when he was so close to returning home. Freya was bad enough. Freya came by the farm a few times, asking for him, but he refused to see her. He felt too guilty for that kiss, and opted for avoidance rather than actually dealing with the situation. By the time he was preparing to board the bus back home, the last thing he expected was Charlotte's father chasing after him.

The broad-shouldered Mr. Tremblay could have passed for a linebacker, even in his forties. A ragtag band of men stood in line, waiting to board the coach, Erwin among them. He wiped the sweat from his brow with a folded handkerchief. The small suitcase stuffed with his belongings felt heavy from the amount of time he had been holding it. From seemingly nowhere, Mr. Trembley hurtled towards him, nearly knocking him to the ground.

"You're not going anywhere, young man!" he shouted. His face shone red with anger.

Erwin barely knew the man, much less what the hell was going on. He tried to scramble away, still clutching his suitcase, as the bus pulled up. After tussling for a good few minutes, Erwin finally escaped the man's grasp. This bus was his last chance to get home or he'd have to wait another week in this godforsaken hillbilly place.

"You're gonna do right by my daughter," Mr. Tremblay huffed, struggling to his feet.

"Your daughter?" Erwin was exhausted and confused.

"Charlotte, you idiot."

"What about her?"

"You got her pregnant."

The other passengers had already boarded by this point. The busdriver, a bearded man with a gruff voice, called out to them. "You coming or no?"

Erwin glared at Mr. Tremblay. "Give me a minute," he shouted over his shoulder. He turned back to Charlotte's father. "She said that?"

"She did," he confirmed. "You were the last one to take her on a date, and if I recall, you brough her back rather late."

Erwin bit his tongue. He wanted to say something snarky about how a girl didn't need to go on a date to get pregnant. He knew Charlotte had been involved with other boys, that he wasn't the only one. He aslo knew he had done nothing that could have possibly gotten her pregnant, so the child couldn't be his. "And she said it was mine?" he managed.

"Are you calling my daughter a liar?"

The bus driver grew aggravated with the delay. "You coming or what?" he asked.

"Guess I'll have to get the next one," said Erwin.

The driver closed the door and the bus pulled away in a cloud of smoke. Both men coughed, trying ineffectually to cover their faces. Mr. Tremblay clapped Erwin on the shoulder, his face softening.

"Come on, let's get back," he said. "We'll get this mess sorted out."

Erwin felt trapped. How could he argue against Charlotte's claims without accusing her of sleeping around? He struggled to think of a way they could both come out of this with their reputations intact, and there was no real way to prove that the baby wasn't his. Not unless it bore no resemblance to him, but even that was doubtful, and it would be months before that could be determined.

The two men made the trip mostly in silence, sitting in the cab of Mr. Tremblay's truck. Erwin cracked his window to let some fresh air in. He reached into his back pocket. "Care for a smoke?" he asked.

"Sounds like a good idea," said Mr. Tremblay, who provided the lighter and rolled down his window as well. "Wish I had a flask handy."

Erwin resisted the urge to laugh. The situation wasn't funny in the least, just awkward as hell. "When we get there," he began, between puffs, "Could I have a few moments to talk to her?"

"Sure thing. I've got to try to calm down the missus. She's more of a wreck than I am. But she'll be better knowing I didn't let you get on that bus."

"I bet."

When they arrived, Mrs. Tremblay was crying over a cup of coffee in the kitchen and Charlotte was hiding in her bedroom.

Mr. Tremblay went in to his wife while Erwin disappeared up-stairs. He found Charlotte in bed, lying facedown in the pil-lows. He sat on the end of the bed and stroked her hair away from her face. Eventually, she rolled over to look up at him.

Her eyes widened for a minute. "It's you," she said eventually.

"It's me." He helped her sit up and reached for her hand. Reluctantly, she let him hold it.

"I thought you were leaving," she said.

"I was. I was ready to get on the bus home and then your father showed up."

"Oh." She wrinkled her nose.

"Oh? What did you tell them, Charlotte? What lies have you been telling?"

She sunk down into the bed again, trying to pull the sheets over her face.

He ripped them from her hands. "You can't hide from this, Charlotte. What did you think would happen?"

Tears sprung from her eyes. "I don't know. When I found out, I didn't know what to do. I said the first thing that came to mind."

"You know it's not mine, right?" he asked, briefly entertain-ing the idea that she was innocent of how human reproduc-tion operated. Maybe she honestly thought it was, maybe she didn't understand. Maybe she wasn't as manipulative as she seemed.

Her cheeks flushed red. "I know that," she said. "I'm not an idiot."

"Then why did you say it was?" He spoke quietly, but with a hard edge. He wanted so badly to shake some sense into her, to yell and scream, but knew her parents were just below and would hear him if he did.

"I don't know."

"What do you mean, you don't know? You just say words without thinking? Without thinking about the repercussions?

You really are a child, Charlotte." He stood and walked to the window, looking out at the maple trees, their leaves dancing in the breeze.

She turned away from him, rolling over in the bed like a petulant schoolgirl faking sick. He looked back at her, so small in the bed, her red curls spread out over the pillows. She was beautiful, but this wasn't what he had wanted. He wasn't ready for this kind of commitment, to live out a lie with a child that wasn't even his. It did make him wonder, though.

"How did you get pregnant?" he asked.

Her voice came to him, muffled and sarcastic. "The usual way."

He grabbed her arm, forcing her to sit up. "This isn't a joke, girl."

She struggled against him, wincing. "Ow, you're hurting me, Erwin."

"Well, good," he replied. "You're hurting me. You're hurting my reputation, trying to ruin my life. I want to know why." His face was inches from hers now, his eyes ablaze with anger.

"I thought you'd be happy," she whispered.

"Happy?" he raged. "In what world would I be happy?" He let go of her arm, letting her drop back against the headboard. "Tell me the truth. What happened, and why am I now suddenly involved."

"Okay, maybe not happy...but I thought you'd be willing to help me. You do like me, don't you?"

"Of course I like you. That's what makes this so difficult."

"There was a man, a friend of my father's," she began. "He had a bit too much to drink."

Erwin's face softened. "Did he take advantage of you?"

"Yes," she finally admitted. "Yes, he did. I couldn't tell. He said goodbye, he was supposed to leave, but he came to my bedroom, instead."

Erwin shook his head. "Say no more, my dear." He pulled her close to him, enveloping her in a hug. He felt a warmth come over him, a sudden, fierce need to protect her, even though the damage had already been done. "I'm sorry," he whispered into her ear. "I am so sorry this happened to you."

Chapter 13

PRESENT DAY

I could tell my brother was listening in by now, because of course he was, but he didn't say a thing.

I had so many questions swirling around in my head, I didn't know where to begin. "But how do you know so much about this?" I asked. "Rumors only go so far. I'm pretty sure they would keep Charlotte's sudden pregnancy more hush hush."

Brandon, using a rag to wipe down the taps, looked over with a knowing wink. "Because the bar is a drunk man's confessional," he explained. "Less religious men need some liquid courage to share their sins, and when they do, they don't care as much who is listening. I don't share the secrets I've heard, but sometimes we've got a crowded bar and a man will start spouting off about a brawl he had years ago, a girl he knocked up, a lost love. You wouldn't believe the things you hear."

Luis leaned across the bar, sipping his coke, still begging for a beer. Eventually I gave in. What harm could one beer do? We played a round of darts and listened to Earl and Dale volley gossip and rumors between them. Brandon humored their crude remarks. Dale joined me for a few rounds of cricket, his aim true and much more advanced than mine. I didn't stand a chance. The darts flew from his hands like trained birds to their designated perches on the board. He played with his own set, rather than the bar darts.

"I think I'm at a disadvantage," I claimed.

"Why are you so curious about Erwin Wilson anyway?" he asked, plucking his darts from the board. At least two had landed solidly in a double and triple mark, the third straight in the bullseye.

I sauntered up to the line, aiming. My first dart sunk in a single 20.

"I'm a writer. It sounds like an interesting story."

"Maybe," he replied. "Just old news around here."

My next two darts went wide, the first barely landing on the board, the second angling toward the floor. I scrambled after them. "Might be interesting to those who don't know, though," I reasoned.

"Erwin did have too many wives, and way too many children," mused Dale.

"So, according to Earl, wife number one was an accident, sort of."

"I suppose you could say that."

"What about the others?" I asked. "I mean, most people don't make the same mistake more than once. At least not intentionally. Do you think he loved Charlotte?"

"Maybe he learned to," said Dale. He shot his final round of darts, beating me soundly, and we returned to our stools at the bar. Luis flipped the TV to a late-night talk show. I punched him in the arm, promising I'd wrap things up soon and we could get back to the cabin for some sleep.

"Or you could buy me another beer," he reasoned, winking at me.

"Kid's got moxie, I'll give him that," commented Brandon from behind the bar.

"Maybe next time, kiddo." I ruffled his hair for good measure. Luis grimaced, but stopped trying.

"But what about the other wives?" I asked, turning back to Dale.

"I heard one was a Russian," offered Dale. "Didn't know a lick of English when she arrived."

"Which wife was she, in the order I mean?" I asked.

"Don't know," said Dale, "but sure was a looker. And a whore."

Chapter 14

KATYA PETROV, 1970

Katya Petrov arrived in America, innocent of the ways of men, wide-eyed and honest, but also without knowing any English other than "Hello" and "Nice meet you." The man who had purchased her kept her hidden from the outside world and she knew little more than the kitchen where she cooked his meals and the bedroom where he raped her nightly. One day, she disobeyed him and before she knew it, she was out on the streets with no money, nothing to eat and nowhere to go. The price of a burned breakfast proved to be steep.

To support herself, she started turning tricks in the alley of Earl's Pub. She would take any cash she could get for servicing the patrons there. No one told because they knew it would get back to their wives that they had been there. One of these patrons was Erwin Wilson.

Erwin, as seemed to be his constant state, was a married man. He had two young boys, who were quickly growing into men. Erwin was no longer a young man, rather a grizzled, nearly-middle-aged lout who spent most of his afternoons drinking while his wife cried over the dishes. She feared for her young boys, Raymond and Delmar, who were only young teenagers, but would soon face the draft. He could do nothing to please her anymore, it seemed, and instead of staying at home with her to watch her grieve the sons she hadn't even lost yet, he left. There was little for him to be happy for. The farm was in a sad state and he could hardly keep it up, even with the help of his sons. Instead, he found solace in drinking and companionship with other unlucky saps at the tap.

One late evening, stumbling out at bar close, Erwin nearly tripped over Katya as she provided oral pleasure to one of the local drunks. He grumbled at her and swore.

"What do you think you're doing down there?" he demanded. "That man doesn't have any money."

She stood, towering over him in her six-inch heels and wiping cum from her lips.

"He pays up front," she explained.

The man, finished with her services, struggled to zip up his pants and ran away down the alley.

"You want?" she asked Erwin. She puckered her lips at him and thrust her breasts in his face. "You like?"

"I have a wife," he grumbled.

"Most do," she urged.

"How did you get here anyway?" he asked. "This ain't exactly the kind of place for girls like you."

"Why do you care?" she asked.

"Just curious."

"Plane." She spat the word out like it tasted bad in her mouth. As if she hadn't tasted other, more foul things just moments ago.

"I've never been on a plane," thought Erwin, out loud.

"Less talk," she said, frustrated. "Blowjob or no?"

He refused her advances and walked home in the dim light of the streetlamps. The several-mile jaunt sobered him a bit, thankfully, but all he could see when he slept that night were her pleading eyes. She looked so dead and empty inside, like the mere husk of a person. He imagined that must be the way she felt, too, living only to service men's most carnal desires.

Given that Erwin frequented Dale's Pub on a nearly daily basis, he often happened upon Katya and her johns, who were also patrons of the pub. Like many of his compatriots, he tried to pretend he didn't see what was happening. The woman had a right to earn money, just like everyone else and just had an unconventional and distasteful way of doing it. Although it may not be legal, she wasn't hurting anyone and the men involved knew what they were getting themselves into. In other words, it was a don't ask, don't tell sort of scenario. Many nights, Katya didn't even enter the establishment, just waited outside. Once the drunk men knew she was there, she didn't exactly need to advertise.

One night, Erwin offered to take out a haul of trash for the bartender, and ran into her leaning against the wall in the alleyway. She wore a skirt so short that you could see the curve of her asscheeks and a shirt so low her breasts were on prominent display. The stiletto heels she wore added a good six or seven inches to her height and her uneven blonde bangs hung into her piercing hazel eyes. At first, she didn't say anything, but as he hoisted the bag of refuse into the dumpster, she made her appeal.

"I remember you," she began. "Man who thinks he's too good for me." She blew a large bubble with the gum she was chewing.

Erwin didn't even look, just dropped the trash bag and turned to head back into the bar.

"Think you're better than your friends?" she asked, strutting toward him.

"I don't think I'm better than anyone," he replied. "I told you, I've got a wife, and I don't cheat."

She smacked her lips, blowing another pink bubble.

He turned to her, popping it with his index finger.

"How old are you?" he asked.

"Old enough," she replied, trying to lick his finger before he could withdraw it. She spat the gum onto the pavement and batted her eyes at him. "How old is your wife?"

"I won't hear you blaspheme her," he said.

"What, is she a Holy Mother?" she asked.

"She's my wife and she deserves some respect."

"Uh huh." She stalked around him like a cat examining its prey before pouncing. "I hear you have many wives."

"I have had a few, yes," he admitted.

She stopped, leaning in so he could catch her scent. She smelled musky, like tobacco and hickory. It was a smell that suddenly overwhelmed him, making him want to reach out and touch her. He felt the excitement rise in him.

"Your wives perform wifely duties?" she asked.

"It's none of your business what I do in the bedroom."

"Oh, but it is!" She placed one long-fingered hand on his bicep. "What happens in bedroom is exactly my business."

He managed to brush her aside, but by the end of the night, when he came stumbling back out that door, she was waiting for him, barely hidden in the shadows. "What's your name, again?" she asked, drawing him to her. "Ernie?"

"Erwin," he replied, not resisting now. He could barely stand up on his own, and leaned heavily against her.

She wrapped her arms around his neck, pulling him in for a long, wet kiss. Her lip gloss tasted like a cherry lollipop. Before he could stop himself, he was kissing her back, drunk with the softness of her lips. She worked her tongue between his teeth and massaged his tonsils with it. Moments later, she unhooked his belt and began with the zipper on his pants.

"For you," she said, as she slid his pants from his hips, "First taste is free. Tough customer." She laughed, throwing her head back for a moment and her thin, white neck shone in the moonlight. She looked suddenly fragile in that moment, like a porcelain vase about to fall and break from a great height. She knelt before him on the pavement, took him into her mouth, and made him forget all of the wives he had ever had.

In the days that followed, she came to him again and again, sometimes even venturing into the pub to lure him out. There were a few times he tried to offer her money, but she would not accept it. He didn't understand the special treatment, but reasoned why pay for something you can get for free. As they became more comfortable with each other, he also became more careless. He would leave home earlier and earlier in the day, on one occasion even stepping out before noon. His wife Hazel had just finished clearing the breakfast table and he was already headed out the door, grabbing his coat and hat from the rack as he went.

"Where are you off to?" Hazel asked. She ran to the sink to start the washing.

"Out," he murmured under his breath, pulling his coat around him.

"Where to so early?" She turned to look at him, her eyes starting to brim with tears.

"Now, don't you do that," he scolded, his voice rising. "Why are you always crying, woman?"

She took a step toward him and thought better of it. Instead, she turned away, slowly moving back to the sink, the familiar movement of washing dishes. After all, this was their routine. He would leave, and she would stay, and she would clean, trying not to cry through it all. She was rarely successful.

"I just wish..." she blubbered. "I wish I knew where you were going."

He paused, let out an exasperated sigh. This woman was getting on his last nerve. He touched her shoulders from behind and she jumped, whimpering like a tiny dog.

"What, do you think I'm going to hit you?" he demanded.

"No, no." Hazel wiped her eyes and returned to the dishes. "Is it so wrong that I want to know where you are? I worry." She didn't look up from the sink this time.

"If you must know, I'm going to Earl's," he said.

"Are they even open yet?"

"If they aren't they will be soon," he replied, and left in a great galumphing rush.

It turned out Hazel was right and he found the door locked. He wasn't there for the booze anyway, the question was whether Katya would be haunting around the place yet. She didn't necessarily keep regular hours, by any means, and he didn't know if she had a place of her own. They didn't exactly talk much, just moans and sighs between breaths, but a thirst burned inside him that only she could quench. The fight with his wife only made him want her more. He walked to the back of the bar and glanced down the alleyway where he usually found her, dolled up and ready for his advances. Always eager, always accommodating, always wet. Even though he knew she still did things with other guys, he felt like she gave him special treatment, that she belonged to him like a loyal pet. But she wasn't there, at least not yet.

He sighed, the hunger boiling in his lower gut, like an aching need that growled to be fed. He ran up and down the alley, looking for any sign of her, a scent, a sigh, a footstep. He even called out her name a few times. Where did she go when she wasn't here? For a moment, he realized that she must go somewhere else to sleep, but where? He turned a corner and finally found her, slumped under an archway with only a cardboard box between her perfect frame and the cold cement. He clutched her to him, and suddenly she seemed so small, so fragile, like a ragdoll thrown away in the corner after she no longer provided amusement.

She slowly woke in his arms, staring up into his face with such amazement that it overwhelmed him. It felt like something sacred, that he had surpassed an unspoken boundary between them.

"Why you here?" she whispered. Her voice was hoarse and broken. As he looked at her more closely, he noticed bruising on her arms and legs, great red welts rising on her limbs.

"What happened?" he asked.

"Big man last night," she slowly explained. "Take what he want for no pay."

"Oh, Katya," he moaned, looking up and down the street, as if the man were still lurking somewhere there in the shadows. "Who was it?"

"Don't know," she said. "Was dark. Couldn't see him."

"He just left you like this?" he asked. He hugged her small frame to him like she was an injured child, not a prostitute. He brushed her hair from her face and examined her again. The man must have raped and beaten her. No woman deserved that kind of treatment - no man should steal what isn't freely given. Tears welled up in his eyes, seeing her so incredibly broken. Before he could help her to her feet, he heard footsteps down the alley and pulled her further into the alcove. Who could that possibly be?

Then a familiar voice. It was Hazel. "Erwin? Are you there?" she called after him. She sounded scared, panicked.

Erwin tried to slow his breath, but his heart raced as he still held Katya. If Hazel should find them, it would mean the end of everything. On some level, he loved both women, but surely, Hazel would leave him if she found out about Katya.

With every step Hazel took toward them, he felt his heart beating in his throat. Just when he thought she might turn back, Katya let out a low moan. Erwin hushed her, placing his hand over her mouth. She struggled against him, pushing him rolling out into the alleyway.

Hazel gasped. "Erwin!" She ran for him, bending down over his body. "Erwin! Are you alright?"

He put his hands over his head, shielding his face from her. He hoped beyond hope that she wouldn't see Katya hiding just a few feet away.

"What is it?" Hazel asked. "What are you doing out here? I was so worried, I just couldn't." She reached for him. "I just had to find you." Then she turned and noticed the other woman, mangled and broken on the ground. "Who - who's that?"

Erwin tried lying. "I don't know. I found her like that."

Hazel moved to try and help Katya and the woman pushed her away, nearly scratching her face.

"I don't need your help, bitch!" shouted Katya. She scrambled to her feet and started limping down the alleyway. "Go home to your wife, Ernie," she nearly screamed. Erwin could hear her sobbing as she pushed herself along, one hand dragging along the wall.

"She seems to know you," accused Hazel, staring after Katya. Her face was a question that didn't need to be asked.

Now it was Erwin's chance to make a decision. To either continue to live the lie he had been living or chase after Katya. In a moment of dumb bravery, he opted for the latter. He called after Katya and left his wife there, on her knees in the alleyway, as rain began to fall from dark clouds. A few months later, their marriage was dissolved and he took Katya as his new bride. They moved a state away to escape the rumor mill and he was able to provide for her financially, if not emotionally.

Chapter 15

PRESENT DAY

"You weren't kidding were you?" I said to Brandon when Earl was through.

"Anything can come out after a few drinks," he agreed. "Good thing the little one here was sleeping, huh?" He motioned to Luis who was snoring away, his head propped up on the bar. I smiled warmly, ruffled his hair and woke him up. He snorted and straightened, looking around like he didn't know where he was.

"Come on, buddy," I urged. "Let's get you to bed."

On the ride back to the cabin, he dozed a little more, then came awake with questions. "What are you doing out here, anyway?"

"I'm trying to write a book."

The car moved slowly along the gravel drive, which diminished to dirt and dust. I took us around a few hairpin turns as the forest gathered around us.

"What kind of book?" he asked. "The last one you wrote was a real smash."

I picked up on the sarcasm in his voice. "I've already told my story so I'm trying to tell someone else's," I explained.

"Uh huh. This Wilson guy."

"You betcha," I replied. "Can you believe he had twenty-three wives?" I tried for a tone of excitement but honestly, we were both very tired by this point.

"Who cares?"

"I do! And by the time I'm done I hope my reader will, too!"

Luis just grumbled and leaned against the door, staring out the passenger-side window into the dark. I didn't expect much of a response, but I tried a few questions of my own anyway.

"So, why are you here? What happened."

"Nothing," he muttered. "I just can't stand those kids. Oh my god, little boys are the worst."

"They can be rough," I admitted. "But you were supposed to be working. Does anyone know where you are?"

"No."

I smacked him upside the head.

"What was that for?" he demanded, sneering back at me.

"They must be worried sick! I'll make a few phone calls tomorrow"

"Please don't make me go back."

"I'm here trying to work. You can't just show up out of nowhere expecting me to take care of you!"

"I can take care of myself. Besides, I didn't know you were here, if you remember."

"Seems a little too convenient, if you ask me."

He didn't respond, just stared off into space. We rode the rest of the way back to the cabin in a strained silence. The only noise came from chirping crickets and stray branches hitting against the sides of the car. When we arrived, he slunk off to bed, while I sat up. I tried to jot down every detail I could remember from the conversations I had at Earl's Pub, noting that they were drunken conversations and their veracity could only be taken with a grain of salt. Eventually, I passed out on one of the armchairs in the living room.

In the middle of the night, I was awoken by a scuffling, flapping noise. I sat up abruptly and looked around. There was very little light in the room, but as my eyes adjusted, I caught sight of something flying to and fro across the ceiling. It fluttered around the windows, then circled back toward me, swooping down toward my head, then back up to the ceiling. I fumbled for a light switch and saw a bat clinging to the top of one of the windows. It swooped around again, flapping frantically, and I screamed bloody murder. I scrambled for the closet door, pulling out a broom and began swatting at it. I didn't have a plan, per se, just to knock it out of the air, but everytime it came close to me, I let out a screech. With it clear in my sights, I swiped at it, missing. As I backed up, I bumped into something, or rather someone and jumped out of my skin.

Luis laughed. "What do you think you're doing?" He snatched the broom from me and moved to open the front door.

I was still shaken from my scare. "I don't know," I admitted. "I have no idea what I'm doing."

Luis shushed me, turned off the light and stepped out on the porch. "Got a flashlight?" he asked.

"Why?"

"It probably got in through a small opening or something, chasing after bugs. If you've got a light we might be able to lure some moths out here."

I stumbled around in the dark for a minute before producing a flashlight from the kitchen. I handed it to Luis, who turned it on and walked out to the porch. I joined him. He set the flashlight up on the far side of the porch, stood it on end until it had collected a few curious moths. We sat on the porch swing and waited. After a few minutes, the bat finally found its way out of the living room, swooping in for some winged snacks.

"Where'd you learn that from?" I asked.

"Been camping a few times with the scouts."

"At least you're good for something." I hugged Luis and he actually let me squeeze him for a moment. "I'll put you to work yet."

After picking up a few insects, the bat flew off and we returned to the cabin. Luis returned to his bunk and I finally crawled into bed. I suppose having him around wouldn't be so bad, afterall.

Chapter 16

The next morning, before Luis woke up, I dialed our mother. At the very least, I felt the need to tell her about Luis, but it had been months since we had spoken. After the first few rings, I almost chickened out, but then I heard a voice on the other end of the line.

"Yes? Who is this?" my mom asked.

"It's Lizzie."

"Eh?" Mom had started losing her hearing recently. You had to practically shout for her to hear you properly.

"It's your daughter, Lizzie."

There was a long silence.

"You mean the woman who tore my family to shreds?" Mom asked.

"Mama..."

"The one who told the whole world her mother had children out of wedlock and then called her sister a whore?"

"I never called Maria a whore."

"You might as well have."

I waited for more lambasting. I had expected harsh words but not quite this harsh.

"No daughter of mine would say such things."

"Listen, Mama." I struggled to get a word in edgewise.

"I'm no mama of yours. You are a disgrace to this family and I wish you had never been born."

I tried a different tact. "I just wanted to let you know Luis is with me."

"Luis? My baby! You stole him from me, too?!"

"No, Mama. He just showed up yesterday afternoon, but he's here, safe with me."

"Likely story."

"He's going to stay with me for the summer. I'll put him to work."

"Doing what? Spreading more lies? Great influence you'll be. He's supposed to be working for real money as a counselor at that camp." Mama exasperatedly sighed into the phone. "He's a hoodlum, anyway. Good riddance."

"Mama, don't write him off just because you're mad at me."

"Mad doesn't even begin to describe - sure, fine, you'll be in good company." She slammed the handset down. Even now, when so many people had switched to cell phones, she maintained a home phone, attached to the wall with a long spiral cord. At least this phone gave her the satisfaction of truly "hanging up," not just swiping to end the call.

I didn't know what I had expected. The last time I had spoken with my mother, it had been over Christmas dinner with little eating but a lot of arguing, that ended in yelling and slamming doors and oaths against one another. I was surprised at the negative reaction toward Luis, though. Maybe he had gotten into some other trouble I didn't know about. As long as he proved helpful, though, I was willing to make do with him as my assistant. Maybe it would prove a good experience for him. I climbed back up to the loft to awaken him, promising fresh pancakes as a reward for getting his butt out of bed. I didn't tell him about the phone call. They could always hash things out later.

As soon as we walked through the door at the Deep Dish Diner, Darlene greeted us with a wide smile, clutching a stack of menus to her ample bosom.

"Who might this handsome young fella be?" she asked.

I provided introductions and we settled into one of the cushioned booths. As promised, I ordered a tall stack of pancakes for us both. Luis' were chocolate chip. Even as a growing boy, he could appreciate a good chocolate chip pancake.

Darlene bustled about, serving up coffee for us. Luis took his with both cream and sugar and I, as per usual, took mine black.

"I heard you two made a visit to Earl's," tittered Darlene.

"That was just last night," I remarked. "Word sure gets around!"

"Maybe not as fast as you think," admitted Darlene. "I stopped out for a nightcap after cleaning up."

"Ok, good. Don't need that rumor getting back to my mama!" I joked.

"How would it?" asked Luis. He didn't seem to get the joke.

"Just saying, she's already mad as hell at me as it is."

"Did you talk to her?" he asked, swirling his spoon through his coffee. It was a light brown now, more cream than coffee, really.

"Yeah, I gave her a ring to let her know where you were."

"Did you have to?" he asked.

"Yeah, you're still a minor, buddy. Didn't want the camp calling the cops reporting a missing person or kidnapping or any of that nonsense."

"I'm not a little kid, Lizzie."

"Doesn't matter, you're my kid brother and I thought she might be worrying about you. Besides, it's not like she's going to come chasing after you. You know she doesn't like driving, much less hours away."

It was true. Though they had a family car, Mama rarely drove in the city. She claimed she couldn't stand the traffic and the rudeness of other drivers. Besides, who needed to drive when you could just take public transportation?

I tried to focus my attention on my coffee, letting the bitter brew soothe my sore throat. Hydrating with some actual water probably wouldn't hurt, either. I tried to look on the brighter side of things, at least now I wasn't alone and would have someone to bounce ideas off of, even if my brother didn't want to fully participate in the research. We ate in awkward silence when the pancakes arrived.

"So, what do you want to do today?" I asked, eventually.

"Not much to do, is there?" he replied.

"I suppose not."

Darlene jumped into the conversation. "You could head over to Weston. They've got a few new shops out that way, you could go antiquing!"

"Antiquing?" Luis scoffed. "Do I look like a middle-aged gay man to you?"

Darlene just stared.

"Luis! Mind your manners," I scolded. "Nevermind my brother, Darlene, he grew up in a barn."

"I mean, Jesus was born in a manger," countered Darlene.

I paused.

"Do you know what a manger is?" she asked. "Needless to say, it's in a barn."

"I meant no offense," I said.

Darlene laughed. "I'm just joshing you. Can I get you two anything else?"

"Some sanity?" my brother asked.

As we walked out of the diner, I considered a game plan for the day. "Tell you what," I started. "How about we head to Weston, check out the town, maybe do a little research. I think they have an academic library worth visiting."

"Sounds like fun," Luis said sarcastically.

"I'll call Michael on the way, let him know my progress."

"Could I listen to the radio instead?"

I acquiesced and soon my ears were being bombarded by a string of half-songs and talk-radio as Luis scrolled through the dial. The scenery at least was gorgeous, more rolling hills and green horizons that stretched out as far as we both could see. It took a good half hour to get to Weston, and the first thing I did when we got there was follow the signs to the community college.

Chapter 17

We walked up to the circulation desk so I could see what reference materials were available. The librarian assured me there were newspaper clippings going back several decades all scanned to microfiche for posterity.

"I suppose I should tell you I'm neither faculty nor a student," I hazarded.

She pushed her spectacles up from the tip of her nose. "You do realize this is an academic, not a public library?" she asked.

Luis snickered.

"I was hoping for limited access. Maybe for a fee?" I pulled open my purse and began rummaging through it for my wallet.

"I might be able to set you up with some sort of guest pass. Will you be in the area for any length of time? We have a monthly subscription for $100."

I gasped and Luis laughed again. "For a library?" he asked. "What kind of crock is this?" Then he turned to me. "Hey, sis, gonna turn tricks for a library card?"

My cheeks grew hot and it was everything I could do to not slap him.

"I'm out," he shouted, throwing one hand up in the air and strutting toward the door.

I chased after him. "Don't you dare embarrass me like that!"

"Well, that shits ridiculous."

"Regardless, there's no need to be disrespectful."

"You're not my mother."

"No, and you should be glad I'm not. I would've slapped you down right then and there."

"Really?"

I paused and continued walking down the sidewalk in silence.

"Really, Lizzie?" He looked so innocent now, like the little brother I remembered tagging after me when I was a teenager and didn't want to spend time with him.

"Probably not," I admitted.

"That's right, sis. You're too much of a chicken." Then he was back to the bravado act.

"You want to grab a bite to eat? I'll call my agent and see if he can help out with the library fees."

"Fine. They got ramen in this joint?"

"I don't think so."

We settled for a corner sandwich shop where the fanciest thing you could find was a BLT and while Luis scarfed his food down I called Michael. I knew I sounded desperate but sometimes that's what a girl needs, not just emotional support, but a little financial help. Despite Luis' joke about turning tricks, we both knew I would never sink to that, especially not for the purposes of acquiring library services.

"Show me the money!" shouted Michael into my ear.

"Heh. Funny you should say that," I replied.

"Why's that?"

"That's exactly what I need."

"You're asking for an advance?" he asked.

"Well, not exactly."

I explained the scenario of obtaining library access - for a fee. He was surprisingly understanding and only asked me to describe, in great detail, exactly what I would need.

"It sounds like you could use an advance," he offered.

"Explain."

"Well, the publisher wouldn't give you one the first time around because you were up-and-coming, not a sure bet yet. This time, you might be able to get some spending money up front, as long as it relates to your research. This would also be with the promise that you will be writing something for me, and soon."

"I get it. So sort of like a loan?"

"Not really. This money comes at no cost to you, but it is being given in good faith. That is, with the expectation that you will be producing another great book in the coming months and that we get rights to it, blah blah blah."

"Of course. I really think I've got some solid leads here. I'm not quite sure exactly where it's going yet, but that's why I need to do some in depth research."

"You get 'em, girl!"

Michael's enthusiasm helped spark my own ambition. We agreed upon the terms of my advance, as well as an initial deadline for my first few chapters. That would mean these copious notes I had taken would need to get translated into real writing, and soon. However, every little bit would help the journey, especially the apparent library research fees I now had to contend with.

"Is there any possibility you could wire me some of the money right away?" I asked, hoping for the best.

"Sure thing, sweet cheeks," he replied, making me blush despite myself. "The official funds should go through in about a week, but I can electronically send over some to keep you afloat in the meantime. How much do you need?"

"Is this straight from your pocket?" I asked.

He admitted it was. We spent a few minutes arguing over whether it was overstepping for me to take his money, rather than the publisher's, but he insisted. By the time the conversation ended, he had transferred a few hundred directly into my checking account.

"Thank you so much, again, Mike. I don't know what I'd do without you," I said.

"No worries. You've got this."

Well, at least, I had the money to make it happen.

Luis and I returned to the community college library, and I laid a several crisp twenties on the desk in front of the librarian. She eyed me, running her eyes over me like I had done something nefarious to obtain the funds, and then had me fill out and sign some forms.

"Will your boyfriend join you?" she asked, glancing briefly in Luis' direction.

"My brother, yes," I replied.

"The monthly pass is only for one person."

Luis snickered at my sigh. I shushed him and laid more bills on the desk. Once she issued our guest passes, she led us to the third floor where the archives were housed.

As it turned out, the Weston Community College library housed microfiche images of the Crawford County Gazette dating back to the early 1900s. The librarian showed us where the film was housed, in labeled boxes along the back wall, and how to load the microfiche machine. She pulled the front handle of the machine to load it, checking that the glass plate was centered for viewing. She unrolled some of the film from a spool, threaded it through the machine and hooked it into the opposite side. Then, she explained how to use an application on the computer to skim through the film, resize the image for viewing, and scan individual articles.

"Is there any way to search for specific articles?" asked Luis.

"Unfortunately, no," she explained. "This is pretty old school, you have to look through everything. But, if you have a general idea of the dates you need, or the type of article, it might narrow your search a little."

"We need to go all the way back to 1935," I explained. "We'll be looking primarily at wedding announcements."

"Do you have a better idea of a specific date? That might help," she offered.

"Not really."

"Well, let me know if you need any help finding what you need, but without much more information it might be hard to find specific articles."

"I know."

When she walked away, I caught Luis staring at her ass and scoffed.

"What?" he asked. "I got a thing for sexy librarians."

We both grabbed a box of film and set up our stations.

"We're gonna be here all afternoon, aren't we?" he asked.

"It's likely," I replied.

The work proved incredibly tedious. At least we could skip ahead to the marriage announcements of each paper, so that saved a little bit of time. On a yellow notepad, I started to compile a list of each of Mr. Wilson's marriages. With the listing came the woman's maiden name, which may prove helpful. I couldn't just search for every Wilson in the phonebook and hope for the best. The announcements also included the towns in which he was married. As I had suspected, many were in Orchard Square or even Weston. At least he hadn't traveled all over the country to marry all those women. With Luis begrudgingly helping me, I started to create a more cohesive timeline, as well as a few notes regarding why he had married each woman - that part would take a bit longer to fill in. I also calculated the age of Mr. Wilson at the time of each marriage.

It seemed that he had a new wife every year or two. The longest wives he had managed to hang on to were Hazel, who he was married to for thirteen years, followed by Melanie (7 years), Laura Bianci and Valerie Thomas (both 5 years) and Miriam Cohen (4 years). If I could talk to any of these women, maybe they could provide some insight regarding the nature of the man. Given all of the near-overlap though, I wondered if he wasn't dating several women on the side at the same time that he was married. I also wondered who had initiated the divorce in each case. Unlike wedding announcements, people don't often advertise their divorces, so the reasoning wasn't as clear. Also, given the number of children listed in Mr. Wilson's obituary - did he have children with all of these women?

Against Luis' protests, we then turned to the phone books and looked up every name for the Orchard Square and Weston wives - searching under Wilson. We didn't expect to find them all, but managed to find a few: Stella and Natalie in Weston, as well as Laura. I would continue to ask around Orchard Square for anything anyone knew, but memories from a second-hand source were just that, second-hand and couldn't always be trusted. I was starting to build a pretty convincing case, though, that Mr. Erwin Wilson was skilled at breaking hearts. But like most things in life, I realized it was likely more complicated than that.

Chapter 18

Before returning to Orchard Square, we swung by the super Walmart to buy a few fishing rods, as well as bait. I couldn't remember the last time I had been fishing, but Luis seemed to know what he was doing, or at least pretended to know. When we got back, we sat out on the dock, casting our lines out into Oatmeal Lake. I warned Luis about the thick mud that gave Oatmeal Lake its name and he promised to be careful should he decide to go swimming out in it.

I opened a beer, took a long swig, and propped my rod up against the cooler. Luis reached for a beer of his own and I swatted him away.

"You let me have one at the bar," he complained.

"That was a freebie," I offered. "Don't learn to count on it."

He finished affixing a wriggling worm to his hook and cast his line. His stretched out much further than mine. "I provided free labor all day," he complained. "You owe me."

"I also bought you breakfast and lunch."

The sun was starting to reach the tops of the trees as we sat and a cool breeze blew across the lake. I could feel myself drifting, my eyes fluttering closed, then open again. Rather than fishing, I would much rather lie in a hammock right now, let the cool air rock me to sleep. It had been a long day and a long drive back. I would be glad to finally rest when the sun set.

"Tell me more about why you're here," I ventured as I stretched out in my lawn chair.

"Can I have a beer?" asked Luis.

"Fine," I gave in. "But just one."

"Score." Luis reached in the cooler and popped the top of a can. He chugged and then let out a massive belch.

"I can see you've been working on your manners."

"Whatever." He gulped the rest of it down, crumpled the can under his heel and moved to toss it out into the water, until I grabbed his arm to stop him.

"Littering, too, I see."

He lowered his hand and dropped the can into the cooler amongst the ice, a few more brews and some bottled water. He burped again, and this time it echoed off across the lake.

"Careful," I warned. "You'll scare the fish away."

"I'd be surprised if we caught any anyway," he complained. "The best time is early morning."

"You want to get up before dawn just to fish?" I asked.

We sat in silence for a moment before I tried again. "So fess up, kid, what's been going on with you?"

He fidgeted with his pole for a minute, reeled the line in and recast into another spot. "I told you, I just needed some space."

"Why?"

"Why did you leave home?" he asked, turning it around on me.

"You got a free beer, you owe me some answers first."

He sighed. If we weren't already fishing, he'd probably walk away from me and leave the conversation incomplete - just unanswered questions spreading out into silence, like the ripples of dragonflies landing briefly on the lake and then hovering away.

"Hmm?" I hummed at him.

"Fine, you really want to know?"

I nodded enthusiastically, my head bobbing.

"After you left, Ma wouldn't leave me alone. It was like all her attention was on me all of a sudden."

"That makes sense." I sat up. "You were the last kid in the house."

"I mean, yeah I was, but I was so used to her just ignoring me. You used to be the problem child."

I laughed. "I haven't been a child for a while now."

"I know, but you were still living at home at least. Why'd you have to leave?"

"You think she would've let me stay? After what I did?"

"I guess that's true."

We sat for a moment, silent. I guess we weren't ready to talk about the why and how of my leaving. It felt like the right thing to do at the time, but now, somehow, I felt like I had abandoned him and that the entire situation was somehow my fault.

I started to say I was sorry when my bobber dipped what must be a great big fish bit and started dragging my pole into the water. I chased after it, scrambling and then yanking the pole backward. Luis laughed at me goodnaturedly, throwing his head back. I began reeling it in, the pole bending downward as I strained against the fish's strength. It continued to pull on the hook, dragging down the line. Then the weight fell off my pole and it was clear the fish had gotten away, taking the bait with it. I swore, took a moment to stomp my feet in anger and defeat, then begged him to load my hook with another worm.

"At least I'm good for something," he said.

"So explain it to me. I get that you didn't want to be home with Ma. But what happened at the camp?" I cast my line back out into the water. The sun was steadily getting lower. If we didn't catch anything for dinner, we'd be eating a pizza I had stuffed in the back of the freezer.

"I wanted to get a new job, maybe working at the shop with our cousin Marcos."

"Working on cars?" I asked. "I thought Ma *wanted* you to work over the summer."

"She did, but she wants me to save money for college. And she didn't want me around Marcos, so I wound up here."

"And you don't want to go to college now?" I asked.

"Not if I can't afford it. Not if I can make more money with Marcos."

"So instead of talking it out, you took the job at with the Scouts and then abandoned it?"

Luis' bobber finally dipped below the surface of the water. The fish were biting at the least opportune times. Maybe he'd be able to keep his on the line, though. As he reeled it in, I could see he had a small bluegill, hardly enough for a few bites. He unhooked the fish, smiling sheepishly.

I shook my head and told him to throw it back. It wasn't worth the effort of deboning and cooking, much less eating. We would eat the frozen pizza instead. We abandoned our perch and put away our gear, as the sun lit the sky with a mosaic of oranges, purples and reds.

"If we wake up early enough," I promised. "We can try again in the morning."

"You plan on waking up early?" he asked.

"What do you think?" I knew I wouldn't. I had a long night ahead of me, mapping out my plan of attack for interviewing some of the women we had researched. But I had to admit eating something other than diner food, sandwiches and pizza would be a nice change. At least I had remembered to pick up some coffee grounds and we could have fresh coffee without needing to stop at The Deep Dish.

"I have a proposal for you," I offered.

"Ew, you want to marry me? I'm your brother?!" Luis joked.

"No, weirdo." I lugged the cooler while he perched both poles on his shoulder. "I think we should split up tomorrow. We'll cover more ground that way."

"You trust me with interviews?" He looked excited at the prospect, despite his best efforts to appear nonchalant. After setting the poles on the porch, he followed me inside with a slight spring in his step.

"Yeah, I'll write up some questions, but I think you can handle it." I reached in my purse, pulling out a small tape recorder. "And I found this - take notes, but you can use it and I can play everything back."

"Cool," he admitted. "Will it earn me another beer?"

"No, but I might list you in the Acknowledgements when all is said and done and published, alright?"

"I mean, I guess that works. It's a deal." We shook on it.

After our dinner of pepperoni pizza and Cokes, I referred to my chronological list of wives and the ones we had found contact information for. We had one in Orchard Square and a few in Weston to speak with, assuming they would agree to speak with us. Given that we didn't know much about the women in Weston, I decided to craft a sort of questionnaire to help Luis out. He would introduce himself as my assistant, not my brother, ask some probing questions to get the conversation started and then have a conversation with each woman. I would call them first thing in the morning and see what we could arrange. Many of them were likely older and retired at this point, so we wouldn't have to worry about scheduling around a work schedule or anything of that sort.

After Luis crawled up to bed, I jotted down some notes, as well as the following questions for his reference in the interviews he would conduct: How did you meet Erwin Wilson? Can you describe your relationship with Erwin both before and after marrying him? What led to your divorce? Were you in contact with him after the divorce? Overall, how would you describe Erwin Wilson - as a man, a husband, a father?

The following morning, I called all of the women to arrange interviews. I was able to reach Stella and Natalie, who agreed to meet with us together. Apparently, the two women were still friends with each other, although they were married and divorced from the same man. Needless to say, I found that convenient but a bit odd. The first I spoke to was Stella, who mentioned she was going to lunch with Natalie and would like to interview her as well. We made a lunch date and I told them I would be bringing along my assistant Luis if they would be willing to speak about Mr. Wilson both together and apart. Stella agreed and I contacted Natalie to confirm this arrangement. Both women seemed strangely excited about the prospect. Unlike Freya, they appeared to have no ill will toward Erwin and were relatively amicable about the entire arrangement. I also left a message for Laura, who didn't answer. I hoped she would call back in the next few days.

Luis chewed on a buttery slice of toast while I made my calls and sipped at my scalding coffee. By the time I finished, the final dregs had gone cold and I poured myself a warm-up. Luis seemed to be intrigued by the way I talked to these women on the phone.

"I hope you were listening, sir," I announced. "You'll be on your own this afternoon."

"I got this," he boasted.

"Uh-huh," I responded. "We'll see."

Chapter 19

We loaded into the car and set off for Weston. On the way, Luis practiced first by reading over the questions I had written the night before and then we both practiced grilling one another.

"Where did you first meet Erwin Wilson?" he asked me.

I spoke in a silly, nasally voice. "We met at work. I was his secretary."

"I see. Was he married when you met him?" Luis prodded.

"He was! But he loved me so very much." I made swooning noises, oohing and ahhing for dramatic effect.

"Did you have an affair?" Luis tried.

"I wouldn't call it an affair," I added. "We were in loooooove." I stretched the word out as long as my breath could manage.

"Ew," remarked Luis.

I reached over to squeeze his shoulder. "Remember, no matter what they say, no judgment. You want them to keep talking. Act like you're interested, even if you're not."

"Fine," he replied, then returned to reporter-mode. "When did you first realize he loved you?"

"When he brought me flowers. They were soooo beautiful, and he told me I was beautiful, too," I continued.

"Did he leave his wife for you?"

"Of course he did. We were in lurve..."

"Lurve?" asked Luis. "You've got to be kidding me. What's lurve?"

"Well, there's love and then there's *lurve*." Now we were just two siblings teasing each other again, rather than roleplaying interviews.

"I don't get it."

"Lurve is like - more than love." I had made this up on-the-spot but the logic seemed to follow. "Fine, my turn."

Luis leaned back and cleared his throat, preparing to put on his "feminine falsetto" voice.

Now I asked the questions. "How would you describe Erwin Wilson?" I tried.

"Oh, he was a looker," began Luis. "Real tall, reaal handsome. I wanted to jump his bones!"

I laughed, despite myself.

"Where did you meet him?"

"Me? Oh, I was a dancer then. He came to see me dance," crooned Luis.

"What kind of dancing did you do?"

"What do they call it - exotic? Yeah, I was an exotic dancer."

"I see, and Erwin was a customer of yours?"

"Yes, gave me great tips and everything," said Luis, his voice rising an octave higher.

"You're a little too good at this," I remarked.

"I mean, I do have two sisters," he reminded me.

"I guess that's true. So what do you think? What was Mr. Wilson's deal?"

"I think he couldn't keep it in his pants."

Based on what I had heard so far, I tended to agree. No matter what excuse the man gave, he seemed to have a wandering eye that could not be tamed. Even with Melanie's depiction of him as a kind and generous man, he had still married a woman nearly sixty years his junior. That just wasn't normal behavior for an old man. Hopefully after we interviewed a few more of his wives, we'd get closer to the truth.

We met with Stella DeVries and Natalie Bernard at a local lunch joint called Frenchie's that served primarily paninis, salads and soups. Stella and Natalie both ordered the all-you-can-eat soup & salad combo, which Stella explained was their weekly Friday tradition. Luis and I both ordered paninis. I thanked both women for their time and briefly explained I was writing an expose on Erwin Wilson and would like their input.

"Why are you so interested?" asked Stella. She wore wide-rimmed glasses with red cat-eye frames that nearly took up her entire face.

"I'm interested in human stories," I explained. "What people do and why they do it."

"Alright," said Stella. "I get that. But why him? He really wasn't that exciting."

"Not exciting? He had twenty-three wives!"

Stella's eyes grew wide. "He made it to twenty-three?" she exclaimed. "My goodness. I didn't realize there were so many of us!"

Natalie nodded along, her long silver-haired herringbone braid cascaded down her back, but started to shake loose with the movement. "We were number five and six, I think," she added.

"I've spoken with his most recent wife, as well as one of his childhood loves," I explained.

"What's the most recent one look like?" asked Stella.

"She's young," I admitted. "But claims he was a kind and generous man."

"Kind and generous," Stella scoffed. "Right. Must've softened a bit in his old age."

"If you ladies don't mind," I explained. "My assistant Luis and I would like to interview you separately, and then come back together for some more general questions. Would that be alright with you?"

"Sure," said Stella. "Why not?"

"I'm fine with that," agreed Natalie. "Which one of you wants to talk to me? Stella's more of a talker than I am," she added.

Given that Stella would likely open up more, I passed her off to Luis and explained he would be using a tape recorder as well. "Fine by me," she agreed, and the two of them moved to another table a few feet away. I fixed Natalie in my gaze and tried to get her to open up, but she was a bit of a walnut in the fact that she was old and wrinkled, and a tough nut to crack.

I asked a few probing questions to get her started, such as was she friends with Stella prior to meeting Mr. Wilson, had they been friends throughout their marriages, etc. The first thing she did was pull a photo from her purse and show me the two of them carousing, both of them laughing and wearing fluffy fur coats. They seemed to be enjoying themselves, and living in the very lap of luxury.

"One thing Erwin Wilson did was take care of us," she explained. "At least financially."

Chapter 20

NATALIE BERNARD, 1974

Natalie Bernard and Stella DeVries had been best friends since the second grade when an oversized bully tugged on Natalie's braids. When she heard Natalie screaming from across the playground, Stella rushed over and stomped on the toe of the boy's shoe until he winced and cried "uncle". From then on the two girls were inseparable, Stella often taking charge when Natalie shied away from more challenging and dangerous tasks. Stella was the first to wear makeup, the first to kiss boys, and the first to know about and claim she had sex. Natalie, however, excelled at smoothing things over when Stella caused waves, and always managed to coerce Stella's parents to shorten her sentences whenever she got grounded. Natalie's parents were stricter and required an earlier curfew, but Stella would always show up, just after Natalie was supposed to have gone to bed, and sneak her out through the window.

One night, the two girls snuck out to meet up with Stella's new boyfriend and his friend, who she tried to set Natalie up with. While Stella always seemed so pretty and almost excessively confident with boys, Natalie could barely muster up the courage to talk with anyone she had a crush on. Stella reassured her, saying that her boyfriend's friend could serve as "practice" and it didn't matter if she screwed up with him. The boys went to a different school so they couldn't cause much trouble for them anyway.

Natalie thought Brian was cute, but not nearly as cute as her current crush, Danny. For the night, however, he would suffice. The four teens piled into Paul's car. Paul and Stella had been dating for a few months and were always sucking face and necking in the back of Paul's car. Stella admitted she dated him mostly for the car, the fact he was three years older and didn't go to their school. She liked the excitement of dating an older boy and the anonymity of not dating someone they went to school with.

"Come on, Nat," Stella urged, as she piled into the front seat between Paul and Brian. "You can sit on Brian's lap. I'm sure he won't mind."

"Can we just sit in the back?" Natalie begged.

"Oh, feeling frisky already?" Paul teased.

"That's not what I meant," she whined.

"Cool it, Nat. He's just kidding. Sure, me and Paul in the front, then. Brian, will you accompany Miss Virgin in the back?"

"You're a virgin?" Brian asked as he slipped in next to her. She could feel the heat of his leg against hers.

"Of course not," she lied, and Paul drove off into the night.

He parked the boat of a car on the outskirts of town. There were few lights out here and you could see the stars stretching as far as the eye could reach. Stella wasn't very interested in stars, though. She quickly crawled atop Paul's lap and they started kissing.

Natalie turned to Brian, feeling a bit uncomfortable. They had just met, afterall. He grabbed her hand and they moved up to the other front seat. As they did so, Paul laid his seat back and Stella reached down for the zipper of his pants. Natalie tried not to notice them. She sat sideways on Brian's lap rather than straddling him. He leaned in to kiss her neck and a tingle ran down her spine. Then he moved on to her ear, sucking and nibbling. She could feel the wetness of his saliva dripping down into her ear and shook her head. It sloshed around like a "wet willy" she would get from her older brother. She grimaced, feeling entirely turned off by the thought.

"Are you alright?" asked Brian.

"Not really," she admitted.

Stella and Paul were fumbling with their clothes, trying desperately to get certain parts of their bodies fitting together just so without getting entirely naked. Paul moaned with desire and perhaps a bit of exasperation. Stella lifted her skirt, pulling her panties to the side and mounting him, letting out a sudden gasp as they made contact.

Natalie looked away, blushing furiously. Brian didn't seem to notice, or at the least, didn't mind what was happening. "I'm not -" Natalie blurted out.

"We can just make out if you want," Brian offered.

"Sure," she agreed. "Just lay off the ears, alright?"

Brian pulled her closer, his lips pressing against hers, and then forcefully pushed his tongue into her mouth. Everything about it felt rushed and rough. There was nothing soft or gentle about the way he held her. As she tried to pull away, he grabbed her left breast and squeezed hard. He finally abandoned her mouth and began nibbling on her neck, then her chest. She cried out in pain.

"You like that?" he asked.

Natalie looked over to where Stella was thrusting her hips rhythmically against Paul, the two of them moaning and gasping in pleasure. She felt strangely turned on and jealous of their lovemaking, but repulsed at the same time. She had never seen people have sex before and there was something so animalistic about it - unsightly and strange. Brian realized she wasn't giving him much attention and then followed her gaze to the other couple.

"You like to watch?" he asked.

"No, no," mumbled.

He pushed her hand down toward his lap and she could feel him, hard and almost pulsing with desire for her. She gasped, a little excited but mostly scared. This wasn't the way the night was supposed to go. They were supposed to be going for a drive. Apparently, that meant something different to the rest of them. She had clearly misunderstood.

"No," she said again, trying to extricate herself from Brian's grasp.

"Don't play hard to get," he teased.

"No, stop," she said, a bit louder this time.

"Stop what?" he asked.

"Just stop," she tried again. This time, she pulled away and reached for the door handle. Thankfully, he didn't try to stop her. She managed to climb off his lap and scramble out of the car.

"Natalie, wait." He followed her for a step or two but then she began to run.

Her legs felt numb, but she somehow managed to move them. She pushed herself forward, nearly tripping on the gravel as she began to run. The air caught in her lungs and all she could do was move as fast as she could, arms and legs pumping in time to her gasping breath. The tall grass ripped against her and she made it halfway down the hill before she had to stop.

She nearly fell forward, her head down with her hands on her knees, gasping for breath. She couldn't go back. Not now that she had made a complete fool of herself. Instead, she started walking. By the time she made it back to her house, the sun was starting to rise and she knew she'd be in all kinds of trouble. Instead of Stella, she'd be the one grounded this time, but at the same time, she was glad she hadn't let Brian go any further. Despite Stella's attitude toward sex, Natalie wasn't ready. After seeing Paul and Stella going at it like that, she felt like she'd never be ready. The whole scenario just left her feeling gross and disgusting for even watching.

When she opened the front door, her mother sat waiting for her on the living room couch. She was drinking coffee and tapping her fingers on the end table, but rose immediately when her daughter staggered in. She enveloped her in a warm, welcoming hug and asked where she had been.

Tears creased Natalie's cheeks, but she couldn't even begin to explain.

"What happened?" her mother asked. "Did someone hurt you?"

"I didn't let him," she sobbed.

"Oh, honey." Her mother hugged her even harder. "Who did this?"

"I don't want to talk about it."

"Alright. Let's get you to bed."

Her mother walked her to the bedroom and tucked her in, smoothing the fly-away hairs from her sweaty forehead. "Just know I love you," she said as Natalie started to finally calm down and drift off into fitful sleep. "But you're also grounded."

"Grounded?" Natalie started awake, sitting upright in the bed. "I didn't do anything!"

"Despite what you say, honey, I know how it is. It takes two to tango. What were you doing out driving around in the middle of the night with boys anyway?"

"It was Stella's idea," she pouted.

"Of course it was, but did you think for a moment that it was a bad idea? That you should say no?"

"I didn't think-"

"That's right. You didn't think." She tucked the sheets around Natalie again, urging her to lay back down. "You need to think about things before you go and do them. I don't want you seeing that girl again."

"She's my best friend!"

"Not anymore she isn't."

A few nights later, while Natalie combed and braided her hair as she prepared for bed, she heard the clink of a small rock against her bedroom window. She glanced down to see Stella smiling up at her as if nothing at all had happened. They hadn't spoken since the incident, not even at school. It had been strange passing by each other in the halls as if the other didn't exist, and now here she was like they were still best friends. Natalie shook her head and Stella put on a comedically dramatic frown. She stomped her feet for good measure. She tossed another small rock, sending it ricocheting. Finally, Natalie opened the window.

"What do you want?" she called down.

"Why won't you come out and play?" asked Stella, smirking.

"You know why," Natalie replied. "I'm grounded, thanks to you."

"Well, why'd you get caught?"

"Goodnight, Stella. I'm going to bed."

"No, wait, Nat! I miss you."

"You miss me? You haven't talked to me in three days."

"I thought you were mad at me."

"I am mad at you." She started to close the window, but Stella had one last plea.

"No boys, I promise. Just you and me, like we used to," she begged.

"I'm tired. I'm going to bed." Natalie closed the window, locking it shut tight.

She watched for a moment as Stella stared up at her, her eyes looking so desperate. Then she pulled the blinds and turned away. Little did she know, it really would mean the end of their friendship, at least right then and there at that moment. Within the next month, Stella moved away with her family without even a word of goodbye.

It wasn't until a few years later that Natalie received a letter from Stella in the mail. Her mother brought it up to her bedroom as the sun stretched high in the sky. It was already nearly noon, but she had let her daughter sleep in on this warm summer Saturday. Natalie stretched and yawned, struggling to sit up. "What is it?" she asked drowsily at the knock.

"I have some mail for you," her mother called from the other side of the door. "Can I come in?"

"Some mail?"

Her mother opened the door and then nearly skipped across the room in excitement.

"Who's it from?"

"You remember your old friend Stella?" she asked, then added, "looks like an invitation. Maybe even to a wedding?"

Natalie reached for the pink envelope, which was addressed to her in curlicue calligraphy of golden ink. "I thought you didn't like Stella."

Her mother sat down on the edge of the bed. "Maybe she's become respectable," she considered, thinking out loud. "I bet it's a wedding invitation, based on the looks of it."

Natalie tore open the envelope and sure enough, that's exactly what it was. On elaborate cardstock with lace ruffles, the details of the wedding were embossed, inviting her to the wedding of Stella Elaine DeVries and Erwin Wayne Wilson. She had no idea who the groom was, but apparently, she hadn't entirely severed ties with Stella and had warranted an invitation. She glanced up at her mother whose face beamed with excitement.

"Weddings are so much fun," she exclaimed. "You should really go. Catch up. I'd love to go dress shopping with you!"

"I don't know," grumbled Natalie. She couldn't get the image of Stella out of her mind, standing in the yard, begging for her to sneak out again. Much less the strange, scary night that had led to their estrangement in the first place.

But her mother was having none of it. She seemed like such a giddy little girl that her excitement proved entirely contagious. "Just think," she giggled. "You can invite Danny as your plus one! Won't that be so romantic? Maybe you'll even catch the bouquet!"

Natalie had been dating her boyfriend Danny for a few years now, but they weren't too serious. Sometimes she considered dumping him but never got up the energy to do so. Their relationship was convenient and comfortable. Bringing him to the wedding might give him ideas but he was also the obvious choice for her plus one. Natalie gave in to her mother's demands, went dress shopping, and picked out a nice demure dress, a dark shade of purple that reminded her of violets. It landed just below her knees and had cap sleeves that didn't show off too much skin. Danny chose to wear a suit and tie and came to pick her up from the house on the day of the wedding. It felt like senior prom all over again, with her mother forcing them into a series of posed photos before she would let them out the front door.

They drove for a few hours to the town where the wedding was being held, to a small chapel up on a hill in what felt like the middle of nowhere. When they arrived, they saw a bride standing out on the lawn posing for photos with her bridesmaids, all wearing pastel green dresses that blew wildly in the breeze. Natalie stared out the window and began panicking. Her breath caught in her chest. She knew it was bad luck for the bride to be seen before the wedding.

"Did we miss it?" she asked Danny. "Are we late?"

Danny finished parking the car and checked the invitation, which he had stashed in the glove compartment. "I don't think so," he said. Then, looking at the time added, "No, the ceremony starts at three..."

"Are you sure?" Natalie stared out the window at the happy bride. She had to admit she didn't recognize the woman but also hadn't seen Stella in years. If it was her long-lost friend, she had definitely put on a considerable amount of weight. She felt lost, like she shouldn't have come, after all. If she couldn't even recognize Stella, she clearly shouldn't be here.

"It's only two-thirty," Danny reasoned. "Unless they printed the invitations wrong, we're early, not late."

Natalie was holding back tears now. She felt so confused. "Are we in the right place?"

Danny referred to the invitation again, glancing at the sign on the side of the church for verification. "Yes. Come on, let's go in. If there's been a mix-up there should be someone inside who can help us."

Natalie nodded and reluctantly followed him in. It seemed like the entire wedding party was outside taking photos now and guests were streaming out. She didn't recognize anyone, but who would she recognize anyway? She doubted Stella would invite many of her old friends, that Natalie would be one of the few exceptions. They walked in and found a few ushers quickly stripping decorations from the pews. Thankfully, Danny spoke for her.

"Hi there," he greeted one of the ushers, a young man who looked to be barely a teenager. "We're here for the DeVries - Wilson wedding?"

The boy shook his head, a confused look crossing his face. "The wedding is over."

Just as they were about to turn around and leave, Natalie finally spotted a familiar face. It was Stella's younger sister, all grown up, with the same smile and face she remembered but without the baby fat. She wore a fluffy pink dress the color and texture of cotton candy. *Thank God,* she thought. *I haven't entirely lost my marbles.* The younger girl, Mary, ran to greet her.

"I didn't know you were coming!" she exclaimed.

"We haven't missed anything, have we?" Natalie asked dumbly.

"Of course not!" exclaimed Mary, enveloping her in a warm embrace. "Somehow the wedding got double-booked. They told Stella she could have the chapel and then we found out just last week there was another wedding! Thankfully, they were still able to squeeze us in, but we have to wait until they clear everything away. Then we're all set. Stella's getting dressed in the basement, but could you help out with decorations?"

"Too bad you can't just reuse the ones from the previous wedding," reasoned Danny.

"Right?!" said Mary excitedly. "It would be so much easier, and cheaper! But Stella thought it was bad luck, and anyway, they were the wrong colors. As soon as these are down, we've gotta put the pink ones up as soon as we can. Good thing everybody seems to be running behind. Except you, of course."

As soon as the purple and blue flowers and ribbons were dismantled, Natalie worked to help Mary get up the pink ones. Admittedly, Natalie preferred the purple, but it wasn't her day and she didn't get a say in the matter. She pretended, some-what successfully, that the pink was perfect, even though it reminded her painfully of Pepto Bismol, or "Pepto Abysmal" as she called it at home. No matter how she tried, any time she had taken the supposedly stomach-settling medication, it had made her throw up instead. The chalky taste probably had something to do with it.

Eventually, other guests began to arrive and find their seats. Natalie ran to take her spot next to Danny. They sat about halfway back on the bride's side. As predicted, she didn't really recognize anybody other than Maria, but that was pretty much what she had expected. She seriously wondered if she would recognize Stella or if she would look like a stranger with her hair and make-up done. They waited in anticipation for the ceremony to begin. Danny held her hand and she smiled up at him. Despite her coldness toward him, he really was a decent guy, but the spark in their relationship had already faded and she wondered how long they could possibly hold on, pretending they still felt a strong connection. Maybe he still did, and that was what worried her. At some point, she would have to give him up, but for now, he felt comfortable and safe, reliable even.

A tall, gangly man sat down at the organ and began playing. The sound filled the entire church, echoing and filling up the eaves. Chatter from the guests eventually quieted and the hymn took over. The groom stood impatiently waiting at the altar, his hands in his pockets. He wore a gray suit and his thinning hair was combed over the top of his head in an unsuccessful attempt to make it look fuller and thicker. He intermittently leaned forward and back on his toes, as if he were ready for the entire thing to be over. Natalie thought he looked a bit old for her friend Stella, but she reasoned he must have a great personality, or maybe some money that made him a more attractive match.

A small girl and boy walked down the aisle, the girl with a basket full of pink petals which she dropped unceremoniously in clumps. The boy, in his tiny suit and polka-dotted bow tie, broke free from her and ran to the groom, who swung him in his arms before planting him back on the ground. The girl ran to a woman sitting in the front row who must have been her mother. The guests tittered, then quieted again as the brides-maids and groomsmen began to walk in.

The first two pairs Natalie did not recognize, but then Mary entered as the Maid of Honor, looking like a radiant pink cloud on the arm of her escort. Once the entire wedding party stood awkwardly at the front of the church, the organist began to strum out the Wedding March and the minister motioned for everyone to stand.

Natalie didn't have a very good view of the bride but was glad to see her dress was fitted and sleek compared to the confectionery of her bridesmaids. Her hair was twisted into an almost impossible updo, no doubt held together with pins, hairspray, and hope. Her father hadn't aged well, but he smiled through his wrinkled jowls nonetheless, proud to display his daughter. She clutched a bouquet of pink roses to her chest, shaking ever so slightly as if she were a frightened chihuahua shivering. Natale tried not to laugh and covered her mouth with her hand. Danny gripped her other hand tightly, squeezing it. Maybe he did care more about her than he could admit, and clearly more than she wanted, or even deserved.

Stella sent her father away with a kiss and handed her roses to her sister. She met her husband-to-be at the altar, held both his hands in hers, and looked up into his face. Natalie didn't know him, but they looked happy, expectant. Maybe this would be a good thing for her friend, and maybe they could be real friends again. Her heart swelled with the hope that the wedding would be a new beginning and maybe they would get a chance to talk at the reception.

Natalie had never been to a wedding before, Stella being the first of her friends to get married. She was amazed at how quickly the ceremony went. A few songs, a reading, the exchanging of vows and rings, and then the wedding party walked out again. She imagined a more religious ceremony would include things like more prayers, a full service, maybe communion, but without all of that extra dressing, a wedding ceremony itself was sweet but incredibly brief. Danny kissed her quickly on the cheek when it was over, announcing his love for her. It wasn't that they hadn't said "I love you" yet, but this seemed imbued with a deeper meaning. She hoped he wasn't getting any ideas. When they returned to the car, they checked the address for the reception and made the drive in near silence.

During the reception, Natalie didn't get the chance to talk with Stella because her friend was seated at a sweetheart table with her new husband in the front of the ballroom. It felt a little like watching a movie, rather than actually experiencing it. The food was pretty standard fare, dry chicken with mounds of mashed potatoes and green beans on the side. She and Danny were seated at a table with people they didn't know and he asked her a few questions about Stella, how they knew each other, and the like but Natalie wasn't really paying attention. She watched her friend from afar, who seemed to be happy, at least that was her hope. What else could she wish for? After the bride and groom's first dance and the father-daughter dance, Natalie nudged Danny and asked if he wanted to leave soon.

"If that's what you want to do," he said, hesitating.

"There's really no reason for us to stay," she replied.

He nodded and went to go grab their coats. At that moment, Stella finally approached her, a wide grin on her face, and pulled her by both hands onto the dance floor. Natalie awkwardly followed, feeling incredibly out of place. They started the electric slide, but midway through, Stella made a noise deep in her throat, and ran from the dance floor. Natalie followed, unsure what was happening or what she needed to do. They made it to what must be the kitchen before Stella retched, throwing up into a garbage can and Natalie ran to hold her hair out of the way. Stella threw up a few more times before raising her head and wiping her mouth with her hand. Natalie gathered her hair and pushed it past her shoulders.

"Let me get you a glass of water," she offered. She checked the cupboards, found a glass, and poured some water from the tap.

Stella groaned, retching again, and struggled to apologize. "I'm so gross," she muttered.

"You're fine." Natalie offered the water and Stella struggled to drink it down. "Just try sipping it," said Natalie.

Stella looked up at her with smudged mascara leaking from her eyes. "You're such a good friend."

"I'm really not," said Natalie, "but I try." She offered Stella a wan smile and eventually, the two women giggled at each other, embarrassed at the situation they suddenly found themselves in. "Drink a little too much champagne?" she asked.

"I guess so," replied Stella.

"Other than the whole throwing up thing, it was a beautiful wedding, nice reception...." tried Natalie.

"Thanks."

"I'm not just saying that," Natalie reassured her. "I really mean it."

"Thanks."

"Let's get you cleaned up, honey."

Natalie dragged Stella to the bathroom, helped her wash her face, fix her hair and makeup, as much as possible. During the process, they hashed out their thoughts and reconnected.

"I can't believe you're married," said Natalie, reapplying lipstick to Stella's smudged lips.

"Me either," admitted Stella. "How did this happen?"

"You tell me."

"I mean, it's been years, and I'm not sad about it."

"I should hope not," said Natalie, smiling into her friend's face.

"We'll be fine. Erwin comes from money. I know he'll take care of me," Stella reasoned. "I just don't know if I'm really ready to be a wife."

"It's a little late for second thoughts."

"Yeah, right? What about you? Got anyone you're seeing?"

"I've been dating Danny for a few years now."

"*The* Danny? The same one you've had a crush on for like forever?"

"The same."

"Well, good for you." Stella managed to slug Natalie in the arm, gently. Just then, Danny arrived at the door to the bathroom, looking for Natalie.

"What's going on in there?" he asked, concerned. "Are you alright?"

"We'll be fine in just a minute," Natalie called to him. She finished fluffing Stella's hair so she didn't look as downtrodden and enveloped her friend in a big hug. "We should get together sometime, after your honeymoon. Call me."

"I will," Stella promised.

Chapter 21

NATALIE BERNARD, 1974

The next time they talked, Stella sobbed into the phone, distraught.

"I thought I loved him," she admitted, "but I guess I just got caught up in the idea of getting married."

"What do you mean?" asked Natalie.

"I wanted to be married so bad, I never even thought if it was the right thing to do."

Natalie had not known the nature of her friend's relationship so she found it exceedingly difficult to give any advice about it. "What do you want to do?"

"I think I want a divorce."

"But you've been married for less than a year. Don't you want to try to work it out?"

"I don't think it's worth it. Actually, he's worth more to me as an ex-husband than a husband."

"I don't understand." Natalie knew nothing about the financial aspects of marriage, or divorce for that matter.

"If we get divorced, I'll get alimony. Especially because of the baby."

Natalie had forgotten about the baby. It seemed like such a strange thing to forget, but Stella had hidden her pregnancy well and had in fact been a few months along at the time of their wedding. Once the baby had been born, it seemed he was always in the care of one nanny or another and Stella seemed to have very little to do with him, except now, when his very existence might mean she would get more money. This was a side of Stella that Natalie was unfamiliar with, one more concerned with worldly pleasures than emotions or relationships.

"I think you should try to work things out, for the sake of your child," Natalie advised, "but do what you think is best. Only you can make that decision."

When they met for coffee a few months later, Stella had another suggestion. "You have no idea how wealthy my almost-ex-husband is, do you?"

Natalie shook her head. She sipped her coffee. "I have a feeling I'm about to find out."

Stella laughed, finished the last of her coffee, and asked for a round of mimosas.

"I'm not sure I need that," said Natalie, trying to decline the drink.

"Nonsense, we're celebrating!" said Stella. "It's on me."

The waitress scurried away to make the drinks and Stella leaned in conspiratorially. She wore a large-brimmed hat with felt flowers that nearly touched Natalie's head as they bowed over the table. Natalie also noticed she wore real diamond jewelry that shone garishly in the early light. "Actually, it's on Erwin." She laughed with glee. "I had no idea getting divorced could be so lucrative. Erwin had to pay for everything, even my attorney's fees."

"How did you manage that?" Natalie asked.

"Well, without him, I'd be practically destitute," Stella explained. "And with the baby. You should really marry rich, Nat. That way when it doesn't work out, it still works out."

"I'm afraid Danny plans to propose."

"I can't believe he hasn't yet," mused Stella, "but he doesn't have much money, does he?"

"No, not really, and I don't want to marry him."

"Well, why not? The two of you are practically married already if you ask me."

Natalie sighed, staring into her coffee like she was trying to read tea leaves. "I don't know. I just-"

"You don't feel anything?"

"Not really."

"I didn't feel much with Erwin. I mean, he's not exactly young and strapping, but I married well and my family approved. I'm sure if you just smiled at an older man, he'd propose on the spot."

"That's ridiculous."

"No, not really. It's a fact. Any man over thirty, definitely any man older than forty, would gladly marry a woman nearly half his age given the chance. You should use your assets while you still have them."

"You talk like you've got a scheme brewing," Natalie said.

Their mimosas arrived and Stella downed hers in a few greedy gulps. Natalie left hers untouched. She didn't think orange juice and coffee would make the best combination for her already nervous stomach. However, she could tell Stella was enjoying herself and that's all that mattered, that her friend was happy. She'd worry about herself later when she was sure Stella was actually thriving and not just putting on a brave front in the face of her divorce.

"I have a grand idea, actually," said Stella, after burping unabashedly. "Ohh, bubbles!" she exclaimed.

As it turned out, Stella's scheme was to have Natalie introduce herself to Erwin, to serve as a distraction while she took as much of his money as she possibly could. It wasn't stealing, exactly, but Natalie viewed it as pretty much the equivalent. She wanted to help her friend but also felt a little dirty about the whole thing. What if Danny found out that she had been flirting with another man? It could surely mean the end of their relationship, but wasn't that what she wanted? She had been hanging on to this thing for far too long anyway, and what harm could she possibly do with a little flirting? It was harmless, really, just a favor to a friend, and it might actually be fun. It had been so long since Natalie had tried to use her womanly wiles for anything - she had grown so incredibly comfortable with Danny that she barely put in the effort to do her hair or wear makeup anymore. They tried to make the meeting seem organic, but it was anything but. Stella arranged to find out Erwin's schedule for the next few days and sent Natalie to their home on the pretense that she was picking up a few things that Stella had left there, just small stuff like some clothing.

When the day arrived, Natalie did everything she could to make herself enticing. She wore a short, tight pencil skirt and a low-cut blouse that displayed her cleavage. She wore a thin gold necklace with a charm that settled just above her breasts, drawing more attention to them. She also wore the highest heels she could comfortably walk in to add that additional boost to her backside, and she practiced walking seductively back and forth in front of her full-length mirror. She even practiced what the two of them had coined the "bend and snap" back in high school, pretending to drop something and then bending over to pick it up. She felt a little ridiculous, especially once she added a thick layer of eyeliner and black mascara, as well as bright red lips. This was a sting operation of specifically feminine nature, and she was prepared for every-thing, or so she thought.

Natalie lifted the lion-shaped knocker at the estate and let it drop, sending a hollow echo through the entire entryway. She had struggled a bit with the marble steps, but arrived at the door a bit breathless and still smiling. When the door finally swung open, a uniformed butler greeted her, asking her name and business. She told him she was a friend of Stella's just stopping by to pick up a few things. He stood aside to let her enter and she had to struggle to keep her jaw from dropping to the floor.

The place was not only massive but also immaculate. From floor to ceiling, intricate tapestries depicted scenes from Greek mythology, Hercules slaying the many-headed hydra, Sysyphus pushing a heavy boulder up a hill again and again, and Narcissus gazing lovingly at his own perfect reflection. On several pedestals, stood elaborate urns also carved and painted with dramatic scenes. If Natalie had more time, she could spend hours fawning over each of them, but she was here on a very specific mission.

"The former Mrs. Wilson's things will be in her bedroom," the butler explained, his expression blank and his voice a low monotone. "You can take the stairs to your left. It will be the first door you come to."

Natalie nodded and started her ascent. She climbed a few of the stairs in the wide spiraling staircase and then turned back to the servant. "Is Mr. Wilson here?" she asked.

"He is in his study," said the butler. "But he would prefer to be undisturbed."

It seemed if she wanted to see him, she'd have to do some snooping, but to keep up the pretense, she continued up the staircase. When she reached the top, she came to a long hallway with several doors. She was awed at the sheer height of the ceiling stretching above and the grandiose red carpeting that reminded her of a Hollywood runway where starlets posed for the paparazzi. She took a deep breath before pushing her way into what the butler had referred to as the former Mrs. Wilson's bedroom. Natalie paused for a moment, wondering if Stella and Erwin had kept separate bedrooms during their marriage, which seemed odd but in a place as large as this, there were no doubt many more bedrooms than were strictly needed.

Maybe Stella had just moved to her own bedroom when their marriage started to fall apart.

Behind the door, Natalie found a large four-poster bed with a dramatic lace canopy extending from the ceiling to the floor. There was so much fabric in the canopy that it almost looked like an elaborate mosquito net to keep out pests. She couldn't quite help herself and climbed into the bed, felt the luxurious pillow-top, and sunk back onto embroidered pillows. She had left the door open a crack and after a few relaxing moments, heard a small knock at the door. She pulled herself upright, straightened her skirt, and cleared her throat. The butler stood in the doorway.

"I thought you came to get some things?" he asked.

She wanted to shout back that he had no right to judge her but opted for a more polite reply. "Do you know where Stella kept her dresses?" she asked.

"I would imagine she kept them in the closet, not wrapped in her bed linens."

She imagined him smirking at her behind his emotionless face, but he stared straight ahead like some kind of well-mannered robot. "Please make haste," he added, then turned to leave.

Once he was out of sight, Natalie heard him descending the stairs. Funny how she hadn't heard him come up them, sneaky as he was, but she was perhaps too engrossed in the comfort of the bed. She looked around and spied another door along the back wall. When she opened it, she found a walk-in closet nearly the same size as the entire bedroom. Well-tailored and dramatic dresses, maybe more accurately gowns, hung along both sides of the closet, and the back was reserved for shelves of high heels and purses, many of them leather and freshly cleaned. Now, where to begin? Natalie was surprised Stella had left so much behind but based on her estimations, there were enough clothes here to last her through most of the year if she wore a new dress every single day. Such a quantity was practically ridiculous. Who would need to dress up this much other than a professional ballroom dancer, or a rich snob who attended charity balls on the regular?

Nevertheless, Natalie selected a few of the dresses without looking at them too carefully and draped them over her arm. She closed the closet door behind her and then the bedroom door as she stepped back out into the hallway. With any luck, one of these doors would lead directly to Mr. Wilson's study. She tried each one as she walked down the passageway, and they all seemed to open to bedrooms, each larger and more immaculate than the last. This house could make one impressive bed and breakfast or even a five-star hotel for that matter. Just when she was about to give up, she heard what sounded like sobbing from behind one of the last doors. She turned the handle and found the door locked. It turned in her hand but would not budge. She put her ear to the door and could tell that the sounds were clearly coming from behind it.

Eventually, she got up the courage to knock. There was no immediate response, but the sobbing seemed to fade a little; it was barely discernible now. She tried again, knocking a little louder.

"Not now, Melville," said a voice. "I told you to leave me alone."

Natalie wondered if she should try again, but didn't want to risk the wrath of what seemed to be a bereaved man. She felt stupid for being here in the first place. She didn't belong here and didn't really want to get in the middle of Stella's feud with her ex. She wondered why she had agreed to come in the first place. "Sorry, I'll just go," she said, barely audible, but her voice still echoed eerily in the great hallway.

"Who's that?" asked the voice, which must belong to Mr. Wilson. The door opened a few moments later to a man who looked half dead. A river of tears ran down his face and his hair, which had been slicked down so carefully at the wedding months ago, now looked wild and bedraggled. His eyes were red and bloodshot. Natalie wondered if he had been drinking. He barely glanced up at her as she struggled to introduce herself.

"I'm Natalie, a friend of Stella's," she explained. "I came for a few of her things."

"*Her* things," scoffed Mr. Wilson. "According to *her,* they're *all* her things, but she's never spent a dime while we've been married." He stumbled back to the leather chair behind his desk and eyed Stella suspiciously. "I told Melville I didn't want to be disturbed and here I am, disturbed."

"I am so sorry, I just didn't want you to think I was a stranger trying to steal things, or something like that."

"Oh, not a stranger, for sure. Just a friend of Stella's helping her rob me blind."

Natalie shook her head, unsure how to respond to the accusation. "I assure you, sir, I am only taking some of the clothing she told me to take. Nothing else."

"Heh," scoffed Mr. Wilson. He reached into a drawer of his desk and pulled out a thick cigar. After snipping the end of it, he lit the fat roll with a zippo. It smelled strangely like a campfire and toasted marshmallows. Natalie stood, balancing the dresses on her forearm, unsure of her next move. Theoretically, the plan sounded perfect, just a bit of continued distraction to keep Mr. Wilson's mind off how Stella really was robbing him blind, but now that she was here, standing in front of him in a skimpy outfit, she felt fairly ridiculous.

"So what else do you want?" he asked, blowing wide smoke rings in her direction. "Care to share a drink?" He winked, finally giving her a good once over and apparently liking what he saw.

She stared back at him.

"I mean, come on, honey, don't just stand there! Either sit and join me or get the fuck out."

Natalie draped the dresses over the back of the chair and picked a glass from the cart sitting next to his desk. She grabbed tongs for the ice and carefully dropped them with a cute little "whoopsie." She bent to pick them up, giving Mr. Wilson a clear view of her assets, and then rose again to drop two large cubes into her glass. She poured two fingers of amber-colored brandy and then moved to refill Mr. Wilson's glass as well.

"I'm sure you've heard all about me," he began. "Only horrible things, I'm sure, if you heard them from Stella. I'm really not that bad of a guy." He reached into his pocket for a worn handkerchief and wiped his eyes, blew his nose with a honk, and replaced it in his jacket pocket.

Natalie carefully carried her drink back to her seat, crossed her legs, and rested the glass on her thigh. It felt cool against her hot skin. She worried her cheeks were flushed. What exactly was she expected to do or say in this situation? She tried to think back to what Stella had told her, that Erwin was a tool and was only good for his money, but he looked pretty vulnerable at the moment. Just a lonely man drinking, smoking, and crying alone in his study. How could she broach the subject of his loneliness without being too harsh about it? She sipped her drink and sat in silence for a moment.

Erwin took another puff on his cigar, ashed it in a pewter tray, and smiled sheepishly back at her. "I mean, do I look like a bad guy?"

"No, sir," replied Natalie.

"Please don't 'sir' me," he said. "I get that from these servants all day. Makes me feel like I'm some kind of a professional asshole. One of those corporate drones."

"Not at all," she had to bite on her 'sir.' Part of it came from his age. She had been taught to give deference and respect to her elders. He couldn't be too much older than her but the age difference was still obvious between them.

"I think Stella is just taking everything out on me. You don't know what it was like, being married to that woman."

Natalie didn't want to commiserate with him. She was steadfastly on her friend's side in this, but he was putting her in a strange position. She didn't want to disagree with the man in his own house. After all, she was the unwanted one here, the unexpected visitor.

"Maybe it would be best if I left," she offered.

"Please," he urged. "Don't. I'm just so-" She waited for him to continue, but he began choking back sobs. He cried so hard that his face turned a bright red with the effort of it. She wasn't sure how to respond, but she couldn't stand the sight of him in such obvious pain, even though she barely knew him. "I'm sorry," he apologized. "I don't know what- I don't know why she never loved me."

Eventually, Natalie set her glass carefully on the front of his desk and walked around to him. She couldn't stand the sight of him so distraught. Before she knew what was happening, she grabbed his shoulders and pulled him into a great hug. As he was still sitting, his head barely reached her chest and she let him nestle his face there, streaming with tears, right in the cleavage she had so carefully prepared for his eyes. But now she played the role of mother, not lust object. She held him like that for several minutes before his sobs subsided. Eventually, he looked up into her face and she saw wells of sorrow there. She wondered if it was more than just the loss of Stella that troubled him and if in fact there were some deeper meaning behind his despair.

As he untangled himself, suddenly embarrassed by his display of emotion, he whispered to her. "Thank you, Natalie. I guess I needed that. A shoulder to cry on."

Not exactly a shoulder, she thought, but I'll give him the benefit of the doubt. "It's alright, we all need someone to talk to sometimes," she managed. She jotted her number on a scrap of paper and handed it to him. "Feel free to call me when you need to talk." She walked out of the office, forgetting the dresses draped over her chair.

When she reported to Stella, she lied and told her that Erwin had been entranced by her stunning good looks and that they had arranged a date. Stella rubbed her hands together and actually cackled, just like a Bond villain. It was a little hard for Natalie to watch, but she didn't dare reveal Erwin's vulnerability to her friend.

During the final divorce hearing, when a judge measured out Erwin's assets, and Stella took a large portion of them, Natalie arrived on Erwin's arm. Stella smiled at the couple, assuming it was only the conclusion of her nefarious ends, but by this point, Natalie had developed a genuine affection for the man. True, she felt a little sorry for him, but it also felt good to be needed, to be the rock he could depend on while Stella ripped his opulent life nearly to shreds. It wasn't until a month later when Stella received her own gold embossed wedding invitation that she realized what had actually happened. She called her friend in a frantic panic, stumbling over her words as she struggled to say them.

"What do you mean, you're marrying him?" she asked.

Natalie remained as calm as she possibly could. "We're in love," she explained.

"You don't know the first thing about love," Stella accused. "You dumped that poor puppy dog Danny and he was perfect for you. Why do you have to go for my sloppy seconds?"

"I won't dignify that with a response," said Natalie.

Stella hung up, huffing and puffing about the ridiculousness of the whole situation. When Natalie finally broke radio silence, several months later, almost a year into her new marriage, Stella was prepared for the inevitable.

"He was so sweet in the beginning," Natalie complained.

"Of course he was," replied Stella. "Because he thought he needed you. Now that he's no longer broken, he has no use for you."

Natalie sighed. "That can't be true. This can't be how it ends."

Stella laughed cruelly. "How many times has this man been married?" she asked Natalie.

"Too many times," groaned Natalie.

"Just make sure you take him for all it's worth. Get that alimony."

Natalie sighed again, dramatic and exhausted at the same time.

"Maybe, eventually, he'll learn his lesson," Stella continued.

"Maybe once he runs out of all the family money," Natalie guessed. "But given what I know, that might take a while."

Before long, the two divorced women were friends again. Over the years, their conversations drifted back to their shared husband - his attractive qualities and his many, many faults, but he was, after all, just a man. What more could they expect?

Chapter 22

PRESENT DAY

By the time Natalie had finished telling me about what I now realized was most likely the most interesting time of her entire life, we had both finished our meals and the waitresses were making another round of warm-ups on our coffee. Despite her claims that she wasn't much of a talker, Natalie had been quite animated in her retelling and got into enough detail that I had struggled to keep up with my notes. Although I was glad I had loaned Luis the tape recorder for his conversation with Stella, I could have really taken advantage of that technology as well.

When we brought the two women back together, they gave each other a knowing look. Stella called the waitress over and ordered two shots of whiskey, offering me one, which I almost accepted. They downed their shots and laughed.

"You know, Nat, I really don't miss those days, do you?" Stella asked.

"Not much," agreed Natalie, "but I do miss my younger body." She touched my shoulder gingerly. "Never get old, Sweetie," she said. "I don't recommend it. Everything hurts."

Stella nodded in agreement.

"I do have a few last questions for you," I admitted.

"Shoot," said Stella.

"Did you continue to receive alimony from Mr. Wilson after your respective divorces and do you receive it through his estate now?"

"Yes, we do," said Natalie. "Who do you think paid for lunch?"

They shared another laugh and I must have done a poor job hiding my true emotions. I have never had a very convincing poker face.

"What?" asked Stella. "You don't approve?"

"No, it's just that..." My words trailed off as I struggled to articulate what I meant.

"Pain and suffering, my dear," Stella suggested. "Pain and suffering. I feel like we each earned it for what we had to put up with."

"Was he such a horrible husband?" I couldn't stop myself from asking.

"Not so much," admitted Natalie. "But not a particularly wonderful one, either."

"Did either of you remarry?"

"And lose the alimony?" asked Stella. "No, we're better off on our own, anyway."

I thanked the two women for their time and for their stories. By the time Luis and I got settled back in the car, he started laughing almost uncontrollably. I didn't see what was so funny.

"Those two are some characters, huh?" Luis asked.

"They had a story to tell, for sure," I responded. "Natalie gave me quite a bit to work with, but I think maybe she was just glad to have someone to share it with. Why, what did Stella say?"

"A lot," said Luis. "Seems like she had everything plotted out from the very beginning."

"What do you mean?" I asked.

"She was just in it for the money."

"Really?" I glanced over at my brother as he dramatically wagged his eyebrows at me.

"Yup," he confirmed, "but don't take it from me." He set the tape recorder on the console between us and hit play. Stella's excited voice filled the car with a slightly different version of her story, one which cast herself in a much seedier light.

Chapter 23

STELLA DEVRIES, 1973

When Stella's family moved away from Orchard Square, they settled in the nearby town of Weston. Stella's mother feared the young girl had gotten a little too friendly with her then-boyfriend and felt a relocation would do her some good. The larger town ensured that there would be better opportunities for her daughter as well. Stella, with her good looks and social skills, quickly found a job as a teller at a bank, and it was through this job that she first met Mr. Wilson.

He came to the bank that first day with a shiny leather briefcase and wearing a well cut suit. Although she could have anyone her age she wanted, Stella could appreciate the appeal of a man who knew how to dress well. He wore a striped blue tie and a pocket square to match. He stood in line, but let others go before him so that she could be the one to serve him. He had filled out a deposit slip and she read his name, neatly printed in black ballpoint pen. He also presented her with his ID.

After examining the documents, she smiled widely. "Everything looks to be in order. How can I help you today, Mr. Wilson?" she asked.

"I'm making a deposit today."

"Alright, I can get that taken care of. Would you like an account balance when I have completed the deposit?"

"Yes, please."

She entered the necessary information and collected the cash from him, which came in a stack of fifties and hundred dollar bills. She counted the bills, verifying that he had given her the correct amount, and then printed the account balance on a receipt. She tried not to ogle the balance amount, but her face clearly brightened.

"You must be very successful, Mr. Wilson," she couldn't stop herself from saying.

"Yes, I am," he replied, somewhat smugly.

"May I ask what it is that you do for work?"

"I run the family business," he replied, without going into any detail regarding what exactly that business entailed. To her, it didn't really matter anyway. As long as he wasn't break-ing the law or in trouble with the feds, money was money.

She handed him the receipts. "Is there anything else I can do for you, Mr. Wilson?" she asked.

"You can give me your number."

She blushed, her face turning a bright shade of pink.

"I'd love to take you out to dinner sometime."

"I think I'd like that." She beamed at him, her whole face aglow with excitement. She took one of the business cards and wrote a number she could be reached at. "You can call me anytime."

Their hands touched briefly as she passed the card over the counter to him. "You can count on it, Stella."

A few days later, Stella primped and prepared for her date. She had gotten one of the new French manicures earlier in the week and thankfully none of her nails had chipped, yet. She blew her hair out into long, beachy waves and applied a pale blue eyeshadow crayon to the edges of her lids. Paired with a bold red lip, she looked a bit more made-up than she was used to but hoped that Mr. Wilson could appreciate the extra effort. Many of the girls at work had moved more toward a natural look, where you could barely discern that they were wearing makeup at all, but Stella, for one, preferred to stick to a more polished appearance. While some women had eschewed makeup altogether, claiming it made them into objects of lust, rather than men's equals, Stella held onto more traditional ideals and didn't want Mr. Wilson to think she was too much of a feminist (even though she definitely supported a woman's right to work and earn equal pay).

She heard the doorbell ring below and spritzed some Charlie perfume on her wrists before running down to answer the door. The sweet, floral scent of jasmine and gardenia wafted around her for a brief moment and she breathed in deeply. This was her moment to shine. If she could win Mr. Wilson's favor, she had a lot to look forward to as a future wife and mother. It might even be a future where she could choose whether or not to work, and having that option thrilled her. Imagine what she could do with her free time if she didn't *need* to work. She might decide to work, anyway, but without the stress of worrying about rent and paying other bills, her life would be so much more luxurious and enjoyable.

Mr. Wilson wore a derby-style hat, which covered the small balding patch on the top of his head, but his blue eyes sparkled mischievously. Without a moment's hesitation, he took her arm and escorted her to his car, a pale blue Pontiac Grand Prix, which shone in the street light. Stella wondered what it looked like during the day - it must be nearly the shade of the sky on a warm summer's day. Like a gentleman, he opened the passenger side door for her, and waited for her to gather her skirts and slide in before walking around to the driver's side. When he turned the ignition, the car growled and then hovered at a low purr she could feel vibrating through her thighs.

A warmth spread across her lap and she smiled, asking where he would be taking her.

"You'll see," he replied, winking. He shifted the car into first gear and they cruised smoothly down the street.

With each intersection they passed, Stella began guessing where they were headed. "Are we going to Chez Louis?" she tried.

"No."

"What about…" She looked further ahead at an approaching sign. "El Pollo Loco? They have the best margaritas," she tried.

"No. I'm taking you to a much nicer place than that."

"You don't have to spend a lot of money on me," she lied.

"Don't you worry your pretty little head about that, darling."

She smiled, content that cost was not a factor for him. She began to grow a little distraught, however, as they drove further and further through town and out onto a dark country road.

"Just where are we going?" she asked, trying to sound calm and unperturbed.

"You'll see," he promised. He pulled a thin cigarette from his jacket pocket and lit it from the built-in car lighter. He rolled his window down a tad and let the cool night air blow in on them, catching wisps of smoke as he drove.

They continued to drive, further and further from all signs of civilization and around a small lake until she saw a few dim lights in the distance. As they approached, she finally saw a sign around the bend. They were fast approaching what appeared to be an out-of-the-way supper club named The Blue Heron. Stella had never been there before and didn't even know it had existed before this very moment.

"I know it's a little out of the way," he said. "But I assure you, it is definitely worth it."

As soon as they walked in the door, a hostess approached them to take their jackets. She greeted Mr. Wilson by name and asked how many their party would be.

"Just me and the lovely lady," responded Erwin.

A large man stepped out from behind the bar, greeting Erwin with a boisterous hug. "How have you been, man? It's been a while since I've seen you around!"

Erwin hugged him back, gripping the man's forearm as he did so. They shared a quick peck on the lips much in the same way the French kissed each other on the cheek. Erwin motioned toward Stella to introduce his friend.

"Ronnie, this is my lady, Stella DeVries." He pulled Stella toward him, wrapping his arms around her. "Stella, this is Ronnie. He's family."

Stella moved to shake hands, but Ronnie enveloped her in a hug instead. She felt a bit smothered and overwhelmed at the moment. "Like a cousin? " she asked.

"Well, not exactly, but close enough," said Ronnie. The two men shared a hearty laugh. "Well, now that we've been properly introduced, step into my office so I can get you two set up with drinks."

The bar was dimly lit but cozy. The bar shone, freshly polished and with brass accents. Behind the bar, a large mirror reflected the bottles back to her, so many expensive liquors she had never heard of before. Ronnie took his place on the other side of the bar. He smiled wide and spread his hands out.

"First drink's on me, buddy. What'll it be?"

"I'll have an Old Fashioned," said Erwin.

"And for the lady?"

Stella shook her head. "I haven't the faintest idea," she admitted.

"Well, what kind of liquor do you like? What flavor profile?"

"Flavor what?"

"Do you like your drinks sweet? Maybe a little sour?"

"Sweet sounds good."

Ronnie flashed her another smile. "I've got just the thing."

Erwin took a stool at the bar and patted the one next to him. She gingerly sat next to him and struggled to cross her legs without falling from the stool. He pulled her closer to him and gave her a peck on the cheek. She blushed as she looked warily around. Despite the dim light, she could see several signed photographs hung on the walls. She didn't recognize any of the faces, though. She considered asking Erwin, but instead sat in silence and watched Ronnie work. He poured liquid from several bottles, added a twist to Eriwn's drink, and started filling a martini shaker for hers. Ronnie worked with such smooth movement that watching him felt like watching a circus performer. He radiated such sophisticated confidence that she felt entirely overwhelmed. By the time he set the martini glass in front of her, she realized she had been holding her breath in anticipation. She sighed, letting the air leave her lungs and taking another deep breath. He poured the drink out for her and she took a tentative sip. It tasted like sweet strawberries coated in sugar. She smiled, delighted.

"What is this?" she asked.

"Exactly what you asked for," he replied.

She and Erwin exchanged polite conversation as more restaurant patrons settled in around them. If anything, Stella felt a bit underdressed. Everyone looked like they were wearing their Sunday Best. Admittedly, she was wearing what passed for one of her fancier dresses. She simply didn't have pearls or a fur jacket, much less an embroidered bodice. Many of the people were older, but all of them looked to be going out on the town, enjoying the atmosphere around them.

Finally, a waitress came to escort Erwin and Stella to their table. They sat at a small table for two with elegant candlesticks. In the dim light and after a few drinks, Erwin looked especially desirable to Stella. She couldn't stop herself from laughing and smiling at every little thing he said. She could feel a warmth rising in her chest and worried that her entire face was beet red. After glancing at the menu, she expressed concern about the prices. Many of them weren't even listed on the menu.

"How do you know how much things cost?" she asked.

"If you have to ask, dear, you can't afford it," Erwin replied, flashing her a smile.

"Can you afford it?" she asked.

"Dinner is on me, honey. Don't you worry your pretty little head about it."

She wanted to be upset at the implication that she couldn't or shouldn't do the math, but there was something incredibly charming about the way he wanted to take care of everything.

"I would buy you the moon if it was for sale," he offered.

"Why would I want the moon?" she asked.

"Why wouldn't you?"

She suddenly felt the urge to use the bathroom and excused herself.

Before she could leave, he leaned over the table toward her, motioning toward the menu. "Do you know what you want, my darling?" he asked.

"Not yet," she admitted, glancing back.

"Can I surprise you?"

"Sure. The drink was a good guess. Just know, I'm not incredibly hungry so nothing too much."

She grabbed her clutch and hurried off to the ladies' room. When she got there, she was surprised to find an entire lounging area there, not just sinks and toilets. There were elegant couches and overstuffed upholstered chairs, as well as a gigantic floor-to-ceiling mirror where a few dazzling women checked their hair and makeup. One of them turned to her, giving her a good once over.

"And who might you be?" the woman asked.

"I'm Stella," she replied. "And you are...?"

The woman didn't deign to answer her question. "Are you here with Mr. Wilson?" the woman inquired.

"Actually, yes, I am. Do you know him?"

The woman laughed and nudged her friend playfully. "She wants to know if I know Erwin," she stage-whispered. "Oh, honey, are you in for a wild ride." She held her hand out, letting her rings glimmer in the Hollywood-style lights. "I'm his ex-wife."

"His ex-what?" Stella gulped. "I didn't know he had been married."

"Oh, a few times!"

"He's been married more than once?"

"Oh, I think I was wife number two. Who knows how many there have been since me? He doesn't like to hang around long, for sure."

Stella stared at the woman, who still held her hand out in greeting. Eventually, she shook it, but none of this seemed real. Her perfect man wasn't so perfect, after all.

"I'm Elenor, by the way," the woman said as they shook hands. "And this is my friend Charlotte." She motioned toward the woman standing next to her. They were both stunningly beautiful and seemed to be well-off based on their long gowns and elaborate jewelry. "She was wife number one."

"Wait a minute, you're friends? Is this some sort of ex-wives club?" Stella stumbled over her words growing more uncomfortable by the minute.

"I was Charlotte's maid and, well, let's just say Erwin's eyes and hands wandered," explained Elenor.

"I don't understand," said Stella. "I need to sit down." She nearly collapsed into one of the overstuffed chairs.

"Oh dear!" exclaimed Charlotte. "Look what you've done to the poor girl, Elenor. You didn't need to just lay that all on her."

While she tried to regain her composure, Stella could feel the two women hovering over her. They clucked and tutted like two old hens pecking away at sawdust. She didn't want to believe what she had just heard. Erwin had married multiple women? And somehow these women were on friendly terms with one another, even though it seemed as though he had cheated? Was this some kind of elaborate joke? She felt dizzy and her heart beat so quickly she felt like it was going to burst right out of her chest. What was happening?

Charlotte, the redhead, looked down at her then, reaching for her hand. "Don't mind Elenor, hon. She's had a few too many." She sat on the edge of a chaise lounge next to Stella.

Elenor huffed and traipsed off to the toilets, leaving the two women in the lounging area.

"I just don't understand," began Stella. A few tears had formed at the edge of her eyes and she struggled to keep them from falling down her cheeks.

"Elenor and I are good friends and have been even before either of us had met Erwin. He isn't a bad man, really, just doesn't know what he wants. In the end, I think we took advantage of him." Charlotte looked away for a moment, straightening her skirts.

"You weren't mad that he made a pass at your friend?" asked Stella, incredulous now.

Charlotte stared at her and scoffed. "Of course, I was mad! But things are what they are and everything wound up alright in the end. I forgave her, eventually, but I don't think I've completely forgiven him."

"How did you take advantage of him, then?"

"That's the rub." Charlotte held her face in her hands for a moment, then, remembering her makeup glanced at the mirror quickly before continuing. "Erwin has a lot of family money, and he doesn't mind spending it. When everything went south, in both our marriages, he was more than happy to pay out some alimony, just to get rid of us."

"Really?" Stella was used to a man who clutched money like a string of pearls, like the most valuable thing he would never give up.

Charlotte nodded, just as Elenor returned. She rose to join her friend and the two women left without another word. Stella stood slowly, examining herself in the mirror again. Just what was she doing here, then? Erwin seemed to genuinely like her, but why pursue a relationship that already seemed doomed? Then again, she could let him take her out, spend some money on her, and have a good time for a while. No one said they had to be serious. She took a few deep breaths and left the lounge.

When she returned to the table, Erwin was anxiously waiting for her. Their food had already arrived, but as she sat, she realized she no longer had an appetite. He glanced over, a worried expression crossing his face.

"Are you alright?" he asked. "You were gone for quite a while."

"I'm not feeling well," she replied, and it really wasn't even a lie.

"I ordered you the Lady's Plate," he offered.

She glanced at the food and saw a small cut of steak with a cream sauce and two small, round lumps of white meat that appeared to be some sort of seafood. Her stomach did a flip-flop.

"It's filet mignon and scallops. Give it a try."

"I'm just not... I don't think I can eat it," she admitted.

"Just a few bites?"

She shook her head.

"I'm sorry you're not feeling well." His eyebrows furrowed. "Would you like something else? You're not vegetarian, are you? I wish you would have told me if you were..."

"No, it's not that." She shifted in her seat, stood awkwardly, and started for the door.

"Stella, what's going on?"

She started to walk away, but it felt like she was slogging through a swamp, her body was moving incredibly slowly. It felt like it wasn't her body that was moving, more that she was watching herself getting up, walking out the door, and leaving. Her brain felt so clogged with impossible thoughts. She just wanted to get out.

She passed the bar and Ronnie tried to reach out to her. "Did you need a refill?" he asked, trying to catch her attention. But it was like he was just part of the background scenery. She kept moving.

Once she made it out the front door, a cool breeze caught her hair and whipped loose strands into her face. She didn't even bother pushing them aside. She realized she had been inexplicably holding her breath and now felt that she could breathe more easily. The tears she had been holding back finally came streaming down her face. What a fool she was. The whole evening was a disaster. What could she have been thinking, going out with a random man she barely knew?

She stood there, leaning against a decorative fence outside of the restaurant, for several minutes. Perhaps she should go back inside. Got herself together. At the very least she would need to let Erwin drive her home, even if this whole night was a bust, but she dreaded the ride. How long had it taken them to get out here? Eventually, she heard the door behind her open but she didn't bother turning around to see who it was.

Erwin placed his hand on her shoulder and she flinched away.

"Are you feeling ill?" he asked.

"I just needed some fresh air," she muttered.

"You didn't say anything. You just got up and left. What's going on with you?"

"I don't know."

He pulled a pocket square from his jacket and moved to dry her tears with it. Numb, she let him do it but didn't say anything. She noticed he carried a paper bag with him.

"I had them bag up our food," he explained. "Let me take you home at least."

She hugged her arms to her chest and shivered.

"Oh, yes, your coat. Let me get your coat."

He disappeared into the restaurant, leaving her alone with her thoughts again. She had really ruined everything. There was no coming back from this disaster and she still needed to sit with him in the car the whole ride home. Why couldn't she just pretend nothing had happened, eat a nice meal, and have a decent evening? Why did she need to be so dramatic?

The door opened again, revealing Charlotte and Elenor. They were practically falling over each other with giggles and they didn't notice her immediately. Stella pushed her hair out of her face and hoped they would continue on their way without paying her any attention. Wishful thinking, apparently, as Elenor wrapped her spindly arms around her. Stella could smell the alcohol on her breath.

"Why so sad, dearie?" the woman cackled. "Man troubles?"

Charlotte pulled Elenor away. "That's enough! Let the poor girl be."

Elenor wouldn't stop, though. "I bet you didn't even get to see his dick yet. So sad. He's pretty well-endowed. You should have stuck it out, at least for the night."

"Elenor!" Charlotte chided her. "Don't listen to her," she said to Stella. "She's had too much to drink. I'm sorry we've ruined your evening."

Stella didn't know what to say, so she didn't say anything. Instead, she watched Charlotte struggle to wrangle Elenor into their car and then slide in behind the steering wheel. She still couldn't quite process what was happening. Were these women really Erwin's wives? They seemed such a mess, she wasn't sure what to believe. Maybe she should just confront him about it. Maybe they were just teasing her and none of it was even true.

As the car pulled out of the lot, Erwin returned, her coat draped over his arm. He helped her into it and walked her back to his blue Pontiac. As they settled in, he glanced over at her with concern. "I'm sorry this evening did not turn out as planned. I hope you feel better soon and are willing to come out with me again."

Stella gulped. "Sorry, I'm not feeling well."

"It's not your fault, dear. I'm glad you didn't try to struggle through dinner. I'd rather have you be honest with me."

He offered her a weak smile and pulled out of the gravel drive. Charlotte and Elenor had already sped away, taking their doom and gloom with them. As Erwin drove, slowly making his way back to civilization, they sat in awkward silence. She desperately wanted to ask him about his previous relationships (marriages?) but didn't know where to begin. Thankfully, he began to talk.

"I hope I haven't done something wrong," he tried.

"No, no," she assured him. "I just...I think I just need to lie down for a while."

"Are you sure?"

She left his question hanging and then decided there was no good way to bring up the issue at hand. She just blurted out the first thing that came to mind. "You're a bit older than me," she began.

"Is that a problem?

"No, it's just...have you been married before?"
Erwin paused. "Yes, I have been married."

"How many times?"

"What do you mean, how many times?" he asked. "Do you think I'm a Mormon or something?"

"No, it's a legitimate question. Why don't you want to answer it?"

"I'll answer it. I'm just not sure you want to know the answer."

"What is that supposed to mean? Why are you being so secretive?"

"What about you?" he asked, turning the question on her.

"I've never been married," she replied.

"Fine, then. I've been married four times."

"Four?" She turned in her seat to stare at him. "Just how old are you?"

"Thirty-eight," he replied.

"And you've been married four times already?"

"I'm very unlucky in love."

"Or maybe too lucky!" she responded.

"Being married four times also means I've been divorced four times."

She paused her interrogation. "I suppose that's true."

"Where is all this coming from, anyway? I don't like to talk about the past. I'd rather focus on the future, or even right now." He tried to reach for her hand, but she swatted him away.

"At the restaurant -" she struggled to get the words out.

"What happened at the restaurant?"

"I met two of your ex-wives!"

He chuckled, but she really didn't find anything funny. "Let me guess, Charlotte and Elenor."

She nodded, her words caught in her throat.

"Those two have been causing problems for me even before I married them!"

They were getting closer and closer to town now, the streetlights becoming more frequent and the buildings closer together. Stella both wanted to know more and dreaded finding out the details of Erwin's previous relationships. Did she really want to join his collection of wives, of ex-wives?

"Is this what's been bothering you?" he asked.

"Yes," she admitted. "I just couldn't wrap my head around it. The idea of you with multiple wives."

"I wasn't married to both of them at the same time," he reasoned, chuckling again.

"Well, I know that. It just... was a lot to get thrown at me all at once."

"Alright, I'll give you that. Tell you what, Stella, let me take you out again, and you can ask me as many questions as you want, about the other women in my life, but know that none of that matters. All I'm interested in is you."

"Fine."

"Is it actually fine, or are you just saying that?"

"It's fine," she replied. "I guess I just want to get to know you better."

"If answering questions about my wives is what it takes, I'll do it. Just know that I'd rather be talking about you, about us, if there's still an us."

"Alright."

"And next time something bothers you, just tell me, okay? I can't read your mind. How can I make things better if I don't know what's wrong?"

She didn't have an answer for that.

"Now, we're almost back to your place. I have just one favor to ask you."

"What's that?"

"Can we pretend for a minute that this date went well and will you let me kiss you goodnight?"

She laughed at his eagerness but honestly wasn't sure if she wanted him to kiss her at this point. She was willing to take the chance, though. Maybe he was a good kisser. "I'll allow it," she managed.

Chapter 24

PRESENT DAY

I reached over the console to stop the tape recorder, giving my brother a knowing look. We were already nearly back to Orchard Square and this woman was still talking?

"So he gives her a wallop of a kiss and everything's fine again?" I ask.

"Not quite," replied Luis. "She has a change of heart when her parents kick her out and she needs the money."

"Wait, her parents kicked her out?"

"When they catch her and Mr. Wilson in the car." Luis winks at me.

"Wait, what?!"

"Don't worry, she didn't go into all the gory details but gave me enough to get a good idea. Her father catches them and they kick her out the next day. She's suddenly homeless, shamed, and has nowhere else to go. Mr. Wilson is a convenient patsy."

"Damn."

I tried to return my attention to the road, but all I could think about was this poor girl suddenly required to rely on a man she barely knows, a man who might very well be bad news. Couldn't she have stayed with a friend, instead? Then I remembered her family had just moved to town and they didn't really know anyone yet. She had few options in that situation. Even if she took advantage of his money, she had some reasonable reasons for doing so.

Luis pulled me from my reverie. "So what do you think?" he asked. "About Mr. Wilson?"

"I think he was more complicated than I originally thought, but I still maintain he was a bit of a womanizer. What about you?"

"Based on what Stella told me? And the way these women are all cashing in on alimony? I feel a little sorry for the guy."

"Really?"

"I mean, he's just trying to live his life. Maybe he shouldn't marry every woman he falls in love with, but they're the ones divorcing him, and profiting from it."

"But if he were just faithful to the wife he has instead of looking for the next greatest thing, they wouldn't divorce him in the first place," I counter. As we continue to argue back and forth, I drive right past The Deep Dish and then have to turn around. "I promised you ice cream, didn't I?"

Luis smiled back at me, and I remembered he was still just a kid, albeit in the body of an almost-man. I noticed the peach fuzz growing on his upper lip. I still saw him as the five-year-old trying to tag along with me everywhere I went. Is it no surprise that he'd come running to me when he ran into trouble, claiming it was an "accident" that he had found me?

I made a y-turn in the middle of the street, and we headed back to the diner. When we got there, it was hopping with customers, including a few I recognized. I spotted Dale and Brandon from Earl's Pub in one of the booths and waved hello. They each had a thick slice of cherry pie in front of them alongside steaming hot mugs of coffee.

"Why don't you join us?" asked Brandon. "It'd be nice to have some fresh conversation."

"What do you mean?" retorted Dale. "Are you sick of me already?"

"I mean, I talk to your drunk ass nearly every day."

"Fine, fine. But you get paid to do it," countered Dale. "And yet, you still meet me for lunch on occasion."

"Because you won't leave me alone," said Brandon, then turned back to us. "Never mind him. He's just an ornery old bastard. Let me scootch over, and you can join us."

Brandon moved to sit next to Dale and then slid his pie and coffee across the table. Luis and I slid across from them. "So, what have you two been up to today?" he asked.

"We were interviewing some old ladies in Weston," replied Luis.

"Now, that's no way to refer to our interviewees," I chided.

"But it's true. They were old. They were ladies. I don't see the problem," said Luis.

Dale chuckled from behind his coffee mug, setting it down gingerly on the table. "I like this kid," he mused. "Tells it like it is."

"So why were you interviewing old ladies?" asked Brandon as he picked at his pie. He frowned, suddenly more preoccupied with the pie than his question. "Darlene!" he yelled across the restaurant.

Darlene came bustling up to the table, noticing Luis and me for the first time.

"Oh, hi, dears, I didn't see you come in!" she exclaimed. "What can I get for you this fine afternoon?"

Brandon interrupted her before we could get a word in edgewise. "Darlene!" he hollered again, even louder.

"What do you want?" she snarked back.

"I thought I ordered this pie a la mode."

"A la what?" she asked. She wrinkled her nose at him.

"Mode," he responded. "With ice cream?" He talked down to her like she spoke another language and couldn't understand him.

I could tell she wanted to yell back at him, but her friendly demeanor wouldn't allow her to. "Oh, yes, I'll get that right away." She jotted something on her notepad and then turned to Luis and me again. "And for you?"

"I'll have a chocolate shake," I replied.

"Can I get a hot fudge sundae?" asked Luis.

"Oh, dear, I think we're out of the fudge," she said, worrying the edge of her apron with one hand. "Would Hershey's syrup work?"

Luis pouted. "I guess so."

"I'm ever so sorry."

Brandon chimed in, interrupting the exchange. "Oh, stop your blubbering, Darlene; chocolate is chocolate. The boy will survive." He changed tact. "I won't without my a la mode, though."

Darlene quivered. "I'll get that for you right away." She scurried away like a little mouse running from a fat cat.

"Do you have to be so hard on her?" Dale commented.

"Have to? No. Want to? Yes," replied Brandon.

"But why?"

"She just gets so worked up about everything. It's a gas to watch her. Besides, it's all in good fun."

"Does she know that?" Dale adjusted his baseball cap, scratching his head while he did so.

"She knows I love her. That's how I express my affection."

"So that's why you always make fun of me?" asked Dale.

"No, I just hate your stinking guts," replied Brandon.

Dale looked taken aback for a moment and then joined Brandon in a hearty laugh. "Yeah, man. I hate you, too."

I could tell the two men had been friends for a long while, the kind of friends who poke and tease rather than come right out and tell each other how they feel. I wondered what their take would be on what we had discovered today, that at least a handful of Mr. Wilson's wives were still living off alimony payments from his estate. Maybe they already knew, and it was old news. Then I wondered how Mr. Wilson's most recent wife felt about the whole thing. She would have the lion's share of the death benefit and remaining estate, but how would she feel about previous wives still getting their cuts? Were all of them benefitting from their divorces?

Luis barged into conversation while I sat musing on my thoughts. There's a reason I'm the writer, always observing and commenting, and he's more of a doer. As he began to talk, I counted myself lucky that he was on my team with this project.

"Have either of you been married?" Luis asked.

"Brandon had a wife, but she passed away," said Dale.

"You know I don't want to talk about that," replied Brandon.

"Well, he asked."

"We don't have to talk about your wife if you don't want to," hedged Luis. He tapped his fingers on the table. "But I'd love to hear about her."

I decided to sit quietly and let this play out. Later, I could talk to Luis about his conversational tactics. He was doing a pretty cool job of sussing out information, but I wasn't sure how it connected to our aims yet. I also reminded myself that not every conversation had to be productive or serve a purpose. Sometimes you could just shoot the shit, and build a connection.

"If you don't want to talk about it, you don't have to," Dale offered.

"No, it's fine. Not like it happened yesterday."

"What happened?" asked Luis.

Brandon prodded at his pie with his fork again, still looking like the cherries had somehow wronged him. He wouldn't eat another bite until he had his ice cream. "She died in childbirth. Along with the baby."

"I'm so sorry," replied Luis, perhaps a little too quickly.

I took the opportunity to jump in. "That must have been very difficult."

"It was hell," said Brandon. "Lost the woman I loved and a child I never knew. My whole family in one fell swoop."

Dale reached over to pat him on the arm in a there, there motion. He sighed. "She was a great woman, your Diane."

"She was, wasn't she?" Brandon looked up for a moment and finally took a bite of his pie.

"I've never been married," offered Dale. "Got close once but never managed to tie the knot."

"How close is close?" asked Luis.

"They were planning the wedding and everything," chimed in Brandon.

Dale looked away.

"What happened?" I asked.

"I guess she changed her mind," Dale replied.

"At the last minute?" Luis asked.

"It was kinda complicated. Long story."

"We've got time," I replied.

"She married your Mr. Wilson instead," Dale muttered.

We sat in shocked silence while Darlene brought our ice cream: a small scoop of vanilla for Brandon, a chocolate shake with sprinkles for me, and a heaping mound of ice cream covered in chocolate syrup, whipped cream, colorful sprinkles and a cherry for Luis. I had suddenly lost my appetite.

Chapter 25

DAPHNE HAMADOU, 2007

Although they had chatted online several times, it wasn't long before Daphne found herself on a plane to America to visit her new boyfriend. It was her first time flying and she clutched her small carry-on bag to her chest for most of the flight. She feared that if she put it in the overhead compartment, she would never see it again, much like she would never see her homeland again if things went well.

She hoped the man she was going to see wouldn't suddenly change his mind and send her back. Afterall, he was an educated American man. She had only spent a few years in school. She also wore long sleeves to cover the scars on her arms from years of working in the cocoa fields. Every little thing he could find wrong with her came to the forefront of her thoughts. She realized that to him, she might just be a commodity he could buy, rather than a complete person with hopes, dreams and more importantly fears.

She held her breath as the plane took off, afraid to even look out the window as the engines roared to life. Eventually, though, she did look and what she saw made her feel so small and a little dizzy. They were up above the clouds now and she could no longer see the land below. It felt like a dream, to be so high in the sky, but the feel of the plane itself was like riding a big bus. The turbulence bounced them around a little, but other than that, if you didn't look outside, you could imagine you were inside the cab of a large bus, bumping along the road. What was missing were the sounds and smells, the bustle of a city. People were so quiet, some of them dozing already, most of the men wearing business suits, traveling for work. The stewardess came by, offering water and soda. She took a bottle of water and sipped it slowly. She knew she wouldn't be able to sleep with her thoughts churning like this.

She could speak English well and cook decent food, but she feared she wouldn't be everything he was hoping for. A social worker had helped her write her messages online, making sure to say the right things. In some cases, she had lied. She definitely hadn't told him about the years of working in the fields, or her scars.

When she was young, her family had struggled to survive and in desperation had sold her to a cocoa farmer. She quickly learned to climb trees and cut down the pods. From there, they piled the pods into sacks and carried them on their heads. She remembered wishing her head were flatter so she could more easily balance the weight. Sometimes, the other children would have to help her lift the sack onto her head but if she ever dropped one, she would be beaten.

When they got back to the farm, they would use machetes to separate the cocoa beans from their pods, holding the pod in one hand and the machete in the other. With practice, she became skilled at using the tip of the blade to expose the beans, but at first she was clumsy and if she wasn't careful, she could slice her arms and hands rather than the pod. When the blood came it seemed as though it would never stop. It came in such a rush of red that she couldn't help but be transfixed by it, running in rivulets down her arm. These scars would never heal completely. The best she could manage was covering them with sleeves.

It was only with the help of the social worker, that she found a new beginning. The woman had helped gather together many of the children from the farm and steal them away from that life. Many of them were even able to return to their families. For Daphne, it was too late. Her parents had died in a fire years earlier, and they couldn't track down any distant relatives. It may have been unconventional, but she had decided to try an online mail-order bride service. Now here she was, starting a new life with a man she barely even knew, and what would she tell him, of her past, of their future together? All she could hope for is something new, something better than what she had known her entire life in Cameroon.

By the time the plane landed in Chicago, she had worn herself out with all her worrying but tried to put a smile on her face. After she made her way through the immigration checkpoint and then customs, it became a strained smile, though. She was tired and just wanted to rest. She was told a friend would be picking her up from the airport instead of her boyfriend, so she looked for the promised sign. Eventually, she spotted a well-groomed man older man in a navy blue suit holding a sign with her name. The sign had been written with large, even block letters that read: Daphne Hamadou - Welcome to America. He wore a black fedora-style cap on his head and wide wire-framed glasses.

She walked up to him and haltingly said, "I am Daphne."

"I am Mr. Wilson," he introduced himself. "We can head to the carousel to pick up your bags."

"I don't have any other bags. Just myself," she explained.

"I think you are plenty enough." He smiled, hooked her arm in his, and escorted her out to a limousine where a driver was waiting for them.

Daphne had seen a limousine before, one late night in the city, but had never ridden in one. Mr. Wilson held the door open for her as she slid into her seat, wide-eyed as she looked around her. Her new husband must have more money than he had let on. Daphne had imagined that everyone in America must have money. After all, they were always buying unnecessary things, but she had not expected this level of opulence. Mr. Wilson slid into a seat farther down the upholstered banquette.

As the limo began to move, Daphne looked around. The inside of the vehicle was lit with white lights that ran the length of the interior ceiling and the windows were tinted so that she could barely see out and no one could see in. There was a television screen embedded in the divider between them and the driver and a full bar along the wall across from them. Even as the vehicle merged into highway traffic, the ride was so smooth it didn't even feel as if they were moving. It was a nice respite from the turbulence of the plane.

"How was your flight?" asked Mr. Wilson.

She smoothed her skirts and set her bag next to her on the seat. "It was fine," she replied shyly.

He reached into the bar, grabbing a glass for himself and a decanter of whiskey. He poured two fingers, no ice, and sipped it gingerly. He sighed. "This is some pretty good stuff," he offered. "Would you like some?"

"Maybe just some water," she said.

He obliged, pulling a bottle of water from the fridge. She unscrewed the cap and drank thirstily, nearly downing the bottle in her first few swallows.

"There are snacks, too. I don't know what they offered on the plane, but I've got more than peanuts here."

"I am fine," she replied.

"Well, if you change your mind -"

"I am fine," she repeated. She wasn't trying to be difficult - she was just exhausted. "How long will it be until we get there?"

"It will be roughly two and a half hours," Mr. Wilson replied. "Three if traffic is bad. In the meantime, you can rest, we can talk, or I could even put on something to watch on the screen there."

She considered her options but still felt incredibly over-whelmed. "Tell me about my future husband," she said. Maybe this Mr. Wilson could help calm her nerves.

He listed off some of Dale's better qualities. He was dependable, an honorable man whose word could be counted on, a good friend, and a decent human being. He did charity work on occasion, served at the soup kitchen, raised money for disabled children, and went to church. But Daphne wanted to know the one thing that couldn't be determined yet: would he make a good husband? Could he take care of her?

"Why didn't he come to pick me up himself?" she asked. "I have been waiting all these months to see him and he isn't here."

Mr. Wilson paused. "He had other things to do."

"Other things to do when his wife is flying all day to reach him? What could be more important than meeting me?"

Mr. Wilson shook his head. The truth was, he didn't know what exactly Dale was doing. If it was working, he could have easily requested the day off. He might be puttering in his workshop building something. He was always tinkering on some woodworking project or other.

"I don't know," he admitted.

"I don't even know what he looks like," she admitted. "He never sent me a picture. I wish it didn't matter but I would like to know if my husband is handsome."

Mr. Wilson wasn't sure how to respond to that.

"I mean, it really doesn't matter. I'm not shallow," she began. "But it would be easier if -"

"If you were attracted to him?" asked Mr. Wilson.

"Yes," she admitted.

They sat in awkward silence for a few moments.

"Is he attractive?" she asked.

Mr. Wilson swallowed hard. Dale wasn't a bad-looking man but was pretty ordinary. He didn't keep himself clean-shaven or work out much. He had a bit of a beer gut. The man had been a bachelor for so long that Mr. Wilson wasn't sure if he knew how to clean up much, but who was he to judge? "I'm not sure how to answer that," Mr. Wilson finally replied.

Daphne imagined a deformed man who had turned to a mail-order bride because no one else would have him. "Is he ugly?" she asked.

"I don't think we should be talking about this."

"He's ugly, isn't he?"

"No, no," Mr. Wilson reassured her. "I don't know. I'm not a woman, I don't know what is attractive and what isn't."

She glowered at him, her eyes narrowing to dark little slits.

"Why don't we watch something?" he tried.

"Like what?" she asked.

"I have a few movies here we could watch," he offered.

He flipped through a selection of DVDs and pulled one from its slot. He inserted it into the player and Daphne could hear it spinning up in the machine. "This is a kid's movie," he warned, "but I think you'll like it."

"Why would I like it?" she asked. "I am not a child."

"I watched it all the time as a kid and I still like it as an adult. Plus, it's about some basic American values - baseball and making lasting friendships."

"You think we don't have baseball in Cameroon?" she asked.

"That's not what I said. Baseball is just a very American sport."

She harrumphed at him and begrudgingly agreed to watch the movie. "What is this movie?" she asked.

"The Sandlot," he replied.

She half expected to let the movie play while she would doze off in her seat. The limo was very comfortable and she was completely exhausted by this point, but instead, she found herself laughing along with Mr. Wilson as they watched the movie. Although the premise was straightforward enough she still found herself asking several cultural questions.

"Do all American children eat s'mores?" she asked at one point.

"Most of them," Mr. Wilson explained. "We like to sit around a campfire roasting marshmallows."

"I'll have to try one, but I think it would be too sweet," she said.

Then, later, "Why did they chew all the tobacco if it would make them sick?"

"American baseball players used to chew a lot of tobacco."

"But why did the kids do it?"

"They wanted to prove they were macho and could handle it."

"Young boys can be stupid sometimes," she replied.

"So can grown men," replied Mr. Wilson.

With the movie as a topic of conversation, their interaction became much more casual and much less combative. Daphne was finally able to relax a bit and let her worries slide into the back of her mind. She didn't forget about it by any means, but it became something that sat on the backburner instead, bubbling away but not requiring her immediate attention. As the drive continued, they finished the movie and then settled into a comfortable space where they began to share bits and pieces of themselves.

"How do you know my husband?" Daphne asked.

"He is a friend of mine, a drinking buddy."

"He drinks?"

"Not to excess," Mr. Wilson reassured her. "Just after a long day at work, or to blow off some steam. There is not much to do in Orchard Square."

"Tell me about Orchard Square."

"It is a small town, mostly farms, a church, a bar, and a few small businesses. I came here from Indianapolis when I was a boy to work and then stayed."

"Why did you stay?"

"I got married."

"So, you are a married man?" she asked.

"Not currently, no."

"I see. You are divorced?"

"Yes," he admitted.

"Do you have children?"

"Yes, but none of them are really mine anymore."

"What do you mean?"

"I don't have custody, but I make alimony payments, child support payments. I will make sure they are taken care of."

"It is difficult growing up without parents," said Daphne. "Even with a mother, I think it would be difficult growing up without a father."

"I've done the best I can to provide for them."

"But have you been a father to them?"

"Not really, no."

"Do you wish you had done more?"

"Sometimes," Mr. Wilson admitted. "It's just.... more complicated than that."

"How far are we?" asked Daphne.

"Hmm?" Mr. Wilson had gotten lost in his own reverie.

"From Orchard Square?"

"We're almost there, dear. Don't you worry." He paused for a moment, considering. "I'm sure you'll be fine, but if you ever need anything -" he pulled his wallet from his pocket.

"I don't need your money," she countered, shying away from him.

"No, no, I wasn't going to give you any." He pulled a business card from the wallet and placed it in her hand. "If you ever need anything, give me a call."

She shoved the card in her satchel and promptly forgot about it.

Mr. Wilson had suggested to Dale that the first meeting with his bride-to-be should ideally be in a public place and that she should also stay somewhere in town, maybe even in nearby Weston, just in case things didn't quite work out between them, but Dale did not heed his warning. He had insisted that he bring Daphne directly to his home. After all, if the two of them were to be married, why would there be any need for that kind of separation at the onset? They had spent months communicating with one another online and had made the decision to marry, and all that remained was the confirmation that marriage was something they still wanted. Dale had paid to fly her all the way out here, the least he could do is offer her some decent hospitality until the details of their marriage were worked out.

Daphne carefully examined the homestead as they approached. While Dale worked as a local handyman, he still owned a decent tract of land which was once used for farming, but now sat overgrown and fallow. He kept a handful of chickens for fresh eggs, a few barn cats, and a shaggy herding dog, who ran wildly through the fields without any cattle or sheep to herd. By the time they pulled up the gravel drive, Dale sat waiting on the porch, beer in hand, rocking anxiously on a rickety old chair. He stood to greet them, trying not to roll his eyes at the limo Mr. Wilson had procured. Mr. Wilson leaped from the limo, leaving her sitting in the cool air-conditioned air for a moment.

"I asked you to drive her up, man," Dale complained. "Who's gonna pay for this?"

"Don't worry," Mr. Wilson assured him. "I've got this covered."

"You're just setting a precedent I can't maintain. I nearly spent my last penny on that flight from Cameroon."

"Doesn't your lady deserve the best? I figured a nice luxurious ride would be nice after her long flight."

"Well, sure," replied Dale. "I just…. Well, let me meet her. I've been waiting months for this." He tossed his empty bottle into the weeds alongside the porch, and it quickly rolled under to join a half dozen others. He wiped his hands on his dusty overalls and stepped down to greet her.

Mr. Wilson returned to open the door for her and she blanched at the sudden heat and humidity. Despite its reputation as a cold place full of snow and ice, Wisconsin could get surprisingly warm in the summer. While it didn't compare to the weather in Cameroon, she was still taken aback. It definitely wasn't what she had expected.

"Daphne!" Dale exclaimed, his entire face lighting up.

She approached Dale with some trepidation and initially extended her hand to him before he enveloped her in a warm bear hug. He held on a little too long for her liking and when he eventually released her, she gasped for air.

"I am so glad you're finally here," he said. "Let's go inside and get out of this heat."

He grabbed her arm and escorted her up the steps, across the porch, and inside to his kitchen where they sat across from each other at a small table. Mr. Wilson followed awkwardly behind, like a forgotten shadow.

"Would you like anything to drink?" Dale asked.

"Water would be fine," said Daphne. She set her satchel on the floor beside her.

Dale pulled down a glass from the cupboard and poured some water from the tap. "I have well water, I hope that's fine."

She nodded. All she really wanted was a chance to lay down after all the traveling. Dale set the glass in front of her and stared at her intently. Mr. Wilson stood awkwardly just inside the door.

"Do you want me to grab your things from the car?" asked Dale.

"She doesn't have any other things," Mr. Wilson replied. "I suppose I should get going."

"Yeah, thanks for picking her up," said Dale. He didn't even bother to get up from the table. "See you around."

Mr. Wilson quietly stepped out, closing the door shut behind him and Daphne suddenly felt trapped in this little house in the middle of nowhere with a strange man she barely knew. A man that was supposed to be her husband in such a short time. What had she gotten herself into?

Chapter 26

DAPHNE HAMADOU, 2007

The next few days were decidedly strange for Daphne. Dale doted on her and seemed to be amazed at her very existence. Every morning when she woke, he served her coffee and eggs, and they sat across from each other at the little table in the kitchen. Eventually, she knew, his excitement would likely wane and she'd be expected to do all the cooking. After breakfast, however, he largely left her alone in the house on the edge of town while he drove his truck to neighbors' houses and businesses to fix odds and ends for them. When he returned in the late afternoon, he would disappear into the garage where he tinkered with other things, various woodworking projects, sometimes the truck, and who knew what else. She could hear him banging around in there, but the one time she tried to bring him some fresh apples she had plucked from trees in the yard, he yelled at her to leave him alone and get back in the house. She felt a bit like a prisoner, with nothing to do and nowhere to go.

During the day, while Dale was gone, she found herself laying for hours on the little twin bed he had set up for her in the extra room. He was reluctant to give her a guest bed, at first, because eventually, the plan was for them to share a bed, but she was traditional and insisted on her own place to sleep before they were married. The first night, she had slept on the couch in the living room, but then told him she needed some amount of privacy and her own space in the house. He had made arrangements to bring a second bed in for her, and the small room on the back side of the house quickly became her refuge. She could lay there and dream of the life she had come from, the life she had hoped to live here, and the reality of what her life had become.

She fingered through the contents of her satchel several times. Among her things was a picture of her parents. When they sold her to the cacao farm, it was one of the few things she had hidden away. Despite the discomfort it caused, she folded it and kept it in the bottom of her shoe. It was surprising she had managed to keep it all these years. The creases in the photo had turned a brilliant white so that when she looked at it, the faces of her parents were broken up and frayed. She could still make out the outline of her mother's silhouette, though. She could barely remember the woman, who looked so self-assured in the photograph, staring straight at the photographer. Now she was the age her mother had been in the photograph. If she had survived the fire, what would her mother think of her now, living in America with a man who was not yet her husband?

A sudden wave of shame washed over her. What a lie she was living. She needed to marry the man and get on with her life. Maybe he would treat her differently if she was his wife. Now they felt distant as if she were just a pet he kept around in the house. She should find the courage to talk to him about how lonely she felt. Maybe she should try to meet other people in town, and offer to join him when he left for work.

As she mused, she stumbled upon a small card she had entirely forgotten about. It was Mr. Wilson's business card. She held it in her palm, staring at it for a moment. He had said she could call him if she needed anything, but talking to another man about her problems would be improper. At the same time, it was her only connection to the outside world. She hesitated. Dale was out in the truck and wouldn't be home for at least another few hours. The cordless phone sat in its cradle on the kitchen wall. She snuck out to retrieve it and then returned to the bedroom, stretching out on the bed with her head propped up on pillows.

She stared at the phone for a minute, daring herself to dial. She looked at the numbers on the business card and punched them into the headset. Holding the phone to her ear, she listened to it ring - once, twice, three times. With each ring, her heart pounded violently in her chest. She heard the door in the kitchen and ended the call abruptly. Dale was home early.

She rushed to the kitchen to greet him. "How has your day been?" she asked.

He looked a bit haggard, his hair poking out in all directions, and he sighed heavily. "Can you make me a sandwich?" he asked.

"Sure," she replied and hurried to the fridge. She pulled out the lunch meat and cheese, as well as some mustard. She tried to focus on the task, rather than Dale, but she wanted to ask him so many questions. Where had he been? What was he doing? Why was he home early? Her unasked questions hung in the air, heavy in the growing space between them.

"I didn't get the contract," he eventually muttered, staring at his lap as he sat down at the table.

She moved to the counter and spread both slices of bread with mustard, the way he liked. "That means you have less work?" she asked.

He glanced up at her momentarily. "That's exactly what that means," he replied. "And less money."

She opened the lunchmeat packet and measured out three slices of turkey. It fell to pieces in her hands and she grabbed more until she could cover the full face of the sandwich. Her hands were shaking and she hoped he wouldn't notice. "Where have you been all morning, then?" she tried.

"I stopped out for a drink," he admitted. "Are you done with that sandwich yet? I need something to soak up the alcohol. Then, I might take a nap." He shook his head to himself. "Today has been a total waste."

"But you have other projects, yes?" she asked. She layered a few slices of cheese on top of the turkey and motioned toward the garage. "Something else you're working on?" She had heard him tinkering away just the day before, sawing, hammering, pounding on what must be wood. She hadn't seen his current project, but he had been working on it for several days now.

"That's just a side project," he grumbled. "Not something I'm getting paid for."

She topped the sandwich with the second slice of bread, slid it on a plate, and placed it gingerly before him. She hoped it would meet his standards. The last time she made him a sandwich, she had used mayo instead of mustard and he had thrown it against the wall. The memory seemed like it was just a bad dream now.

He ate hungrily, barely looking up from the plate. "Thank you," he said, once he had finished eating and wiped his lips. "I think I just need to lay down for a while."

She nodded, gathering the sandwich ingredients and putting them quickly and neatly away. At least she was good for something, but she felt a little like a tool rather than a person at the moment. "Do you need a blanket?" she asked, trying to remain useful.

"No, just a few hours of rest should do me," he replied. "Maybe you can tidy up a little?" he asked. "Just don't use the vacuum."

She nodded. She didn't think the place needed cleaning at the moment, but she would oblige. At least it would give her something to do while he slept.

He retreated into his bedroom, closed the door behind him, and fell heavily onto the bed. Within minutes, she could hear the loud wheezing of his snores. She retrieved a broom from the hallway closet and started sweeping the floors. She collected dust bunnies into neat little piles and then gathered them up in the dustpan, depositing them into the trashcan in the kitchen. Once she was certain the floors had been thoroughly cleaned, she listened again for the sounds of Dale sleeping. His snores had grown fainter but they were definitely still there, his heavy breathing echoing from the bedroom.

She returned the broom to its place and snuck into her room. The phone still sat nestled between her bedsheets and her pillow. She could try to call Mr. Wilson again, but didn't want Dale to overhear her conversation. Although he was fast asleep, her room shared a wall with his and if he woke, he would surely hear her. She opted to go out to the porch instead. She hoped the phone would work out there as well.

She grabbed the headset and tiptoed out to the front door. She opened the door, then the screen door behind it, and walked barefoot out onto the porch. She quietly closed the doors behind her and settled onto the rickety rocking chair. A cool breeze played with her hair and brought the earthy scent of dirt and grass to her nose. She leaned back, rocking, and let herself fall into a trance. Despite her fears, this was a beautiful place. The howl of a distant coyote brought her back to reality.

One of the tabby cats crept through the grass, eyeing her. It jumped up onto the porch and slowly made its way toward the chair, then wound figure-eights around her ankles. She picked it up and placed it in her lap, but it clawed away from her, jumping back down and scurrying under the porch. She sighed. None of the animals had taken a liking to her, not even the over-eager sheepdog who preferred to spend his afternoons lounging in the shed. He had sniffed at her a few times, but wouldn't allow her to pet him. Likewise, she collected eggs from the chickens but they ran from her in fear, clucking obscenities as they went.

She stared down at the phone in her lap, daring herself to call again. The numbers ached at her fingertips and eventually, she dialed, her heart leaping up into her throat again. Instead of Mr. Wilson's reassuring voice, she heard the high-pitched singsong of a woman. "How may I direct your call?" she asked.

Daphne gulped, trying to keep her fear from warbling her voice. "I'd like to speak with Mr. Wilson," she tried.

"Alright, just a minute, hon."

She heard the line click onto hold and a piano concerto tinkled through. After about a minute, she considered hanging up but managed to stay on the line just long enough for a male voice to answer.

"Hello?" said Mr. Wilson. "Who is this?"

Daphne spoke softly, barely audible.

"Daphne!" Mr. Wilson boomed, excitedly. "How have you been, my dear! I haven't seen you in town. How is Dale treating you?"

She struggled around a sob. "I feel trapped," she admitted.

Without much forethought, she told him everything, all of the fears and worries she had been holding inside for the past few weeks. She knew she shouldn't be telling another man these things, but he was literally her lifeline to the outside world. Other than Dale and Mr. Wilson, she knew no one and had contact with no one. Mr. Wilson tried to reassure her and offer tips for how she could talk to Dale about how she felt, but nothing could calm her fears. She cried harder, becoming a blubbering, incomprehensible mess, and grew so distraught she didn't even notice when the front door opened behind her.

"Daphne? Are you alright?" asked Dale, placing one worried hand on her shoulder. She flinched at the touch of his hand. Then he saw the phone. "Who are you talking to?"

Before she could end the call, he snatched the phone from her and shouted into the receiver. "Who is this?! Why are you making my woman cry?" He paused, listening for a response. He turned to Daphne, who struggled to hastily wipe her tears from her face. "What's going on here?"

"I can explain," started Daphne.

"Erwin?" Dale shouted into the phone. "Why are you talking with my woman?"

Dale didn't want to hear an explanation from either of them. He hung up the phone and snatched up what fabric he could grab from the sleeve of Daphne's blouse. He dragged her, protesting, into the house, swearing as he did so. She cringed and tried to slip free from him, and he grabbed her shoulder instead, squeezing her arm so tightly it ached with pain.

"Please, don't," she begged him, the tears streaming down her face, but he only grabbed her harder, pulling both arms behind her back. She clenched her teeth and tried to break free but the more she struggled the harder he clenched her. Within moments he was pushing her down the hallway, using one hand to hold her wrists and pushing the other into her back.

"Why are you talking to other men, you whore?!" he spat.

"I'm not -" she tried, the words falling ineffectually from her lips. Fear flashed through her eyes. She crumpled against the weight of his words.

He pushed her toward the little room in the back of the house. When he finally reached the door, he let go of her wrists for a moment to fling it open but followed it with a swift kick to the back of her knees so that she stumbled forward into the room. She fell to the floor, landing with a loud thud that shook the house, and he slammed the door behind her. She lay there, unable to move for several minutes, her body shaking. Her limbs remembered this, even if her brain had blocked it out, what it felt to be treated like a broken object, a doll no longer wanted. While she shook and sobbed on the floor, blood dripping from her bottom lip where she had made an impact, she heard a key in the door. He was locking her in, and now she was his prisoner.

He held her in the room, without an offer of drink or food, for the rest of the day. A few times, she heard the rev of the truck's engine, its wheels crunching down the gravel driveway, but otherwise, she waited in pain and silence. She watched the birds landing in the apple tree from her tiny window, jealous of their freedom. That night, she tried to apologize, crying out "I'm sorry" repeatedly, but he paid her no heed. She managed to sleep, but terrifying dreams plagued her. She spent the rest of the time lying in bed, staring at the ceiling. How long could he keep her like this, she wondered, and had he ever cared about her in the first place? What kind of man could do this?

In the morning, while she counted the spiders building webs in the eaves, she heard the key in the lock. She didn't bother sitting up. After all, what could this mean but that he wanted to hurt her more? Instead, he tiptoed to the bed and reached for her. At first, she flinched away, but then she saw his face, pale and sad. His eyes shimmered with uncried tears. She let him gently push the hair from her face and sat up against the pillows.

"You know I love you, right?" he asked.

She nodded without answering. She had cried herself hoarse and hadn't tried to use her voice for some time. If she were to speak, she wasn't sure if she'd be able to form the words.

"Come," he beckoned. "Let's have breakfast. Like old times." He reached for her hand and held it, limp and weak in his own strong fingers. "I made your eggs just the way you like them, and coffee."

She wasn't sure what had caused his change of heart but she rose cautiously from the bed and trailed slightly behind him as he led her to the kitchen. As promised, he had laid the table for breakfast, and the eggs smelled terrific. Her stomach growled in anticipation, but when she sat, she found she couldn't begin to lift the fork to eat. It felt like a trick he was playing on her, and she didn't know what to expect. Would he poison her?

He smiled weakly at her from across the table. Alongside the coffee and eggs were orange juice and fresh melon. He had folded a napkin neatly under her fork and placed a few yellow flowers in a vase next to her plate. Slowly, he added cream and sugar to his coffee and then sipped it, staring at her. "Aren't you hungry?" he asked.

She lifted her fork and made an effort to scoop up some scrambled eggs, then mechanically brought them to her mouth. Everything felt so surreal now, like she was dreaming. She looked cautiously at him, then back to her food. It did taste good. It wasn't like she wasn't hungry. After she had taken a few more bites, she relaxed a little and managed to drink some of the coffee and a few sips of the orange juice.

"You know," he began. "If you were good, I wouldn't have to punish you."

She looked into his face and saw he was completely sincere. He felt he was in the right and that she had somehow wronged him with nothing more devastating than a phone call.

"I have something for you," he offered. He got up and left the kitchen, not even looking back at her as he went.

For a moment, she became very aware of the door beside her, the door which led outside to the front porch. While he was out of the room, she could easily flee, but where would she go from there? The truck sat idle in the driveway, but she didn't know how to drive it. Besides, how far could she get before he would be after her and catch her. The last thing she wanted was to be locked away in the bedroom again.

Dale returned with something small clutched in his hand. He bounded into the room with excitement. "I hope you like it," he exclaimed.

She set her coffee down and stared at him in disbelief as he opened his hand and showed her what had been his grandmother's wedding ring.

"I think it's time you had this."

He reached for her left hand and tried to wedge the small ring onto her finger. After several attempts, he finally gave up. Her finger was much too big for the piece of jewelry. Eventually, he slid it onto her pinky instead.

"Now everyone will know you're mine," he said, smiling up at her.

She grimaced. After all, that was how he viewed her now, as property. She tried to remind herself that this was still better than the life she would have had in Cameroon. She tried to be thankful, but her heart ached. She felt so utterly betrayed.

As she cleared the plates and began washing the dishes, he paged through the newspaper. Once the plates had been put away, he turned his attention back to her.

"I think we'll do something new today," he said.

She didn't respond, just listened tentatively.

"I want you to come with me on my rounds."

She wasn't sure if this was a good thing or a bad thing, but she was eager to finally leave the house. "That sounds nice," she managed.

Then he added the real reason for his suggestion. "That way I can keep an eye on you."

Chapter 27

PRESENT DAY

I had managed to slurp my milkshake to the dregs, but I couldn't believe Dale could share this story with us in such an open and honest way. Surely, he must feel ashamed for the way he had treated his mail-order bride. Despite the fact that he had found her in an online catalog, she was still a person with dreams and desires, wants and needs. Nevertheless, it was an intriguing story.

"How did you know the way she thought, what she felt through all of this?" I asked. It was a legitimate question. Even with the passage of years, a person could only develop so much empathy.

"I'm not done with the story yet," Dale said. "But if you must know, months after she left, I found a small journal in her room, under the bed. It was written entirely in French, but I got it translated." He shook his head, staring down at the remnants of his pie, poking it dejectedly with his fork. "I thought I was protecting her," he explained as he downed the last few sips of his second cup of coffee. "But I had no idea what I was doing," he admitted.

Brandon put one arm around his friend. "I hate to say it, buddy, but it's probably a good thing you never married her."

Dale sighed, "I know. You're right."

Luis, who was also just finishing his ice cream, piped up. "I think sometimes people are just horrible to each other. They forget that other people are human, too. They get so wrapped up in their own little worlds that they forget, and then they become so ugly."

Dale nodded. "If you've already got that figured out, son, you'll go far in life."

Luis gave him a wide grin. "But you were pretty horrible to her, I think."

"Truth is, I didn't deserve her."

"So, then what happened?" I finally asked. Clearly, things were going south and fast. Could this story possibly have a happy ending for any of them?

"I thought I could own her," admitted Dale. "She was mine and no one else's, and I intended to keep it that way. But my attempts to keep her close only made other people aware of what was happening. The day I brought her along, I pretty much had her stay in the truck. I didn't need her to help me, I just needed to keep an eye on her."

"Was it a hot day?" I asked.

"What?" Dale's face suddenly fell, as if he was realizing for the first time just exactly what he had put that woman through.

"Did you make that poor woman sit in a hot truck all day?"

"Well, I -" Dale shook his head. "I suppose I did. I went to the first few stops, and then decided I would take her with me for a lunch here."

Darlene approached the table, asking us for refills on coffee. I decided to get a cup, Luis got ice water and the men got refills. "I remember that day," she added. "Dale was here with this beautiful black girl I had never seen before. Her skin just shone and her hair was slicked back into this great tuft on the top of her head." She finished filling our drinks and slowly stepped back. "I could tell she definitely wasn't from around here, and she didn't eat much either, just kinda picked at her food a bit."

"Alright," I said. "Then what?" I kept hoping for that happy ending, and I still wasn't sure if I was going to get it.

Dale continued. "We finished eating and I paid. I told her to wait in the car while I went to the john. By the time I came out, she was gone."

"What do you mean, she was gone?" Luis asked.

"Later, I found out Erwin had stopped by. He saw her sitting in the truck and started talking with her. He just loaded her into his big fancy car and drove off," explained Dale.

Brandon nodded in agreement. "I remember that night. You came into the bar mad as hell."

"Yeah, he finally had the guts to come clean. Told me over the phone that it was for her safety."

"Based on what you've told us," I said. "It sounds like that was the case."

"But he couldn't be a man about it and just confront me face-to-face," complained Dale.

"I don't think that was really an option, buddy," said Brandon.

"Then, she just married him instead of you?" I asked.

"Eventually," explained Dale. "She shacked up with him for a while. I'm not sure what their arrangement was. I found my grandmother's ring in my mailbox one day. It was so strange. I thought I had it all figured out but I didn't have a clue."

"Well, it sounds like you eventually got on friendly terms with him again," I said.

"Sure. After she was gone, we shared a pint, hashed it out," said Dale.

Brandon chuckled. "So many things get worked out over a beer."

Dale nodded. "You know, it's been a long while since I thought about Daphne."

"Why didn't you tell us about her the night we stopped at Earl's Pub?" I asked. "You told us about some of Mr. Wilson's other wives."

"Just too painful. I didn't want to think about it."

Chapter 28

It was only the afternoon but already felt like it had been a long day. We said our goodbyes and Luis and I went back to the cabin. I collected the tape recordings, jotted down a few notes, and then laid down for a nap. The cabin was still and quiet when I woke and the sun was already glowing red in the west. Luis wasn't inside, so I stepped out on the porch, half expecting to see him sipping a forbidden beer on the porch swing, but he wasn't there either. I looked out to the lake, thinking maybe he had taken a canoe out, but the lake was smooth and clear, not a single ripple in sight. He had simply disappeared.

Within moments my heart felt like it would burst from my chest and I could hardly breathe. I had been so wrapped up in getting the story that I hadn't paid enough attention to my brother. How could he just leave like that? I mean, he had arrived all of a sudden, but I thought he was as committed to this as I was. I thought we had agreed that he would help me and I'd even put him in the acknowledgments, but what could I expect from a sixteen-year-old? Apparently not much.

I checked my phone for a signal and thankfully, I still had a few bars out here. I dialed his phone once, twice, three times. I let it ring and ring and ring. He didn't answer. Maybe he had no service. Maybe his phone was dead. I couldn't believe he would just disappear with no note, no word of goodbye, no nothing. And now night fell around me, the sky growing darker and darker with each moment. I kept frantically calling as I sat on the porch swing, but eventually gave up and slumped into an uneasy sleep.

I woke early with the first few rays of light and started sketching out a search plan. I thought of the places I had been to with my brother and where he might be. Maybe he had decided to be responsible and return to the Scout camp across the way. I drove over, spoke with one of the counselors, and they admitted they hadn't seen Luis since he ran away. They still harbored a grudge against him for abandoning his post, but hadn't heard from him.

So I drove over to The Deep Dish. After all, I needed something to eat and he might very well have stopped on his way out of town. Darlene was pleasant and cheery as ever but her face fell when I told her my real reason for being there.

"Have you seen my brother, Luis?" I asked as she poured me some steaming coffee.

"Not since yesterday afternoon, dear. Why do you ask?"

I shook my head, struggling to form the words. "I think I lost him."

She wrung her hands, twisting them through her apron. "I'm sure he'll turn up," she offered. "Can I get you extra whipped cream for that French toast?" I could tell the only language she could really speak was food.

"No, I just need to eat quickly, think of the places we've been, where he might possibly be."

"I'd try Earl's Pub for sure," she offered.

"Are they open this early?" I asked.

"Let's see." She checked a gold watch on her wrist. "They should open around 11, 11:30. Depends on what time Brandon gets there to unlock the doors." She motioned toward my breakfast. "Give yourself some time to eat. You don't need to scarf it down."

My French toast was already more than half gone, but I could take a moment. I glanced around the diner and saw a tall man sitting in the corner who I had never seen. He was just sitting there drinking coffee and staring at me from across the restaurant, but I wasn't being too covert in the way I glanced at him, either. He probably wasn't staring, just wondering why I was taking an interest in him. I looked away, but could still feel his dark eyes upon me.

When Darlene returned with a warm-up of coffee, I asked if she knew him.

"No, he's not from around here," she replied. "Just passing through, he says. I could introduce you if you like." She seemed to like the idea of bringing random people together, but entirely misunderstood my intentions.

"No, no, that's fine," I said. "I was just wondering."

"Are you sure? It's no problem, really."

"No, it's fine. Can I just get the tab?"

"Sure thing."

I glanced at him again and caught the man looking at me. I began to feel uneasy. First Luis disappears off the map and then this strange man appears to stare me down. I couldn't place him either. Part of me wanted to overcome my fear and just approach him, but the rest of me felt assured it must be nothing. I was just on edge because of Luis. I was anxious and worried and couldn't think straight. Eventually, I'd find Luis holed up somewhere, caught in a bit of teenage mischief and everything would be righted again.

I paid the tab, took one last glance in the direction of the strange man, and noticed he had left already. See, I told myself, nothing to worry about. It was just my imagination. If anything, he was staring at me because I was staring at him, and there was nothing more to it than that. I slipped behind the driver's seat of my car and quickly rolled down the windows. I had air conditioning but preferred the fresh air. Already, summer had begun to swell with heat and anytime I found myself outside midday, I felt hot and sweaty. The humidity made the air cloying and heavy. I checked the time, just a little after 11. I supposed I could drive down to Earl's Pub. If nothing else, I could take a little walk to kill the time until the doors opened. Maybe listen to some music on the radio to clear my head.

Sure enough, when I arrived, the doors were still locked and I had some time to kill. I found a bench just outside the bar and decided to sit there in the shade of the overhang. I tried Luis' number once more, hoping for a miracle, but the line just rang and rang with no response. I tried shooting him a quick text. Teenagers these days are so quick to ignore actual phone calls. "It's Liz. Where are you?" I typed, but once again received no response. I imagined him in an Uber with an unsavory driver, kidnapped and locked in a basement. My brain ran through several disastrous scenarios before Brandon pulled up with his rusty red truck.

He approached me smiling. "Had a rough morning?" he asked.

"Actually, yes." I stood to greet him and he wrapped me in a friendly hug. I felt comforted for just a minute. "Have you seen my brother?"

"The twerp you were palling around with yesterday?" he asked. He turned to unlock the door behind him as we spoke.

"Yeah, Luis. He just got up and left yesterday while I was napping. I have no idea where he is."

Brandon harrumphed as he flipped on the lights. "No, last I saw him was with you." He tested the taps, pulled out a rag to wipe down the bar, and unlocked the till, all in one smooth motion. He must have done all these things a thousand times before. "I'm sure he'll turn up."

"In the meantime, I'm turning gray over here." I sighed, letting the air fly out of my lungs and then taking another deep in-breath. Maybe no news was good news. It was better than hearing Luis had tried to come to the bar last night and drink. I didn't think Brandon would serve my brother without me, but who knew? This place seemed a bit lax in its attitude toward youngsters drinking.

"Since you're here, can I get you anything?" Brandon asked.

"Got a shot of Malort?" I mused. Malort is a Chicago classic that many say tastes like a combination of sweaty gym socks and week-old urine, but the very unique flavor would bring me a bit of familiar comfort now.

"Ma-what?" he asked.

"Nevermind. It's a Chicago thing."

"Gotcha. How about some Wild Turkey?"

"That'll do."

He poured two shot glasses of the amber liquid, we clinked them and each downed our shot.

"Anything else I can get ya?" he offered. "Sounds like you've got a day ahead."

"That's for sure." I didn't even bother sitting on a stool. "I think I should head out, maybe head to Weston. I'm trying all the places I took him around here."

"I'm sure he's fine," Brandon said, trying to reassure me. "While boys can get themselves into trouble, it's usually nothing too hard to get out of. He seems like a good kid."

"Thanks. Just let me know if he stops by," I said, reaching for a napkin. "If he does, call me at this number." I grabbed a pen from my purse and jotted down my cell number.

"Sure thing. Good luck." He picked up the shot glasses and set them in the sink, then started wiping down the bar with his rag. "I'll be here if you need a drink later."

"I might take you up on that."

I went back out to my car, wincing as I slid across the hot driver's seat. This time I closed the windows and turned on the AC. This was definitely putting a damper on my investigation, but my brother took priority. As I drove out to the county highway, I dialed my agent, Michael. It would be nice to hear a familiar voice, and I should probably update him on my progress. He answered after the first ring.

"What's kicking, beautiful? You got some words for me yet?"

I wished I had better news for him. "Not just yet."

"It's been a few weeks. Why haven't you written?"

"I've been collecting intel. And now I've hit a bit of a snag as well."

The highway was gloriously empty, with soft, rolling hills rising on either side of the road as I drove. I felt like if I could just keep driving, maybe I could run away and pretend my life made sense. With Luis missing, I felt so lost again, so alone.

"Explain," he chided. "Some of the old biddies are not talking? Do I need to rough someone up?"

As I started to explain, I realized I hadn't even told him about my brother's unexpected visit, so I had to give some background first. "My little brother came to visit unexpectedly so I put him to work."

"I see. Reinforcements!" Michael could be so animated about everything. "Or distractions?"

"A bit of both," I admitted. "But now he's gone and run off and I need to find him."

"So mostly distractions, then."

"It would seem so, but once I find him, which I'm sure I will soon, I have some interesting developments."

"Do tell."

"So it seems Mr. Wilson was mostly a philanderer, but also an unintentional philanthropist."

"Now that's a mouthful. What do you mean?"

"So, some of these women might not have necessarily married him for the money, I mean I'm sure it was a bonus, but they're benefitting from it."

"How so?"

"Alimony. Child support. They're sucking off him like leeches. Or rather, they were."

"Alright, alright, I can dig it. If you've had that many wives, you're not necessarily marrying them all for the same reasons. And I like the sound of it, for a cover blurb."

"The sound of what?"

"Philanderer turned philanthropist. It's a mouthful, but also has a nice ring to it." It figured that Michael would find a way to make light of it.

"And there's something else," I added.

"Oooh! Intrigue!"

I couldn't help but chuckle at his excitement. "I just heard about another wife that he essentially stole from a friend, but of course, it's more complicated than that."

"Alright, I'm listening."

"She was a mail order bride."

Michael audibly gasped on the other line. "And?"

"The friend wasn't treating her right, so he stole her away, and then married her himself."

"Good, good. I like where this is going."

"But for now..." I sighed loudly. "I need to find Luis."

"Understandable," said Michael. "But when do you think you can get me something? Right now, we're just riding on good faith here. I can only talk you up so much before the publisher expects the goods."

"I get it," I said. "I've got a job to do, you've got a job to do, we've all got things expected of us. But right now, I need to find my brother."

"Keep me updated," said Michael. "And good luck. Teenage boys can be a major pain in the ass," he added.

"Yes," I agreed. "Yes, they can." I hung up and returned my attention to the road. The sign for Weston was just ahead.

Chapter 29

My first stop was at the university library, although I did not expect to have much luck there. What teenage boy would run away to visit a library? But I wanted to make sure I covered all my bases, and it had been one of the places we had visited. It had only been about a week ago but felt like ages since we had visited, since I had requested my advance from Michael and shelled out the $100 for a library card. The same friendly librarian sat at the information desk, her hair curled in tight little ringlets. She glanced up at me through her red cat's eye glasses.

"And what can I help you with today?" she asked, with far more perky energy than I could muster at the moment.

"I'm looking for a little Hispanic boy, about yay tall." I held my flattened hand up to indicate his height, starting at about my shoulder and then realizing he now towered over me. I reached my hand up further, and then laughed at myself. "I suppose he's not that little anymore."

She smiled. She had probably fielded several more odd questions already today. Despite the advent of the internet, people always expected librarians to be a fount of endless knowledge. "When do you expect him to come in?" she asked for clarification.

"Honestly, I doubt he's here, I'm just grasping at straws." My face fell then, and I struggled to fight back tears. "He ran away yesterday afternoon. At least, I think that's what happened."

"I can give you a call if he shows up," she offered.

"Don't bother, I'm sure he'll call me when he comes back to his senses," I said.

"Did you have a disagreement?" she asked. "Was there a reason for him to run off?"

"That's just it." I shook my head in frustration. "Everything was fine, or I thought it was. Maybe there's something I'm missing."

She smiled up at me, eager to help but offering no help whatsoever. I sighed. This was a dead end, and I might as well try the next place, the cafe we had visited the other day. I felt like I was running around in circles, getting nowhere in the process.

"Thank you again," I said.

As I turned to walk away, I spotted a familiar face. It couldn't be. The stranger from the diner sat just a few tables away, staring at me with those piercing eyes. If I had more energy, if I had more courage I would approach him, ask him what his problem was and why he was following me. Instead, I tried to brush it off. It must be my imagination, I thought. It couldn't be the same guy, I was just seeing things.

I walked the other way, pushed out the door, and pushed him to the back of my mind. I needed to find my brother. What was it they said about the first twenty-four hours a child was missing? I suppose he wasn't a little kid anymore but I still had no idea what had happened and was beyond worried thinking about him.

The muggy air had become even heavier with moisture and clouds gathered above. It looked like it would start raining at any moment, so instead of walking to the cafe, I drove the few blocks in my car. The windows fogged up quickly and I could barely see but didn't bother turning on the defroster because it really wasn't that far. I looked around the small cafe and saw immediately that Luis wasn't there but forced myself to stand in line with the other customers. If nothing else, I needed something to eat.

By the time I got to the front of the line, I had read over the entire menu at least three times, but nothing sounded particularly appetizing. My stomach was doing flip-flops.

"What is the soup of the day?" I asked the girl behind the counter.

"We have our usual chicken and rice and broccoli cheddar. Today's special is stuffed bell pepper."

I'd had stuffed bell peppers before, but never in soup form. It was worth a try. "I guess I'll have that."

"Cup or bowl?" she asked.

"Just a cup please, and maybe some crackers."

"Oyster or saltine?"

"Saltine." Maybe I'd be able to settle my stomach.

It was approaching late afternoon already and I was getting nowhere in my search for Luis. I found a small two-top table near a window and stared out at the raindrops as they began to fall, heavy on the pavement. The sky grew dim, and the bare bulb lighting in the restaurant sparsely illuminated the space. They brought me my soup and I spooned it up slowly, nibbling at my crackers and trying to push away the gnawing guilt growing in my gut. How could I have lost him? What had I done to make him run away?

Just as I finished the last few spoonfuls of soup, my phone rang. It was an unknown number, but I nearly jumped out of my seat, rushing to answer it.

"Hello?"

The voice on the other end was a female, so not Luis. She spoke quietly and quickly and I could barely make out what she was saying.

"I'm sorry?" I tried.

She sighed deeply, and then repeated herself, a little more clearly this time.

"This is Laura, you called me last week asking for an interview about Mr. Wilson. I'm staying at the Morpheus Hotel if you'd like to meet, say around 6?"

So it wasn't anything about Luis, but still promising. I struggled to shift back into interviewing mode. "Yes, yes, that would be fine."

"We can meet at the bar. I find that liquor helps loosen lips, don't you?"

"Sometimes, yes."

"Alright, see you then, dearie."

I hung up, excited and disappointed at the same time. At least I'd have something to distract me for a while. I finished my food, tried another desperate call to Luis' cell with no success, and looked up the address for the hotel. It was on the other side of town, so I had a bit of a drive, but I still had time.

It was still raining but had slowed to a drizzle, a haze of fog covering the streets. I drove slowly and carefully, my thoughts alternating between worries for my brother and my plans for interviewing Laura. If I remembered correctly, she had been smack dab in the middle of Mr. Wilson's wives, number twelve or thirteen. Even after all this time, I still couldn't quite wrap my head around the number of women he had married. It felt like something was still missing, a piece of the puzzle that I hadn't found just yet. I had these conflicting views of who Mr. Wilson was, a flirt, a philanderer, a wayward soul, a white knight. Most of the women I spoke with bore him no ill will, but that was partly because he had paid them each off, in turn, and his estate continued to pay them. I'm sure just a spoonful of sugar helps the medicine go down, and in this case, that sugar was money.

As I drove, I noticed a long black car, a sedan with brilliant blue LED headlights behind me. The glare of the lights in my side mirror and review nearly blinded me. I've always hated cars with obnoxiously bright headlights. In the city, especially, they seem entirely unnecessary. Hopefully, he'd stop follow-ing me soon and I'd be able to focus more on my own driving than shielding my eyes. That was a wishful hope, though. He seemed to be gaining on me, tailgating. I watched as he fol-lowed ever closer behind, following me around one turn and then another. Was I actually being followed? I swore, tapping on my breaks in the hope that he'd take a hint and back off a little, but he continued following close and panic rose in my throat. I imagined the strange man with piercing eyes trailing me, stalking me, plotting to rape and murder me.

Of course, I couldn't see the driver past those headlights. One last turn into the parking lot of the Morpheus and finally he was gone, the car nowhere in sight. I breathed out slowly. I would be fine. I was just on edge because of everything that had happened recently. Now I just needed to check into the hotel. I figured I might as well spend the night in Weston at this point. I still had a little time before my meeting with Laura. Maybe I could try to relax for a while. I chuckled at myself. Yeah, like that was going to happen. My brain was still a whir of activity.

I checked my account online. I still had a good portion of the advance available, so I splurged for a King-sized suite and picked up my key from the concierge. By the time I got up to the room, I was eager for one of my long afternoon naps but feared I wouldn't wake from it in time. Instead, I propped my-self up on the half-dozen pillows in the bed and flipped on the television.

There wasn't much on and the hotel didn't get many chan-nels. I spent some time watching a cooking show, then settled for an outdated episode of Maury. It was one of the paternity test shows, where women dragged men on to prove that they were the father of an illegitimate child. Much of the time, they were, but sometimes they weren't. Regardless of the outcome, there was always a good deal of yelling, screaming, crying, and overall drama regarding the paternity of these children. I always wondered why people wanted to air their dirty laundry in public like that, but it could be surprisingly entertaining.

Before I knew it, my alarm was blaring. Apparently, I had managed to doze for a bit, anyway. I turned off the ringer, flipped off the TV, and rolled out of the oversized bed. I took a quick look at my clothes, a bit rumpled from sleeping in them, but not entirely wrinkled. I hadn't brought anything else with me, so they'd have to do. Maybe tomorrow I'd go shopping.

I took the elevator down to the bar and glanced around. There were two young women giggling together at one end, both of them much too young to be the former Mrs. Wilson. It appeared she had not arrived yet. I ordered myself a whiskey sour and settled onto one of the bar stools. I made polite conversation with the bartender, who barely looked old enough to drink himself, and waited.

When Laura Wilson arrived, it was with dramatic flair. I had heard the phrase "dripping with pearls" but never before had I witnessed it. She wore several long strands around her neck, which cascaded down to her waist, as well as twisted bracelets of cream and dangling earrings which ran to her shoulders. If I didn't see it with my own eyes, I could not have imagined it. The pink dress she wore was almost entirely engulfed by her jewelry. She placed her white clutch on the bar and beckoned to me. "I would prefer to sit in a booth, dear, if you don't mind. Barstools are so uncivilized."

I acquiesced and she settled herself into one of the plush semicircles flanking the bar. I brought my cocktail over, which I had been gingerly sipping. If nothing else, this promised to be an interesting evening, if I could just keep my worries for Luis at the back of my brain. She ordered a Gibson and when it arrived, twisted the onion garnishing it with two fingers, like it was just another, much larger, pearl for her to play with. I wanted to ask if all the off-white orbs were real, but I also didn't want to insult her. Before I could broach any subject, she pulled the onion from its toothpick and plopped it into her mouth. Then she began telling her story.

Chapter 30

LAURA BIANCHI, 1990

Laura was a hopeless romantic who had her heart set on a young man who wanted nothing to do with her. At the abortion clinic, they sat her in the chair, and she felt strangely lightheaded. She had her mind set on getting rid of it, had refused to think of the baby as anything more than it, and had even joked among friends about the alien growing inside her. But what she wouldn't let on was that this small cluster of cells growing inside her was the only connection she had left to the man she loved. It didn't matter that he didn't feel the same; it was still her only claim to him. She imagined their baby looking just like him - the same sly smile and bright eyes. It would be a boy, she had decided, although, of course, she didn't know. They asked her if she wanted an ultrasound picture, but she refused. It was just too painful. The only thing she asked was if the pregnancy were twins. Would two babies have changed her mind? Did she believe it was life growing or just a clump of cells?

She would need to make another appointment for the actual procedure, but this decision was too heavy for her. She wanted her baby daddy to make it for her, but he wouldn't. Freddie was a good kid that way. He said it was her choice because, ultimately, she would be the one to live with it. But it was a choice she felt she couldn't make. She would lie awake at night, tortured by the thought of it. So she tried to pretend it wasn't happening. She didn't make a choice, even when she most likely should have. She chose not to choose, and she waited too long to choose. There was an upper limit to her denial, eventually, a point at which she could no longer look in the mirror and pretend she wasn't pregnant, that she was just gaining weight. That she was just sick and tired, bloated and sore, and all the things a woman is when she is pregnant. She didn't marvel at the wonder of her own body, didn't rejoice when she started to feel the baby squirm and kick. Each of these moments was just another heartbreak, another reminder that she was alone with this.

Her days passed like endless sighs, marking moments that became weeks and months. She could no longer control her emotions, ranging from giddy highs to obsessive lows. Some days she would lie in bed, wishing she were dead and that she could sleep forever, just forget everything that had happened. At some point, a woman came to visit, a woman who said her name was Miriam. She offered hope when Laura so desperately needed it.

A knock came at the door, midmorning, and Laura's subconscious incorporated it into a dream. A masked man knocked, knocked, knocked, and Laura, still deep in sleep, answered it. The man had no face, just a blank white space where a face should be. She took one look at him, faceless, wearing a long black robe, and screamed and screamed. Miriam knocked again, and Laura woke, feeling groggy and terrified. The very real knock reverberated through her entire apartment. Laura pulled her pink terry cloth robe around her, slid her feet into fuzzy bunny slippers, and shuffled to the door. Before opening the door, she looked through the peephole to see a woman who looked a bit like a Jehovah's Witness.

"Who is it?" she called.

"My name is Miriam."

"I don't know you," replied Laura.

"Consider me a friend. Freddie sent me."

Laura sighed, her heart aching, and she felt like her stomach would drop out of her. Who could this be? A new girlfriend? Nevertheless, she unhooked the chain and turned the bolt. She stood, one hand on the door and the other on her hip. "And who might you be?"

Miriam snaked her way in, smiling like a billboard advertisement. She handed Laura her business card. Laura barely glanced at it, but she could feel the thickness of the paper it was printed on and the embossing. Laura closed the door behind the professionally dressed woman.

"I work for an organization that might be able to help you," Miriam explained. "Is there anywhere we can sit?"

"Next room," said Laura. "Kitchen table." She flicked the light switch, and a single bulb sputtered above the table.

The two women sat across from each other, and Laura let her bathrobe fall open. She wore an oversized stained t-shirt with no bra and basketball shorts. Miriam crossed and recrossed her legs.

"You want my baby?" asked Laura. She let one hand rest on her swollen abdomen. "Adoption agency?"

"Not exactly," said Miriam.

"Good, because I might as well keep it at this point." She stared off into space, her mind blank.

"How are you doing?" asked Miriam.

"How do I look like I'm doing?"

"Have you been going to your doctor's appointments? Have a plan for the care and feeding of your baby?"

"I've got two hands and two tits," Laura smirked at her. "I think I've got it covered."

"Do you have a source of income?"

"Not exactly. But I'm sure I'll qualify for WIC and food stamps."

"Those only cover the bare minimum," explained Miriam. "My organization may be able to help you more than that."

"There's that word again. Organization." Laura looked directly at Miriam this time, sizing her up.

"I gave you a card." Miriam pointed at the business card Laura had tossed on the table. "Take a look."

"Why so secretive?" asked Laura. She glanced down at the card, more carefully this time, and realized it didn't have Miriam's name on it, but instead read: Mr. Wilson's Wives. Below the words were the digits for a phone number. "What is this? Who is Mr. Wilson?"

"Someone who cares," said Miriam.

"Cares about what?" asked Laura. "About me? I don't know any Mr. Wilson."

"You can meet him if you would like."

"I don't understand. You said Freddie sent you."

"He did." Miriam began to stand, straightening her skirt as she did so. "Freddie understands he can't provide for you, but Mr. Wilson might be able to help."

"What is this about wives? I don't want to marry anyone. Is this a cult?"

Miriam had already moved to open the front door before Laura could catch up with her. "Give it a think," she said. "Then, call the number, and I'll set up a meeting for you."

"I still don't understand," said Laura.

Miriam looked back before starting to close the door behind her. "Call the number." Then, she was gone, and Laura still wasn't sure she was properly and fully awake. The whole incident seemed so incredibly strange. All she had were more questions than logic could answer, but it would be several days before she would dare call the number on the card Miriam had given her.

Laura spent the next few days questioning her sanity. Between the obvious dream and the not-so-obvious meeting with Miriam, she needed to know more. She tried calling Freddie because, after all, this woman knew him, but she received no answer. That wasn't entirely surprising but didn't sit well with her either. Why would Freddie send this strange woman to her door without warning? Who was she, and who the hell was this Mr. Wilson? And what was up with the wives thing? The more she thought about it, the more she considered that she might have stumbled upon a polygamous cult or nefarious organization that just wanted to take the baby from her.

Her hands shook as she dialed the number, then she waited impatiently for someone to pick up on the line. Her breath came in jagged rasps. Worst case scenario, she could just hang up. It was relatively risk-free at this point. She recognized the voice that answered, a calm voice that soothed her nerves.

"So, what have you decided?" asked Miriam.

"What was I supposed to decide?"

"Would you like to meet Mr. Wilson?"

"Um, sure, I guess," said Laura.

"How's tomorrow afternoon at about 2 p.m. sound for you?"

"I guess that will work."

"Come to Wide Awake Cafe then. Do you know where that is?"

"Yes, it's about a block from my home."

"Good. And wear something nice. A dress if you have one."

"Alright."

"Mr. Wilson will see you then."

"Wait!" gasped Laura. "I have so many questions!"

"All will be revealed," said Miriam, then hung up the phone.

Laura sighed. What had she gotten herself into?

The next afternoon, Laura squeezed herself into a bright polka-dotted dress she had purchased a few weeks ago in the Maternity section of Target. In such a short time, it stretched taut over her ever-growing waist and barely fit her. She stuffed her swollen feet into a pair of old tennis shoes, laced them up, and walked to Wide Awake Cafe. When she got there, she was already short of breath and struggled to push the door open. The bell above the door rang, and the first person she saw was Miriam, who quickly escorted her to a table.

"So, where's Mr. Wilson?" Laura asked.

Miriam hushed her and poured her a tall glass of cool water. "He'll be here soon."

"Anything you can tell me about him?"

"He's a very kind and generous man." Miriam smiled, showing a row of perfectly straight, perfectly white teeth. "Trust me. He helped me and will help you, too, if you agree to certain conditions."

Laura started to stutter out a question, but Miriam raised a finger to her lips. "Patience. All will be revealed."

* * *

Laura drank her water as she waited for Mr. Wilson. Miriam sat, tapping her fingernails on the table but saying nothing. Eventually, a large man dressed in a tailored gray suit came to the front door. Miriam stood and crossed the cafe to welcome him in. The man unwrapped a scarf from his thick neck and followed Miriam back to the table. Before sitting down, he offered Laura his hand and introduced himself in a low, soft voice. "Nice to meet you, Laura. I'm Mr. Wilson, but feel free to call me Erwin. I hope this will be the beginning of a great friendship."

His hands were warm, and his handshake was confident. Laura took him for a successful businessman, though she wasn't sure just what business he was in. "Nice to meet you," she said, echoing his greeting. "Now, will one of you explain to me what is happening?"

Erwin and Miriam laughed together as if they were in on a private joke. Laura looked from one to the other and shrugged her shoulders. "Anyone?" she asked.

Miriam turned to Erwin before the conversation continued. "Can I get you anything, hon?"

"Some tea. Earl gray, if you've got any."

"Sure thing."

After Miriam left to prepare the tea, Erwin turned to Laura conspiratorially. "I understand you are seeking assistance regarding your situation."

"My situation?" asked Laura, feeling a bit uneasy. She chewed her lip.

Erwin motioned toward her pregnant belly. "You are with child, are you not?"

"What a quaint way of putting it," said Laura. "Yep. I'm preggers, alright."

"And the father?"

"Wants nothing to do with me or it."

"Do you know the gender yet?"

"Does it matter?" she asked.

"Not particularly, just a polite thing to ask."

"Miriam didn't tell me much. She was pretty darn cryptic," explained Laura. "Are you looking to buy the baby, or what?"

"Oh, I don't traffic in babies." Erwin chuckled. "Wouldn't that be a messy racket!"

"I suppose." Laura felt slightly turned off by his use of the word 'racket.' Who did this guy think he was, some kind of mobster?

"No, I work with women. With making their lives better."

Miriam returned with the tea and a saucer with a spoon and honey. She sat beside Laura with a small smile, crossed her legs at the knee, and waited patiently while Erwin slowly stirred the honey into his steaming teacup. Laura looked from Erwin to Miriam, trying to determine their relationship. They looked like they had been working together for some time now. Maybe Miriam served as his secretary?

"I mean, everybody wants a better life; that sounds promising, but just what are you offering me?" asked Laura.

"Security," replied Erwin, "for you and the baby."

"What does that mean?" asked Laura.

"Financial security," explained Erwin. He smiled at her again, and his blue eyes twinkled.

Miriam leaned in. "Everything you need to manage your life as a new mother," she explained. "All the necessities for your new child, and then a monthly stipend for you as well."

"What's the catch?" asked Laura. "What do I need to do?"

"Oh, this isn't a job or anything like that," Miriam added. "You won't be asked to do anything against your moral or ethical code. You don't have to do anything you don't want to."

"But I'm sure I have to do *something*. You wouldn't just be giving away money from the goodness of your own heart, would you?"

"Of course not," said Erwin. "This is where it gets more serious."

"Serious, how?"

Erwin and Miriam exchanged a look before Erwin answered.

"To get this financial security, you need to marry me."

Laura sat in shock for a few moments. Mr. Wilson and his partner let the idea sink in.

"And I don't have to do anything I don't want to do? Including-" she gulped, feeling a bit embarrassed that she was asking "- wifely duties?"

"Exactly," said Miriam.

"Can I think about it?" she asked.

"Of course," replied Mr. Wilson. "But this is a limited-time offer, as there are other candidates."

"I see." Laura chugged the rest of her water and got up to leave. Her head was swimming with the possibilities and a million questions she couldn't even begin to ask. As she began to walk away, Miriam got up and followed her.

"I hope you will consider Mr. Wilson's business proposal," she chimed in as if this were an ordinary Tuesday and they had been discussing entirely ordinary things.

"You mean his proposal?" asked Laura. She was at the door already.

"Of a sort," admitted Miriam. "You will call me? One way or the other?"

"Sure," replied Laura, although she had no idea how to respond to the situation. It would take a while to wrap her head around it.

That night, Laura dreamed of her baby. She dreamed of her boy with Freddie's eyes and chubby cheeks, toddling around and giggling. She dreamed of him crawling, learning to walk, and then running from one end of the living room to the other. Then she dreamed of Mr. Wilson tossing a ball to him, playing catch in the summer sunshine and laughing, the way he had laughed with Miriam, like the two of them had a secret. She dreamed of Mr. Wilson carrying her baby boy on his shoulders, so tall and proud, the boy happy to have a father in his life, one she could grow comfortable with over time, one who could provide for her and her child. She woke up smiling and called Miriam. She was ready to take a leap of faith for her baby.

Chapter 31

PRESENT DAY

I had so many questions I didn't even know where to begin. Was Mr. Wilson's Wives some sort of organization created to help women? And Mr. Wilson spearheaded it with the help of another woman? This wasn't why he had married all his wives, but it sounded like it could account for many of them.

"What was that marriage like?" I finally asked.

"Like any marriage, I suppose, but after Mr. Wilson, I never did marry again." Laura pushed the bracelets on her left wrist further up her arm, moving them out of the way. "I didn't need to. He didn't lie when he said he would take care of me. He took very good care of me."

"But did you love him?"

"Eventually, I think I did, in my way. It was easy to love him, even though that wasn't the original plan."

I wanted to tiptoe around the next question, but nothing was particularly delicate about it. "Did you love him the way a wife loves her husband?"

"You mean, did we have sex?"

I nearly choked on my drink. "Yes, that's exactly what I mean. I was just trying to be -"

"Sex is sex, girl. If I can't talk about it at my age, when can I talk about it?"

"Well, did you?"

"Yes. He was my husband. Grown people have needs, don't they?"

I dropped that line of questioning and tried another tactic. "If you fell in love with him, why did you divorce him then?"

"It was part of our agreement, and I didn't love him in that no-holds-barred I'll-die-without-you kind of way; it was more gradual, more... We had mutual respect. When the time came, we each went our separate ways, better for having been together."

"And he did this with several other women?"

"I assume so, but I didn't exactly keep tabs on him. As I said, we went our separate ways."

"But he continued to pay you?"

"Alimony and child support, yes. That was the deal, and he made good on his promises."

"Do you still receive payments?"

"Yes, from his estate."

Then I blurted out what I had been wondering about after talking with the last few of Mr. Wilson's wives. "Did his most recent wife know about all this?"

"As I said, I didn't keep tabs on him, but I would imagine she would have to know something. Or maybe he told her his money was going to some charity. Not every wife gets mixed up in her husband's financial affairs, especially if he has more than enough money to go around."

"I suppose that's true."

"Are you married?" she asked suddenly.

"No, I'm not," I replied, not expecting the cross-examination.

"Well, why not? You're pretty enough. Young, clearly industrious."

As she listed my supposed qualities, I felt like a pig brought to market. Even my mother hadn't questioned me in such a blatant way, but that probably had something to do with the fact that we weren't talking at the moment. "I guess I just haven't found the right guy," I eventually replied.

"Have you tried?" she asked.

The truth was, I hadn't. I had one steady boyfriend through college, but when he dropped out, I quickly dumped him. I wasn't interested in staying with someone without a degree, and his lack of follow-through wasn't very promising, either. But that's none of her business, and this line of questioning made me very uncomfortable.

"I thought we were talking about you," I countered.

"Alright, alright," she relented. "Fair enough. I don't mind sharing my story, but what is all this for anyway? Just what are you trying to do?"

"I read about Mr. Wilson and all his wives in his obituary. I found it interesting and wanted to know more, so I've been interviewing some of his wives to try to get the full story."

"Once you have what you think is the full story, what do you plan to do with it?" she asked.

"I plan to write a book about it."

"A whole book about it? Wow, that's something." She clasped her hands together. "I never thought my life was that interesting, that someone would want to read about it."

"No? I think it's fascinating."

She leaned in closer, conspiratorially. "At least the parts with Mr. Wilson in it, right?"

"I suppose so."

She sighed. "I will say he was an interesting man overall. Not like anyone else I'd ever met."

"I wish I could have had the opportunity to meet him," I admitted. "I really do."

"Who knows? You might have wound up one of his wives!" Laura laughed while my face grew hot. It was true that the drinks were starting to get to us now and make us more open to conversation.

"I don't think so," I replied, then smiled. "But who knows, right?"

Laura and I shared another cocktail, and then she excused herself for the evening. I was about to gather my things and leave when the bartender walked over with a third whiskey sour. I glanced around, noticing a few more people sitting at the bar, primarily young people and a few middle-aged men nursing their drinks.

"I didn't order this," I explained.

"It's from the gentleman at the bar with the gray jacket, who says he'd like to talk to you."

I reluctantly accepted the drink and searched for the man in question. A few wore suit jackets, one black, another a navy blue. Then I spotted him, a gray jacket and a pair of dark, menacing eyes that looked far too familiar. This time, emboldened by the alcohol, I walked straight up to him.

He smiled as I approached, not anticipating my animosity.

"Just what do you want?" I demanded. I slammed my drink down on the bar. The bartender, now back behind the bar, glanced up for a moment before returning to his cocktail-making - he must have assumed we were having a lover's quarrel.

"Well, your attention for one," the man replied, smiling. "Looks like I've got that, at least."

"Why have you been following me?"

"Oh, you noticed. I must not have done a good job, then." He smirked. "You weren't supposed to notice."

"What is this all about?"

"I hear you're writing a story..."

"And what do you care about it?"

"I'm one of Mr. Wilson's children, and I want you to cease and desist."

Despite my frustration, this sounded like a conversation that needed to be had. I sat on a stool and took a long swig of my drink. "Alright." I sighed heavily. "Explain yourself."

He introduced himself as Bruno Wilson and launched into a diatribe about how it was none of my business to be poking and prodding in other people's personal lives. I assured him everything I had gathered so far had been freely and willingly given.

"You're a pretty girl," he mused. "I would hate to see anything happen to you or your family."

My thoughts flashed back to Luis, who I had been trying so hard not to worry about for the past few hours. "What do you know about my brother?" I asked.

"Your brother?" His expression changed abruptly from a confident smirk to a confused grimace. "I don't know anything about your brother."

"You mean you didn't kidnap him to get to me, to make me agree to drop everything?" I was starting to feel a bit irrational, but the more I thought about it, the more sense it made. Surely, he had taken Luis and was going to use him for leverage.

"What kind of man do you take me for?" he spurted. "I would never do such a thing. I meant I would pursue you legally, take your money. I could sue you."

"Oh," I said dumbly, feeling deflated. It seemed my theories were entirely off-base. I tried to build up some steam again, though, to argue. "Just who do you think you are, anyway?"
"Someone with a lot to lose if you were to continue snooping around."

"How is that?" I asked.

"If you'll stop jumping down my throat, I might be able to tell you."

Chapter 32

BRUNO WILSON, 1998

Bruno's parents separated before he could ever remember them having been together. After the divorce, he and his mother moved from Orchard Square to Weston, and he only saw his father on rare occasions. For a short, glorious time during his childhood, it was every other weekend. A driver would pick him up and drive him to his father's sprawling estate in the country, and he would spend the weekend there. His father would often be busy doing whatever he did for business, and Bruno would spend a lot of time with his at-the-time stepmother, Millie. She didn't last long, but neither did these regular visits. She also had a baby, who only served to irritate Bruno because, of course, the baby got most of her attention.

He was often left to ramble about on the rolling hills, hiding in great copses of trees. Although he was alone in his adventures, he often found something messy and entertaining, as young boys often will. Once, he found an entire nest of blue robin eggs that had fallen from a tree. One of the eggs had cracked open, and he could see a mostly-formed baby bird inside. As he pulled the shell away, he could see that it was dead already and would never cry out for worms or learn to fly. It looked alien to him, a small sack of skin without feathers and eyes sealed shut against the light. Other than its fragile body, the baby bird was entirely beak. If it had survived, had hatched in the usual way, it would have spent its first waking moments hungry and begging for food, its beak upturned. It made him think of the baby back at the house, constantly crying to be fed, changed, and held - so helpless and needy. Too bad it couldn't just fall out of a tree and be silenced like the baby bird.

He rolled this idea around for a while, realizing that if the baby fell from a great height, it would be silenced. He knew instinctively that this was a wicked thought, but as he continued to roam and forage that afternoon, he frequently returned to the idea until he had developed a plan. He didn't mean to follow the plan, but thinking about it made him feel powerful. With a swift movement, he could toss the baby from a second-story window, and then they would have to pay attention to him again. There would be no baby.

As the sun began to set on the horizon, turning the sky into a multi-hued masterpiece, he returned to the estate. His father would surely be home for dinner at least, and he would finally have the opportunity to show him the many varieties of mushrooms he had gathered. Some of them might be good for eating. Bruno was getting better at identifying them using a book he had found in his father's study. He had found several batches of chicken-of-the-woods and puffballs the day before.

When he arrived, however, his father had not yet returned from work. His stepmother said she was tired from taking care of the baby all day, and all she served him was a bowl of pea soup. She didn't even offer bread with butter to go with it. Bruno spooned up the green liquid, making faces at it.

"Come on," urged his stepmother. "It's not that bad."

"Have you tried it?" he asked impertinently.

"Of course I have," she replied. "I made it. It tastes just fine. I think I managed to get the seasoning right this time."

Bruno groaned dramatically and slurped down more soup. "If my father were here, he would demand meat with his dinner."

His stepmother glared at him. "Well, your father isn't here, and you'll eat what I serve you. I know I'm not your mother, but you will obey me when you're in my house."

"It's not your house," Bruno countered. "It's my father's house."

They both knew she was on borrowed time because Mr. Wilson went through wives like water.

She signed, all fight gone out of her. "Just eat," she managed. "Your father will be home shortly, but he'll be missing dinner."

They began eating in silence, soon shattered by the baby's wails. She sighed. She had been hoping the baby would sleep a bit longer so that they could eat in peace.

"You better silence your little goblin," said Bruno, not even looking up from his soup.

"What did you say, young man?" she admonished him.

"Oh, nothing. The baby's crying. You should go get her."

"That's what I thought you said," she replied.

She scurried away, and as soon as she was out of sight, Bruno placed his bowl under the table for the dog to lick clean. He was willing to go hungry if it meant he didn't have to eat more of that green monstrosity posing as soup. When his stepmother didn't return to the table immediately, he left his bowl on the kitchen counter. He grabbed his satchel from the back door and quickly climbed the stairs to his father's study. He had some mushrooms to identify.

About half an hour later, Bruno had laid out his trove of mushrooms on a towel across his father's desk. He dutifully studied each and tried to identify them using the guide, comparing their appearances to the sketches he found there. He heard the doorbell below but was so engrossed in his work that he barely noticed it. He did notice, however, when the baby started screaming again. He tried to ignore the baby's screaming but found it incredibly distracting and could no longer concentrate on his mushrooms.

He marched down the hall to the baby's nursery to find it fussing in the crib. Its little face contorted, eyes squeezed shut, mouth wide open, skin a brilliant red with the effort. It reminded him of the dead bird, its flesh all pink, its body mostly beak, but that baby was silent at least. He muttered to himself, swearing under his breath. If only the baby would be quiet. After a brief moment's hesitation, he reached in to pick it up.

The baby was surprisingly heavy for such a small parcel. He leaned it heavily against his shoulder, bouncing it a little as it cried into his ear. He sighed heavily. Where was that no-good stepmother of his? It was her job to take care of this, not his. He walked with the baby down the hall, still bouncing it on his hip. When he returned to the study, it was still screaming, its face red and streaked with tears. The baby was so full of want, he thought, so greedy for attention, such a suck of time and energy. Before he knew what he was doing, Bruno found himself standing near the open window, just feeling the baby's weight, imagining what it would feel like to "accidentally" drop it to the ground below.

He started to lean out the window, when his stepmother came into the office. He leaned back in, cupping one hand under the baby's butt.

"Finally bonding with your sister, I see." She smiled.

"Half-sister," he reminded her.

"It's good to see you taking care of her."

"Why weren't you taking care of her?" he shot back.

She looked taken aback. "Your father just got home, young man. Why don't you go say hello?"

The baby cried even louder, clutching him with its tiny, grubby fingers. He frowned down at it, gnawing hate growing ever larger inside him. If only he could silence it. He leaned toward the window again, stretching his hands out to dangle the baby out the window.

His stepmother screamed. "What are you doing?!"

His father rushed up the stairs to see what all the shouting was about. He looked at the scene in progress and strode toward his son. The man towered over him, enormous and menacing. "Bruno, what are you doing?" he asked.

The boy glanced at his father but looked right past him. He kept his attention on the baby, screaming even louder now. It would be so easy to just let it slip from his fingers, to let gravity do its work. "It needs to be quiet," he said eventually, through gritted teeth.

His stepmother couldn't stop screaming, begging him to stop. Her cries joined the baby's, and suddenly the great sound became too much for Bruno. He just wanted this all to end, for it to finally be over and for peace and quiet. He imagined the baby curled up on the ground, a silent remnant of the life that had once demanded so much, finally cold and still.

"Bruno," his father called to him, catching his attention. "Bruno, think about what you're doing."

As the baby squirmed and cried, and his stepmother continued to beg, Bruno felt electrified. He was the cause of this. He was the center of everyone's attention. The buzz and excitement felt fantastic.

"Fine then," said his father, as a gruffness came into his voice. "Go ahead," he chided. "I dare you."

Both Bruno and his stepmother turned to Mr. Wilson in confusion.

"You heard me," he continued. "If you think you're such a man that you have the power to end another's life, Bruno, you go right ahead. If you can carry that weight on your conscience, do it."

"What is wrong with you?!" the woman screamed, directing her anger at her husband this time.

Bruno looked back at the baby and finally saw it for what it was, a small, tiny human struggling to survive, unable to communicate its needs except through crying. He looked even closer and saw she was even kind of cute, with chubby cheeks and wide eyes, nothing like the ugly baby bird, dead in its shell. He started to pull the baby back to his chest, and his father tackled him to the ground.

* * *

After the incident with the baby, Bruno didn't visit his father as often. His father was busy, and his stepmother didn't trust him. Besides, Bruno developed his own interests, got a job at the local mechanic's shop tinkering with motorcycles, and simply didn't have time to devote to dear old dad. For his part, his father didn't make much effort to stay in touch with him, either.

As his mother grew older and Bruno grew more desperate, he began to steal from her. Small things at first, coins from her change jar, a few dollars from her purse. He used the money to buy whatever alcohol he could get his hands on. It wasn't long before he had developed a habit and drank most nights, then most mornings. Eventually, he turned to pawning her jewelry. He reasoned that she never wore any of it and wouldn't miss it much.

One afternoon, while his mother played bridge at the community center, he rummaged through the bottom of her jewelry box, hoping for some last remnant or keepsake that he could sell. He had already stolen most of her larger pieces, the long, looping necklaces, and dangling bracelets. There may have been a ring or stud earrings in the bottom velvet drawer. Instead, he found mementos: ticket stubs, a few faded photographs, and what amounted to lint in his eyes.

Regardless, he thumbed through these quickly, just out of curiosity. His mother had been quite attractive as a young woman. In one of the photos, she wore a lacy negligee, her long, blonde hair cascading down her shoulders and over her breasts. It was strange to see her this way, so young and vulnerable. He quickly flipped to the next, a wedding photo with his parents, both dressed pretty casually. She wore a white sundress, and his father wore a suit with no jacket. The only reason he even knew it was from their wedding was that they lifted their hands to show off their wedding bands to the photographer.

Then, he came across another photo of his mother as a teenager kissing a man he didn't know. The man was quite a bit older than her, but he could tell from how they embraced that it was a romantic kiss. Who the hell was this? Someone she had dated before his father? Why would she keep it? The man had black hair, like him, which was strange. Bruno had always wondered why his hair was so dark. His father had light brown hair, and his mother was blonde. As far as he knew, no one else in the family had dark hair. Was this man his actual father?

Wedged in between the small stack of photographs was a business card, worn at the edges. It was blue ink printed on a cream background and looked expensive. The text read: Mr. Wilson's Wives and included a phone number. There was no other information. Bruno flipped it over. There was nothing printed on the back, either. What was this? What the hell did it mean, Mr. Wilson's Wives? He knew his father had had several wives over the years, but why would he have a business card? Was it some kind of a joke?

When his mother returned from playing cards a few hours later, he put a kettle on the stove to boil some water. When the pot started whistling, he poured out two cups and started steeping the tea. He placed one on the table next to his mother as she worked her way through a crossword puzzle.

"Hey, ma," he called to her.

"Hey, what," she replied, irritated at being interrupted.

"I need to talk to you."

"So talk," she demanded.

"It's important," he added.

"Fine." She set her pencil down, looked up from the cross-word, and glared at him. "You've got my undivided attention. What do you want?"

"I found something."

"Well, stop being so cryptic. Spit it out." She turned to her tea, dunking the tea bag a few times. "Must be important; you made me tea."

He sat across from her at the small kitchen table and pulled the picture of the strange man from his pocket. "Mom, who's this?" he asked as he slid it across to her.

"Where'd you find this?" she asked. As she glanced at it, she smiled, remembering.

"It was in your jewelry box," he admitted.

"Have you been snooping through my things again?" she asked.

He avoided the question and asked his own instead. "Who is that man you're kissing?"

"That's Edward," she said. "Edward Jones." She fawned over the picture for a moment.

"Who was he to you?"

"Well, he was my boyfriend, if you can't tell from the picture."

"Before Dad, I'm guessing?"

"Yes, before your father."

"What can you tell me about him?"

She squeezed some lemon into her tea, removing the tea bag and stirring it. For a moment, Bruno thought she might not answer, but eventually, she began to speak. "What does it matter?" she asked. "It was all such a long time ago. What do you care?"

Chapter 33

ROSE SCHMIDT, 1984

Rose struggled to keep up with her peers regarding dating and kissing boys. The desire was there, for sure, but she didn't always have the follow-through. When her first boyfriend finally asked her out, she suddenly became so shy she could barely speak around him. They would spend hours holding hands on the bus, to and from school, casting long glances across the classroom throughout the day, and yet when he spoke to her, she could barely form the words to have a decent conversation. Eventually, he broke up with her in favor of a much more courageous companion, and she was left wondering what exactly had gone wrong.

Meanwhile, her friends Jennifer and Melissa regularly shared their exploits every Monday morning after a weekend of dates. Rose wondered how much of their stories were true and how much was exaggerated, but it wasn't long before they were comparing notes, and Rose always came up short.

"What did you do all weekend?" asked Melissa as they stood at their lockers.

Rose pulled her long blonde hair into a hasty ponytail, glancing in her locker mirror as she smoothed flyaways with her fingers. "Studied for the chemistry test. Watched my little brother Saturday afternoon."

"Boooring," chided Jennifer. She huddled in close, dropping her voice a few octaves. "I studied anatomy with Robert."

"You mean you?" asked Melissa, not daring to say it aloud.

"Yup," Jennifer chirped. "He wasn't joking when he called it a snake."

Rose grimaced. "Ew. That's disgusting."

"You wouldn't think it was so disgusting if you were getting some," said Melissa.

"I don't want some if it involves snakes."

"It's not a real snake, silly," replied Jennifer. Giggles erupted from her perfect pout. The red lipstick she had just applied shined garishly.

Melissa couldn't help herself. "It's a trouser snake!" she nearly shouted.

One of the female teachers walked by just then, carrying a stack of papers against her chest. "Ladies," she said. "The bell is about to ring. You should stop gossiping and start getting to your classes."

The girls calmed themselves and replied in unison. "Yes, Mrs. Patterson." They shut their lockers behind them and scampered off to chemistry to take their exam. Rose was the only one of them remotely prepared for the test.

Later that week, bright pink flyers announcing a party at David Martinson's house floated through the halls. Teachers attempted to confiscate them, snagging them as they saw them and stuffing them into trash cans, but there were just too many. As the girls walked out into the sunlight, Jennifer pulled one down from a bulletin board, tossing the tack at their feet.

"Looks like we've got something to do this weekend!" she squealed. The flier advertised that David's parents would be out of town, and there would be free booze and a live band, most likely some of their classmates fooling around with electric guitars and a drum kit.

"My parents are going to visit my mom's folks this week-end," Rose tried to explain. "I have to watch Matty."

"Sucks to be you," said Melissa. "Isn't Matty old enough to watch himself, anyway? He's gotta be at least ten by now."

"Yeah, leave the little twerp at home," suggested Jennifer. "You don't even have to give your parents an excuse for sneaking out. They won't even notice you're gone."

"But what if something happens? Matty might set the house on fire; besides, he's a huge tattle-tale. He'll tell them I wasn't home."

Jennifer opened the door to her red Cadillac, her pride and joy. The other girls piled in, Melissa taking shotgun. Rose stretched out in the backseat, her thin legs spread across the upholstery as they hatched their plan. Melissa suggested tying Matty up, leaving him locked in a closet for the weekend. They all laughed at that but knew it wasn't a real plan.

"Maybe we just need to find someone else to watch him," tried Jennifer. "Like a hot babysitter or something, so he won't tell either. Bribe the boy."

"Where are we going to find a hot babysitter?" asked Rose. "Anybody who's anybody will be going to that party, not agreeing to watch my baby brother. Besides, we'd probably have to pay for it, and I don't have any money."

"Do you have to be home right away?" asked Jennifer. She was nearing Melissa's house. "I think we should go for some ice cream."

"My mom doesn't get home from work until after five," Melissa replied.

Jennifer pulled into the parking lot, packed with teenagers just getting off school. She spied Robert sitting on one of the benches out front, so as soon as she parked, she squealed and ran to sit on his lap. Within moments they were sucking face, leaving Melissa and Rose to wander into the shop without her.

Rose groaned, pinching her stomach. "My mom says I need to lose weight, but I can't seem to give up sweets," she complained.

Melissa glanced at her friend, sizing her up. She scoffed. "Your mom's the one who needs to lose weight," she said. "Come on; we're fifteen. You don't need to go on a diet."

"I gained five pounds over the summer," Rose continued. "I can't even fit into some of my favorite t-shirts."

"You know what else you gained over the summer?" Melissa asked as they sidled up to the counter. She paused for a beat. When Rose didn't answer, she blurted out, "Boobs!"

Rose blushed, elbowing her friend in the arm. She glanced down as if to be sure that was the truth. She had grown curvier in the past few months, but none of the boys seemed to notice, so she didn't consider herself curvy enough. She wondered if any frozen yogurt options were on the menu but didn't spot any. She'd just get a plain vanilla cone, maybe.

Speaking of curvy, she thought, as a big-breasted girl bounced up to the counter to take their order. Kimberly Johnson was a few years older than them and a townie. Instead of going to college, she worked after graduation and still lived at home with her parents. Supposedly, she was saving up to go to beauty school, but rumor had it she slept around regularly and had more than one boyfriend at any given time. She wore her hair in braided pigtails and garish makeup, making her look a bit like a circus performer.

"What can I get for you?" she asked. She smiled wide, showing her teeth.

Melissa ordered a banana split with extra chocolate syrup and whipped cream. Rose ordered her vanilla cone. As Kimberly bustled back to start making their treats, an idea came to Rose.

"What about Kimberly?" she asked Melissa.

"What about her?"

"Busty babe to babysit my brother," she said.

"That's a mouthful," replied Melissa.

"Exactly."

Kimberly returned to the counter, smiling stupidly at them. Now, how could Rose convince her to babysit? What could she offer that would prove enticing enough? Her parents had just gotten a new entertainment center - that could be enough. Then she thought better of it.

"I hear you're planning to go to beauty school," she said, trying to make conversation.

"Yeah," replied Kimberly. "I want to work at the salon with my cousin. She says she gets great tips."

"Do you need a guinea pig?" Rose asked.

Kimberly set their ice cream on the counter. She looked utterly confused. "A what?"

"Like someone to practice on?" Rose tried.

Melissa glanced at her friend, incredulous. "What are you doing?" she whispered.

"Making a deal," Rose whispered back.

"Oh, yeah, I need some practice for sure. Are you offering?"

Rose glanced down at her long hair, pulling it in front of her shoulders for Kimberly to see its entire length. "I've been thinking about getting a trim," she lied.

Kimberly's eyes lit up. "I'd love to get my hands on your hair!" she exclaimed. "Can I do your makeup, too?"

"Sure, I'll let you make me over," Rose offered.

Kimberly squealed, then sobered a bit. "What's the catch?"

"I need a favor. Are you busy tomorrow night, say around 7?"

Kimberly thought for a moment. "Well, I'd normally be going out with Brad or Tony."

So she DID have two boyfriends?! thought Rose. Of course, she'd be busy. Why wouldn't she be?

"But Brad is gone for the weekend, and Tony's come down with the flu, so I'm free," Kimberly continued. "What's the favor?"

"I need someone to watch my brother. He's ten and can look after himself. Just make sure he doesn't do anything dumb, like burn the house down. You could even use the new entertainment center my dad just installed."

"Really? I love little boys," Kimberly replied, then caught herself. "I mean, they're just so cute. I don't love them, not like that."

"So it's a deal?" Rose asked. "You'll watch Matty tomorrow night, and I'll let you do my hair and makeup."

"Sure thing," replied Kimberly. "I'll come by about a quarter to six. Just one question."

"What's that?"
"Are you sure you're okay with a bit of a trim?"

Rose gulped. Anything for the cause, she reminded herself. "No problem. My fate is in your hands." Literally, she thought to herself.

The night of the party came, and Kimberly arrived early, eager to give Rose her makeover. She brought an entire duffel bag of beauty supplies and set to work right away.

"There isn't enough time to give you a proper perm," Kimberly admitted, "But I might put your hair in hot rollers. Are you still down for a cut?"

"I guess anything goes," said Rose, a bit reluctantly. She shut her eyes tight through the entire process. She had been growing her hair out for the past few years, but Kimberly wouldn't go too short, would she?

"You can open your eyes, silly," admonished Kimberly as she spun Rose around to look in the mirror.

As it turned out, the cut brought the length of her hair to just about her shoulders. Rose ran her fingers through it. Her head felt lighter without all that heavy hair weighing it down.

Kimberly beamed. "You like it?" she asked.

Rose hesitated, considering. "Actually, it's not bad," she admitted.

Kimberly started twisting it into hot rollers, which had been heating in their case on the counter.

Matty poked his head in then, making faces at the two girls. "What are you doing?" he asked, whining.

"I'm fixing your sister up so she can look pretty tonight," explained Kimberly.

"Huh," Matty snorted. "Where's she going?"

Rose placed a finger to her lips, hushing him. "Promise not to tell Mom and Dad?" she asked.

"I'm not promising anything."

Rose sighed. She knew this wouldn't be easy. It would be a miracle if she managed to get away with it, but she was willing to take the chance. "I'm going to a party," she whispered.

"But who's gonna stay with me?"

Kimberly added another roller to Rose's hair. "I'm going to stay with you." She smiled alluringly, which was hard to do without giggling.

"Okay," Matty replied.

"Okay?" asked Rose, unsure what that meant in little-boy terms. "You promise not to tell?"

"Where'd you find her?" asked Matty. "She's hot. Most of your friends are U-G-L-Y." He spelled the last word out like a playground taunt.

"I have friends you don't know," Rose replied.

"If I get to hang out with her, it's a deal." He skipped from the room, whistling.

"Some brother you've got there," said Kimberly, laughing. "He'll make a fine gentleman one day."

"Yeah, right."

Once Kimberly finished with the rollers, she started applying makeup. Rose rarely wore any; if she did, it was usually just a little gloss on her lips. Kimberly started with a thick layer of concealer under Rose's eyes and then covered that with a liquid foundation that made her look tanner than her naturally pale shade. Then she swept some deep pink blush over the apples of her cheeks up to her hairline.

She pulled out a few eye shadow palettes and picked some bright shades. Because Rose was wearing a sleek black dress, she reasoned, she'd be able to wear any makeup color. The hues she chose were hot pink and bright, electric blue. She started with the pink on the inside crease of Rose's eyelids, feathering out to the eye's middle, then finished with the blue on the outside, both above and below her lash line. She added two thick coats of mascara. When Rose blinked, she could see her own eyelashes, which were so dark and thick.

As Kimberly undid the curlers, she teased Rose's hair until it was a great, voluminous cloud. Rose had to keep pushing it back from her face just to be able to see, but the dramatic curls were definitely eye-catching. She could hardly recognize herself as she glanced in the mirror, but she liked what she saw. She looked like some kind of movie star, glamorous and ready for the red carpet.

"One last thing," said Kimberly, not letting her get up from the chair just yet.

She applied a few layers of bright pink lipstick and then gloss over top. Soon, Rose's lips shone the shade of a Barbie convertible - they were just so pink! Kimberly let her out of the chair then and let her take a good look at herself. All-in-all, this hadn't been a bad deal, thought Rose, she had found someone to watch her snotty little brother, and now she was picture perfect for the party. It had been a bit of a gamble but was worth it in the end.

Just then, Matty came running down the hallway. He glanced at his sister, leered at her, and said, "You look...weird." Then he continued down the hall, dashing off to his bedroom.

The girls turned to each other and laughed. Little brothers could be so silly sometimes.

Chapter 34

BRUNO WILSON

Bruno had finished drinking his tea a while ago and was sure his mother's tea had nearly gone cold. As she reminisced, her face shone. As she remembered the girl she used to be, she started to look more and more like herself, despite her wiry gray hair and the wrinkles creasing her cheeks.

"This is wonderful and all, Ma, but when are you gonna get to the good part?"

Rose glanced up at her son. "The good part?"

"Yeah. I get it. You were an ugly duckling who got a make-over. I'm assuming you eventually made it to this party. What does any of this have to do with Edward Jones?"

"Well, that's where I met him, silly." She smiled.

"But he looks so much older than you in that photo."

"That's because he was," she replied. "He was Robert's older brother. He had to be at least twenty. Oh, and I was smitten."

"But why -" Bruno raised his voice, nearly shouting at her as he said the words. "Why do you still have his photo?!"

She flinched. "I can't hang on to my memories?" she asked.

Bruno stood to loom over her. No more beating around the bush. He had to know. "Is it maybe because this man is my real father?!"

Tears came to Rose's eyes and began to stream down her cheeks. "Please," she begged. "Please don't yell at me."

"Is he?" Bruno demanded.

She looked up at him then, like a young child, trembling. "Yes, he was. No one was ever supposed to know, not even you."

"But why?!"

"He loved me and left me, and I was pregnant at sixteen. Your father, the father I chose for you, helped me when no one else would."

"You mean Erwin?"

"Yes."

Bruno took a moment to roll this around in his head. He was a grown man and hadn't even known who his real father was. "I'd like to meet him," he decided. "My real dad."

"You can't," she said softly. "He's dead."

Bruno fumbled with the remaining photographs, the shiny business card still wedged between them. He pulled it out and set it on the table before his mother. "Can you explain this?" he asked.

She glanced at it, her eyes growing wide. "You found that with my things?" she asked.

"Yes, with all these lousy photographs," he said. "More secrets?"

"I suppose you could say that," she murmured. "That card, that organization isn't supposed to exist."

"Organization?"

"Mr. Wilson's Wives," she whispered. "It saved my life."

Chapter 35

PRESENT DAY

Bruno reached into his jacket pocket and pulled out a business card. He slid it across the bar to me. It was yellowed and worn at the edges. At one point, it must have been folded in half.

"What is this?" I asked, without looking at it yet.

"Take a look," he said.

I glanced down, and sure enough, it was a cream-colored business card with delicate blue lettering. It said "Mr. Wilson's Wives" and listed a phone number. There was no other information included on it.

"It was a real thing?" I asked.

"It still is," he assured me.

"What do you mean? Mr. Wilson is dead," I said, stating the obvious. "He can't have any more wives."

"The organization still exists."

"What does that even mean? What is this organization? Why bother telling me all this if you want me to stop investigating?"

Bruno leaned back, taking a sip of his drink. "I want you to understand why."

"What does it matter?"

"Look," he leaned in again conspiratorially. "I understand that this is your bread and butter. You're a writer and like digging into other peoples' business. I get it." He sighed. "So I can't expect you to abandon your work without understanding why."

"So what do you propose?" I asked.

"Go ahead and call the number. Pretend to be a woman in need."

"A woman in need?"

"Most women who turned to the organization had found themselves in a situation. They were pregnant; they needed to get away from an abusive relationship; they needed someone to stand up for them, to help them out."

"Alright, I think I see where this is going."

"Pretend to be one of those women. Call this number and see what it's all about. Then, you'll understand."

"Understand what, exactly?" I asked.

"If you write about this, you could ruin many lives."

"But everyone I've spoken to has spoken to me freely. I haven't forced anyone's hand. No one had to share their story, but they did," I argued.

"You haven't thought about the children," he explained.

"What children?" I asked.

"Mr. Wilson's children. Legally, he has dozens of them, but if you were to conduct paternity tests, not all of them are his. Including me. This could have some real repercussions."

I sat with that for a moment, running it over in my mind. It could mean his heirs didn't get their share of the inheritance or there would be shame on them for being born illegitimately. Although I'd like to think these things didn't matter as much anymore, they were a real concern for some. It could mean breaking up entire families. Maybe some of the children, like Bruno, didn't know the identity of their true fathers. But in the end, wasn't the truth more important?

"This is exhausting," I admitted.

"You're telling me!" he agreed. "You know how hard it was to track you down? You were going every which way today!"

I laughed, but it was devoid of mirth. Poor Luis. I still had no idea where he was or what had happened. "I was looking for my brother. He ran away yesterday."

"He ran away?" Bruno asked.

"Yes," I admitted. "Just poof, gone. No warning, no note, no nothing."

"So that's why you thought I was a kidnapper."

"Exactly."

"Would you like another drink?" he asked.

"No, thank you. I think all I need now is a good night's sleep."

"Alright, just one thing," he said. "Call that number, as I said. I think it will change your mind about whether or not to continue working on this story. What are your intentions anyway? You want to write a big news feature or something?"

"I'm writing a book," I said. "Or I was. But actually, I haven't written much of anything."

"No harm, no foul then," he reasoned. "If you haven't even written anything, there's nothing to get rid of."

"Sure. You have no idea how research works, do you?"

He grinned sheepishly. "No," he admitted. "Not really."

Despite everything, I wished him goodnight and retreated to my hotel room. It was late, and I was exhausted after running around trying to find Luis, interviewing Laura Wilson, and then (unexpectedly) Bruno Wilson. I knew I should call my agent about this new development, but I decided to try calling that mysterious number on the business card first. That would have to wait for the morning.

I stretched out on the king-sized bed and sunk into the pillows. Even spread-eagled, I couldn't reach across the length of the bed by myself. I thought King mattresses are much too large, even for two people, much less one. Even though I was thoroughly exhausted, I spent an unreasonable amount of time staring at the ceiling, letting my thoughts race. What would I do if I couldn't find Luis? What would I do if all the research I had done for my next book proved to be for nothing? I would have to start over from scratch with an entirely new idea. At the moment, I didn't have enough energy to do any of it.

I don't know how long I lay there, but it felt like an eternity, and I still couldn't fall asleep. Eventually, I turned the bedside lamp on and propped myself on the pillows. I switched on the TV, and somehow there were still reruns of Maury running paternity tests on the screen. What was it that Bruno had said? If the truth came out, it could upend the lives of so many of Mr. Wilson's children. But wasn't the truth more important? Wasn't that what I was supposed to be about, telling true stories? My family never seemed to understand that either. They couldn't grasp why I would want to share private information in such a public way.

When I wrote my memoir, *The Women of My Family*, I never intended to hurt anyone. Far from it. I wanted to share the small miracles that made up our life. I saw no shame in how my mother and sister became single parents and how neither married. I saw them as strong, independent women who could care for themselves. I didn't realize these were stories they didn't want to share with the world. I never even thought to ask if it was alright for me to share them.

Were my plans to write about Mr. Wilson's wives shaping up to be the same? It was their story to tell, after all, not mine. I had put so much work into this, though, so much time and energy. I couldn't give up now. Despite my best efforts to sleep, I was still awake after hours of thinking. I could see the sun rising over the horizon, and birds began chirping. At 4:30 a.m., they became a cacophonous symphony, each greeting the new day I couldn't stop coming. I had only one plan: call the number on that business card and see if I could learn the truth.

What did all of this mean? What was this organization Rachel and Bruno had told me about, and what exactly did it offer to women? Was Mr. Wilson the type of man who would rescue women? Or was he simply taking advantage of their vulnerabilities? In the end, what did all of my research amount to?

Chapter 36

I took a quick shower, and when I emerged from the bathroom, I could hear the coffee pot percolating, the lovely, bitter smell already perking me up. I poured myself a large mug and gulped it down eagerly. Then I sat at what sufficed as a small desk in the hotel room. I suddenly felt homesick for my own office space back home: my plush office chair, my ergonomic keyboard, my ceiling fan. These simple creature comforts made it so much easier for me to write. I had brought along a laptop for this venture, of course, but it just wasn't the same. And now I had to make a phone call I didn't want to make. This could make or break my story, I knew. These were the kind of secrets that drew readers in, but they were also the kind of secrets that could ruin lives. Suck it up, buttercup, I told myself, reached for the phone, and dialed.

"Good morning!" said the chipper voice that answered. "Thank you for calling Mr. Wilson's Wives. How may I direct your call?" she asked.

The very real existence of this organization still shocked me. Wouldn't they undergo some sort of rebranding after Mr. Wilson's death? I suppose it was all relatively recent, but it seemed ludicrous.

"Hello?" she chirped when I still didn't say anything.

"Yes," I managed at last. "I need some help."

She took me through a few intake questions, like a reproductive clinic, and eventually transferred me to someone else. The story I told was that I was a pregnant teen in danger of losing housing and in an unsafe living environment. I had been raped, I said, but my religious beliefs meant that I would need to carry the baby. It was a dark and sordid lie, but I figured it would get me access to whoever was offering services to these young women. Did they refer girls to other providers, or were they a one-stop shop? Was the solution always to marry Mr. Wilson? That, too, sounded entirely ridiculous, but when I thought of just how many wives he had over the years, maybe that was the typical solution. Eventually, the hold music paused, and someone else came on the line.

"I'm so glad you called, Liz," she began. "The sooner we sort things out, the sooner you can continue with your life. It sounds like you have been through quite an ordeal."

"Yes," I agreed.

"My name is Miriam."

I wondered if she was the same Miriam Laura had met when she first learned about Mr. Wilson's Wives. If so, she must be pretty old by now, but she was still very much involved. I wondered who the young secretary was and just where they were located.

"The next step is for you and me to set up a meeting," Miriam explained. "Would you be available this afternoon?"

I realized the jig would be up immediately if we met in person. I was not a pregnant teen. I could pose as an older sister, but not a teenager. I didn't think this one through all the way.

"This afternoon would be fine," I managed. "Where would you like to meet?"

"Are you familiar with the Wake Up Cafe?" she asked.

"Yes. That would be fine," I agreed.

"Meet me there at 2 p.m."

"Will I be meeting Mr. Wilson?" I asked. The words sounded dumb to me as soon as they left my lips.

Miriam laughed goodnaturedly. "No, dear. It will just be me, but I'd love to meet you in person before we proceed."

"Great," I said.

I hung up the phone and wished I was about ten years younger and twenty pounds lighter. Well, I guess there was pregnancy weight, but my girth didn't sit in the right place to be a pregnancy. How exactly was I going to pull this one off? Miriam would likely see through me immediately. She could give me the benefit of the doubt, but I doubted it. I had a few hours to worry about it, at least.

As I tried to plan ways to make myself look younger, my cell phone rang. I jumped in surprise when I realized it was my sister Maria. I hadn't spoken to her in months, and she had specifically told me that she didn't want me to be part of her life any longer. What could she possibly want? It must be some sort of emergency.

"Hi, Maria," I answered the phone. "Is something wrong?" I asked.

"I should say so!" she replied. She sounded exasperated, like she had been arguing with someone all morning.

"What's going on?"

"You should know Luis is here. No thanks to you."

I let out a sigh of relief. "Oh, you found him!" I exclaimed.

"You lost him?" she asked. "What was he even doing with you?"

"He needed some space, I guess. I told him he could stay with me for a while."

"You did?"

"I did. I told Ma about it."

"You did?"

"Yeah, I did. Why do you all think I'm too irresponsible to handle anything?" I asked.

"Because you are. You lost him, didn't you?"

"That doesn't matter now," I said. "I'm so glad to hear he's safe."

"You know how he got here?" she asked accusingly.

"No, I don't. I've been looking for him. The little brat didn't even leave me a note or anything. He just got up and left."

"He hitchhiked. Do you know how unsafe it is for a young boy to ride in a car with a stranger like that?" she asked.

"It's no worse than hailing a cab," I reasoned.

Maria paused, letting the silence hang between us. "You should know Cecelia is having her quinceanera next week," she said, eventually.

I smiled. I remembered Cece as an infant, toddling around and getting into mischief. How could she be fifteen already? But I had been cut off from the family. Maria had made it clear she didn't want anything to do with me.

"Am I invited?" I asked.

"You know you ruined *la menarca* for her?"

"What do you mean I ruined her first period?" I asked.

"She read your book. The party wasn't a surprise anymore; it wasn't a celebration we could share as a family. You had to share it with the whole damned world."

I thought back to my own Period Party. My mother and sister had made red velvet cake and decorated the house with red balloons. It was a special time, welcoming me into my womanhood, but it was also incredibly embarrassing. Luis had been so uncomfortable with his older sisters celebrating their first periods. He wanted nothing to do with it.

"You could have still had the party," I reasoned.

"It just wouldn't have been the same." Maria paused as if she were reloading her ammunition. What else did she have to fire at me? "Maybe you'll even find some way to ruin her quinceanera."

"How would I do that?" I asked. "More importantly, why would I do that?"

"I don't know. You're such a fuck-up. It's like because you're unhappy, you have to bring everyone else down with you."

"That's a low blow, even from you," I said.

"Well, I just called to let you know Luis is fine. No thanks to you."

"Thank you for that. Any chance I can talk to him?"

"No, you've been a bad enough influence already."

With that, she hung up. Maybe I'd try to call the boy myself later. I didn't know if he even cared about my research into Mr. Wilson's Wives, but I wanted to talk to someone about my discoveries. While my agent, Michael, would be the logical choice, I wanted to talk with someone with no stakes in the game, and that would be Luis. Despite the panic he had caused me, I missed his mischievous grin.

At this moment, I felt so alone, so rejected. Why did Maria's words hurt so much? I think it was because she and I used to be so close. We had shared a bedroom for years, borrowed each other's clothes, and told each other secrets. And now she wanted nothing to do with me. The best I could get is a courtesy call. I couldn't even get an invitation to my niece's party, such a monumental step in her life. Maybe Maria would change her mind. For now, I needed to figure out how to fool Miranda into thinking I was a pregnant teen.

I tried to remember my teen years. How awkward I had been, how dysmorphic I had felt in my body. I had been much thinner then, almost scrawny. I'm convinced that my thinness contributed to the fact that I didn't start puberty until almost fifteen myself. My sister teased me that I must be a boy because I still hadn't gotten my period yet, and I was already about to enter high school. Maria got hers quite early, at the tender age of barely ten. I was grateful when it finally came, and then immediately wished it would just go away. The whole thing was a painful, messy hassle I didn't have the energy to deal with. I was grateful, however, that I had my first period before my quinceanera. In a Hispanic household, it is customary for the quinceanera to mark a young woman's transition from girlhood into womanhood. I would have felt like a fraud if I hadn't even had my period by then.

But none of that mattered now. What mattered was fooling Miriam. What could I do to make myself look younger? My twenty-five years had worn on me and had molded me into a sarcastic, disillusioned adult. I tried to think of the type of girl who would always be carded when she walked into a bar. Though I had never done any serious acting, I was cast in a few plays. This was another role to play. And with the help of hair, makeup and wardrobe, I could pull it off. My thoughts flitted to a movie I had seen as a kid, *Never Been Kissed*, with Drew Barrymore playing the lead - a young reporter who fashioned herself as a teen to go back to high school undercover. If she could do it, I could do it, I reasoned. Never mind the fact that the story was entirely fictional.

I went down to the tourist gift shop in the hotel to see what I could find. I opted for an oversized pink Wisconsin sweatshirt, a pair of sunglasses, and some sparkly lipgloss. These would work in a pinch. I changed and pulled my hair back into a messy ponytail. Here goes nothing. My stomach was doing flip-flops already.

Chapter 37

A lump grew in my throat as I drove toward Wide Awake Cafe. What was I doing? There was no possible way Miriam would take me for a pregnant teenager. The entire venture was a lost cause.

As I drove, the weight of everything came crashing in on me. There were only so many hours in a day, and the deadline for my synopsis and first few chapters was fast approaching. Even if I made it back to the hotel in the next few hours, that would leave me little time to write, and I hadn't slept in the past 24 hours. I turned up the radio, searching for something more upbeat to listen to and keep me awake, but the tears started sliding down my cheeks. I had spent the whole summer chasing this wisp of a story and had gotten nowhere, even after weeks of research and interviews. I was no closer than I had been at the very beginning. Instead, I was sick and tired of the whole thing and felt inclined to give it up and start over with something fresh or quit altogether.

I turned the volume louder, trying to drown out my thoughts, but the tears kept coming. Frantically, I wished the negative thoughts away, but they lingered at the back of my brain, my interior dialogue becoming increasingly insistent. You can't do this. You are a failure. Why would you even try? What made you think you were a writer? I could barely see the road through my tears, my mascara nearly blinding me. I wiped my face with my sleeve and tried to collect myself at the next stoplight. I took a few deep breaths, but then my breath started coming quickly, in and out like a rapid gulping between sobs. I couldn't ask for another extension. They had already given me part of my advance, and I had already spent it. I needed to produce anything to prove that I wasn't a fraud. I needed to accomplish the impossible, and I had no more time left. I was so tired and hadn't even eaten since lunch yesterday.

I pulled onto the highway, my hands shaking now, my breath caught in my chest, my right foot pressing the pedal to the floor as I sped toward the cafe. I tried to think of Michael and what encouragement he might give me, but I had failed him. He wouldn't have anything positive to say now. I was surprised he hadn't yelled my ear off yet. He'd leave when I told him in a few short hours that I had nothing to show for all my work. He wouldn't want to be my agent anymore. He wouldn't support a loser, like me. Who would?

My hands began to shake so violently that I could barely hold the wheel straight. My breath came and went so quickly, that my hands and feet started to feel numb. I couldn't slow my thoughts or concentrate on the road. My chest felt heavy, a great pain radiating like I was drowning and couldn't get enough air. I pulled off at the next exit, drove until I found a parking lot next to an office building, and stopped the car. What was happening to me? I couldn't drive, at least not safely. The pain in my chest grew, my heart beating far too fast, and I couldn't breathe. I felt like I was dying. I was in the middle of nowhere, had no idea where I was now, and was dying.

I called 9-1-1 and tried to explain what was happening, my voice cutting in and out as I struggled to breathe. The woman on the line asked me where I was, and I had to admit I didn't know. She explained that they needed an address. I swore under my breath.

I looked at the building in front of me and couldn't see a number or an address. Keeping her on the line, I got out of the car, searching for street signs. My legs were wobbly, and my fingers were numb. Eventually, I reached a nearby intersection and read the signs to her. Although I hoped she could stay on the line, she assured me an ambulance would be on its way and hung up. I wanted to return to my car but feared that if I did, they wouldn't be able to find me, so I eased myself to sit on the damp grass under the street signs – Washington and Rose Lane. I hugged my knees to my chest and struggled to breathe until I heard the sirens and reluctantly tottered to my feet.

The EMT approached me, verified my name, asked for my symptoms, and strapped me to a gurney. I looked like a complete disaster by this point and felt like I was losing my mind alongside my life. Pain radiated from my chest, my lungs heaving, my hands and feet shaking and numb, and I felt so incredibly cold as I tried to focus on not dying. While one of the men drove, the siren blaring, the second sat with me, trying unsuccessfully to calm me down. He asked me to try to breathe more slowly, to breathe in for a count of four, hold my breath for a count of four, and breathe out for a count of four. I tried, unsuccessfully, to follow his directions, but the whole time all I could think was, oh, God, I'm a failure, I can't keep my shit together, and now I'm dying, I'm dying, I'm dying.

By the time we got to the hospital, my breathing had slowed a little, but I still felt cold and numb, and it felt like an elephant was sitting on my chest. The weight was unbearable. They rushed me into one of the emergency rooms and left me alone while I waited for a nurse. When the nurse finally pushed the curtains back, she came with a clipboard and a slew of questions. I still found breathing difficult and talking even more impossible, but I answered. She asked if I had taken any prescription medication or any drugs. She took my blood pressure, which had skyrocketed. She asked what I was doing before I started feeling unwell.

"Driving," I replied. "I was upset but couldn't catch my breath." Correction: still couldn't catch my breath.

"Do you have any dizziness or pain?"

"Both."

"Alright, try to breathe slowly and try to calm down."

As if I had much control over that.

"I'm going to start an IV and give you some lorazepam. It should help."

"What's wrong with me?" I asked. I felt like I was having a heart attack.

"Have you ever had severe anxiety before?"

"You think this is anxiety?"

"Most likely a panic attack, but we'll get you settled down and back on track."

I felt like a derailed train, but I eventually slipped into a shallow sleep as I lay there in the cool darkness as the meds started working their magic.

When they woke me to run some additional tests, blood-work, and the complete workup, I could breathe, and my limbs started to feel normal again. "We're just checking all our bases," the doctor explained, "although it appears you have had a panic attack, Elizabeth. For someone who has never had one, it can feel like a heart attack and be very scary, but you'll live."

Unfortunately, thought my inner critic.

"You'll need to schedule a follow-up with your primary care physician and likely seek some therapy if you don't already have a therapist."

"I don't," I muttered.

"The nurse will also go over some coping strategies for you in the meantime before we send you on your way. How are you feeling now?"

"Exhausted."

"Go ahead and get some rest. She'll return with your lab work, and we'll go from there." He patted the bed reassuringly. "Take it easy in the meantime."

After I had been released, they didn't want me to drive myself, but I also had no one I could depend on to pick me up. Eventually, they had a police officer drive me back to the hotel. It was my first time in a cop car, and I didn't even have a crazy story to tell. Not a fun one, anyway. I left my car in the random lot with plans to return for it later. I had been in the hospital so long that the sun was already rising over the horizon. Thankfully the officer didn't try to strike up a conversation because I wasn't in the mood to talk, and it was everything I could do to keep my eyes open. I thanked him for the ride. By the time I reached my hotel room, I stumbled in the door and made my way to the bed like a zombie. I didn't even bother to take off my shoes. I just collapsed from utter exhaustion.

Chapter 38

18 MONTHS AGO

When I arrived at Michael's building, the streetlights illuminated the sidewalks with a yellow glow. As I walked up to the front door, he was already closing it behind him. He wore a slim gray suit coat, and his hair looked disheveled, like he had just gotten out of bed. I resisted the urge to fluff his hair and instead greeted him with a warm smile.

"Hey there, stranger," I said.

"Hey there, sweetheart." He returned my smile and grabbed my arm, escorting me. "I'm sorry the reading for *The Women of My Family* didn't go as planned."

I let my arm go limp in his, relaxing for the first time that day. Our relationship had always been fun and flirty, comfortable even when I felt stressed. "Where to?" I asked.

"Have you ever been to Dillon's?"

"Can't say I have. Is it swanky?" I glanced down at my sweatpants and oversized hoodie.

"A bit, but there isn't exactly a dress code. They'll take your money no matter what you're wearing."

"Good."

It was a walk of a few blocks, and our back-and-forth banter let me catch my breath for a moment. He had a way of helping me relax that was a real lifesaver. The light above Dillon's glowed a neon blue, and Michael held the door for me as I slipped inside. The entire place was covered in a soft blue felt, ceiling, walls, and floor.

"I feel like I'm inside Cookie Monster," I whispered to him.

"That's a weird image, for sure."

I grimaced. "I mean, soft, blue, fuzzy?"

"I suppose."

Stranger still, there was no cocktail menu.

"It's kinda like jazz," Michael explained. "You pick an alcohol, a style of drink, or flavor profile, and they do the magic."

"Sounds like too many choices."

"Not really, they make most of the choices for you. I've never had a bad drink here, either."

"I bet you take all your girlfriends here," I teased.

"You mean my authors? I don't have a girlfriend."

"It's good to know I still have a chance."

He laughed. We ordered drinks. He had a sweet rum-based cocktail they set on fire, and I had a bourbon styled like an old-fashioned with orange liquor and walnut bitters. We sipped our drinks, settling into a small, dimly lit booth. I recapped the day's events, sighing, trying to distance myself from the pain I felt. I hadn't thought about how my book would affect my family or what their reactions would be. Even while writing the memoir, I had somehow distanced myself from the fact that I would be publicizing their very private lives. I admitted to Michael that I had no idea how to move forward, especially given my mother's demand that I move out.

"I could help you find a studio," he offered.

We had ordered a second round of drinks, and the alcohol was starting to get to me. "I might be looking for an apartment; I don't think I have enough funds to afford a studio on top of it," I complained.

Michael laughed. "A studio apartment, silly."

"Oh. Yeah, that's probably all I'd be able to afford now, until the royalties start rolling in."

"Sensible girl. But that's a worry for tomorrow. As I said, you're welcome to crash at my place tonight."

"You have a guest room?"

"No, but I have a leather couch."

We tripped our way back to his apartment, arms linked. I felt wobbly but managed, remembering I hadn't even eaten dinner.

"I know it's a big ask, but do you think we could grab food on the way back?"

"That is a big ask," he said. "Not much open at this hour."

"I'm sorry. I just realized I haven't eaten."

"Well, we'll see."

All we might manage would be a lonely hot dog cart on the way, but Michael kept an eye out for an actual restaurant.

"Why didn't you say something earlier?" he asked.

"I didn't think of it," I replied.

Thankfully, we found a little boutique-style restaurant called Chez la Crepe. It had been ages since I'd eaten any breakfast food, and crepes sounded terrific.

"Looks like they're only open 'till midnight, so we've gotta eat quick, but I think this will work," he said.

We settled into a purple vinyl booth and glanced at the menu. I was surprised to see more than chocolate, banana, and strawberry crepes. They also served savory options, such as ham and cheese (*jambon du fromage*) and egg with spinach (*l'oeufs et épinard*). I struggled through the pronunciations as we ordered. I had taken a few French courses in high school, but it had been years since I'd spoken the language. Ultimately, I opted for Nutella with banana and nuts and tried to wait patiently for the waitress to return.

"Maybe we'll get you sobered up a bit," said Michael. "Don't want you to accuse me of taking advantage."

"Yes," I agreed. "We wouldn't want that." I laughed. Though I found him attractive, I never planned on going down that avenue with him. I had learned not to mix business with pleasure the hard way. As a teenager, I may or may not have dated the assistant manager at the grocery store I cashiered at. Somehow, that hadn't entirely made its way into the memoir. It was a short-lived affair, anyway, "affair" being the key word. It turned out he had been married the whole time.

As soon as our food arrived, I dug in. "This is just what I needed."

"Well, good," he replied. "Glad I could help you out."

"Are you sure you're alright with putting me up for the night?"

"If I wasn't, I wouldn't have offered."

He paid the tab, and we walked the rest of the way to his apartment. Before I knew it, we were riding up in the elevator. I struggled to stand upright. I could barely keep my eyes open between the liquor and the crepes. He helped me and motioned to the couch, which would be my bed for the night.

"That looks pretty comfy, but do you have any blankets?" I asked.

"Of course, Princess." He pulled a purple-and-black afghan from the hall closet and an extra pillow.

"*Graci*," I replied as I gratefully took them from him.

"Don't you mean *merci*?"

"Same difference." I slid my sneakers off and curled up on the couch, pulling the afghan over my legs. As soon as I settled in, a fluffy white cat leaped onto my lap. "And who might you be?" I asked as I scratched under his chin.

"That's Muffin," answered Michael. He stepped out of his oxfords and dropped into the armchair.

"Oh, are you a girl kitty?"

"Nope, still a dude, just a girly name."

"I see. I didn't know you had a cat."

"Cats, plural. Simon is skulking around here somewhere."

"Why does he get a more dignified name?"

"I adopted them from the shelter. They came with their names." He stood to swat Muffin away and made his way toward the bedroom. "I hope they don't bother you too much."

"I'm sure I'll be fine." I snuggled down into the couch. "Thank you again for this. I'm so exhausted."

I slept for what must have been an hour before the cats returned, nocturnal monsters that they were. To them, I was an obstacle course worth jumping back and forth on and bouncing off of. I shooed them away, to no avail. Even when they weren't directly attacking me, they were chasing after shadows, skittering across the floor and destroying any chance at a good night's sleep. Cautiously, I crept down the hall and into Michael's bedroom.

He lay curled up on one side of the bed, heaped in blankets and breathing softly. I closed the door behind me and made my way to the end of the bed. If I didn't lay next to him, maybe he wouldn't even notice I had come in. I stretched across the foot of the mattress and, in exhaustion, fell straight back to sleep.

In the morning, he woke me with a swift kick to the ribs. I let out a yelp, and he awakened, still groggy and very confused.

"I thought you were sleeping on the couch," he mumbled. "What are you doing in my bed?"

"The cats wouldn't let me sleep."

"Come up here, silly." He patted the pillow next to him.

Reluctantly, I pulled myself up further into the bed.

"It's too early to be up," he said. "I'm going back to sleep. We'll go apartment hunting later."

"Okay." I turned my back to him, and we slept that way until the sun rose higher in the sky.

Chapter 39

PRESENT DAY

I didn't wake until mid-afternoon after what must have been the fifth or sixth time my phone rang and went to voice-mail. I scrambled half-heartedly across to the bed and dug my phone out to answer it. It was Michael, of course.

"Why aren't you answering your phone?" he demanded.

"Why do you think?" I mumbled.

"Are you hung over?" he asked, sounding shocked.

"Yeah, I'm on a bender," I replied.

"Really?"

"No, I'm just avoiding your calls."

"Why? Don't tell me you don't have your chapters ready."

"I don't."

"Well, why not?"

"It's a long story. One I haven't written."

"Well, help me out here, Lizzy. You've got to give me something." I could hear the desperation in his voice. "The publisher has already given you a good-faith extension on this. And an advance, sight unseen."

"I was at the emergency room last night." I tried to prop myself up on some pillows. I had the worst morning mouth and was in dire need of a shower. Every part of me felt filthy.

His voice quickly shifted to a tone of concern. "What happened?"

"What is it that celebrities go to the hospital for? Exhaustion?"

"Alcoholism. Drug addiction." He managed a small laugh. "Is there something you're not telling me, Liz?"

"I can't handle it," I admitted. "I had a panic attack."

"Oh, my little brother used to have those all the time," he said. "No biggie. You got this."

"No. I don't," I tried to explain. "I'm lost and don't know where I'm going. I'm sorry I let you down." I tried not to cry, but a few tears escaped my eyes. "I don't know what to do."

"Where are you now?" he asked.

"Still the middle of bum-fuck nowhere."

"No, seriously. Where are you? What hotel, what city?"

Reluctantly, I told him, and he promised to meet me for dinner, that we'd work something out. If nothing else, a more manageable plan of attack.

"The last thing I want is to see you fail, Liz. I know this has been rough on you, but I'm here. Not just as your agent, as your friend."

"Thank you, Michael." I hung up and went promptly back to sleep.

That night, we met at the restaurant in my hotel and shared a nice dinner and some drinks. The conversation stayed light for most of the evening, but eventually, we got down to brass tacks. Although he remained supportive, we developed a plan for me to move forward. He negotiated for my first few chapters to be extended again, with one caveat.

"You don't need to have it finished, Elizabeth. Just started. Get something on the page, something worth reading." He reached out to touch my hand, and I let him. It felt warm and comforting.

"Alright. I promise."

"By Friday?"

"Yes, I can get started even if I don't have anything concrete. I can get you something."

"That's all I need."

He ordered another round of drinks and dessert and acted the perfect gentleman. A small part of me wished he wouldn't have, though. We were saying our goodbyes at the door to my room, and I let slip what could almost be misconstrued as an invitation but then tried to blame it on the wine. He left, and then I was left alone again with my thoughts.

Absent-mindedly, I checked my phone. There was a missed message. I played it back on the speakerphone, hearing Miriam's worried voice echoing back at me.

"My dear Liz, I hope that you are alright and just forgot to meet me this afternoon. Call me back as soon as you are able," she said. "I look forward to your call, day or night. Don't worry about business hours or anything like that. My number is -" and she rattled off a string of digits. I still felt too exhausted to do anything productive, but I would call again in the morning. Maybe I could still manage to get everything back on track.

Chapter 40

When I finally called Miriam back, she was so kind and understanding that I couldn't keep up the lie with her any longer.

"Let me be honest with you, Miriam," I said over the phone.

"What is it, dear?" she asked.

"I'm not a pregnant teenager needing your help," I admitted.

"I know," she replied. I could imagine her laughing at me.

"If you knew, why did you keep up the ruse?" I asked. "Why waste your time?"

"I talked with Bruno the other day," she explained. "I wanted you to get the full Mr. Wilson's Wives treatment and see that there is nothing underhanded or nefarious happening in our organization. We are here to help young women through whatever tough situation they have found themselves in. Now tell me, Elizabeth, what exactly are you aiming at with your research?"

"Good question," I muttered, more to myself than her. "I just wanted to get to the truth of it. Why did Mr. Wilson marry so many women, and what kind of man was he? I thought it would make an interesting story to write about."

"I'll agree with you there," she admitted. "It is quite an amazing story, but you don't seem to realize that Mr. Wilson isn't the interesting one here. He was just a man with a lot of money. I'm the real brains behind the operation."

"What do you mean?"

"Would you still be willing to meet with me?" she asked. "It's a bit of a story, I'm afraid, and I hate talking on the phone for any length of time."

I still felt a bit tired and weak from the events of the past day-and-a-half, and the medication they had given me had left me feeling a bit drowsy, dizzy even. My better judgment insisted that I avoid any driving. Maybe I could get her to meet me here instead.

"I'm staying at the Morpheus Motel in Weston," I explained. "Would you be able to meet me at the restaurant here? I have been feeling a little under the weather and don't think I'm up for driving now."

"That would be no problem," she agreed.

We made plans to meet in the early afternoon at the hotel restaurant. She had piqued my interest. Was Mr. Wilson just a patsy all along? A hapless man who so many women duped? How much did he know about what was going on? I decided to give Michael a quick call.

"Good morning, beautiful," he answered. "Are you feeling better today? Have the gremlins allowed you to get some sleep?"

"Gremlins?" I asked.

"The brain gremlins," he replied. "They like to crawl around in your thoughts, making everything dark and negative. They're pretty awful creatures."

"No, the gremlins have left me alone. So far."

"Do you need me to come by and beat them off with a stick?"

I laughed, despite myself.

"There ya go. That's the Elizabeth I remember."

"I'm going to have a second go with Miriam today," I told him.

"Great. Round two - fight!"

"I mean, I hope there won't be any fighting."

"It's just an expression. You've got this."

"Thanks." I still hadn't told him about my conversation with Bruno. How could I? He'd lose his mind if I told him I was even entertaining the idea of scrapping the story. "After this, I promise to get some pages for you."

"You better. You do realize that not only is your livelihood on the line here, but mine, too? After I got you on the hook, I let go of some of my other fish. You need to keep being a big fish for me."

"I'll try," I said.

"No try, only do," he replied.

I hung the phone up, feeling better about the situation. I still didn't know what to do, but at least I had another lead. Miriam might be the linchpin that held everything all together. If that were the case, I might finally be able to put all my theories to rest and rely on the truth of the matter. While I could take my readers along for the ride, with all my suppositions and ideas about what was happening and why Mr. Wilson had married these women, if there was one central factor, or even primary reason for the epic number of wives he had, that could be my focus. In the end, it seemed like things were more transactional than I had initially believed, and somehow Miriam was the key to everything.

* * *

I settled in early, ordered a hot chocolate, and sat sipping and contemplating. The restaurant at the hotel was small and quaint. Oak doors with glass panels opened to the patio, where a gentle breeze wafted in. If I weren't meeting someone, I would be more likely to sit outside in the sunshine. Despite my original intentions, I had spent too much time inside this summer. I thought I would go hiking, maybe even canoeing out at the cabin, but instead, I found myself sitting indoors, begging old ladies to tell me about their lives. Not that it wasn't exciting and didn't keep me entertained, but I had thought I'd be writing some profound, thought-provoking thing like Thoreau's *Walden*. But who was I kidding? That wasn't my natural inclination. I liked human nature so much more than nature.

When Miriam arrived, I spotted her right away, partially because she was the only person other than the staff in the restaurant, but also because of what she was wearing. A bright red pantsuit with a black-and-white striped button-up shirt. She looked stunning, much more like a businesswoman than a social worker. She stopped one of the waiters on her way to the table, ordering a double shot of espresso. She joined me at the table and smiled, her teeth perfectly straight and brilliantly white. She extended her hand to me.

"You must be Elizabeth," she said.

"And you must be Miriam," I replied.

"Indeed I am. So, let's set a few things straight from the get-go," she began. "While I have spoken with Bruno, I do not necessarily share his sentiments, so you needn't worry about that."

I nodded. I wasn't sure what I had expected in that regard, but I figured that if she was willing to speak to me, she was willing to share her story, in general.

"However," she added. "I do think you should pay him heed. The man does have a point, after all. The information we are dealing in could be detrimental if it became more widely known. As an individual, I don't mind sharing with you, but it might be a different story if you publish everything."

"I understand," I said. "There's no pressure at this point," I added. "If I go forward with this, I will seek explicit permission from anyone I have spoken with. I would hate for it to be a nasty surprise to anyone."

She smiled. "Indeed. No one likes nasty surprises, do they?"

The waiter arrived with her drink and offered a refill on mine. I decided to switch to English Breakfast, and they brought me a small silver pot of boiling water, a tea bag, and a small dish of honey.

"You don't drink coffee?" asked Miriam.

"Oh, I do," I assured her. "Or I did. Trying to take it a little easy today."

"I see. Well, now that we're done with that nasty legalese, let me tell you a story."

I repositioned myself in my chair, ready for anything.

Chapter 41

MIRIAM COHEN, 1976

When Miriam first met Mr. Wilson, she was interviewing for a position as his accountant. Although his family was wealthy, he had recently come into a greater amount of money and needed someone to help him manage it. A great uncle had passed away and, having no children of his own, had given his estate to Erwin as an inheritance. This estate included a large sum of money and a residence out in the country. Erwin simply didn't know what to do with it all. Miriam had come highly recommended by a banker friend, and they met over coffee to discuss her credentials and the position requirements.

"So you have found yourself with more money than you can manage by yourself," concluded Miriam as she sipped delicately at her second cup of coffee.

"That's the gist of it," Erwin admitted. "My friend, Mr. Hemmingworth, told me you have been managing his estate quite thoroughly but that he is looking for a change."

"Oh, so he thinks he can pawn me off on you?" she asked.

"No, not at all, it's just. Well, he mentioned your rate, and I think he simply cannot afford you any longer. The man is about to retire, you know."

"Of course I know," she replied. "I know everything that man does. If he even thinks about sneezing, I know about it."

Erwin laughed. "Sounds like you've got a good head on your shoulders."

"I do," she replied. "So, why should I come work for you, Mr. Wilson?"

"Please, call me Erwin."

"Oh, are we on a first-name basis already?"

"I don't deal much with formalities."

"Fine, then, Erwin, what do you have to offer me?" They negotiated her rate as well as the terms of her employment. It was all accomplished rather quickly because she had come prepared with knowledge of his situation and a decent idea of what she expected of him in the employment arrangement.

She asked him about his great uncle, the progenitor of these unexpected funds, various charities he might donate to, and other ways he could invest to grow his fortune. She also asked about the estate in Orchard Square. Would he be living there, or would he sell it?

"I have only seen the estate once, as a boy during a family reunion," he said. "But I look forward to exploring it again. I might very well live there."

"Are you sure you don't want to sell the space? It might require a lot of upkeep."

"It might help me get a new wife," he offered.

"In reviewing your finances, I did want to ask about that. You have quite a few alimony payments in the works here. Would you be willing to go to court to get those cleared up?" she asked.

"Cleared up?"

"I mean, is it necessary for you to pay for those?"

"It's not very much," he said. "Not in the grand scheme of things."

"But if it's an expense you could easily get rid of, why wouldn't you?"

"Honestly, Miriam, I feel like it is the least I can do. I have wronged each of those women in one way or another. I think of it like penance."

"Are you a religious man, Mr. Wilson?"

"Erwin."

"Sorry, are you a religious man, Erwin?"

"Not particularly, but I still want to make good with those I have wronged."

"I see," she replied, but she didn't. She had never understood alimony. Those women had lost their husband's income, but that didn't mean they had the right to suck him dry once they divorced him. They should be required to provide their livelihood. As a woman, it wasn't always easy, but she managed to care for herself just fine. "Would you mind if I ordered dessert?" she asked him.

"No, of course not. That sounds like a wonderful idea. Whatever you want, my treat."

"Oh, you don't have to," she began, then trailed off. If he was offering, she wouldn't refuse the offer.

However, by the time their pie a la mode arrived, the dull ache that had started in her abdomen had become throbbing pain. She excused herself and hurriedly made her way to the bathroom. She clutched her stomach when she got there and resisted the urge to throw up. Opening one of the stalls, she nearly collapsed to the floor once she got inside.

The pain itself wasn't a surprise, only the timing. She thought she had almost a week until her period would arrive, but it seemed she wasn't that lucky. The cramping was always debilitating, and she usually scheduled herself off for at least a day or two. When her period didn't come as scheduled, however, she would be reduced to this puddle of a woman, unable to accomplish much of anything. She struggled to position herself on the toilet and forced herself to breathe more slowly, pushing the air rhythmically in and out of her lungs. To her surprise, the bleeding hadn't even started, just the cramping. When it came, it would come with a heavy flow and large clots. She wanted to be home for that, rather than out in public, so she could deal with any unexpected mess. In the meantime, she needed to make it back out into the restaurant, if nothing else, to excuse herself and make her way home.

When she finally returned to their table, Erwin looked her over with concern. "Are you alright?" he asked. "You ran out of here like a bat out of hell."

"Well, I'm no demon. I assure you of that." She tried to laugh it off but even laughing proved painful. She looked at her plate, frowning at the pool of melted ice cream. So much for dessert, although she didn't feel like she could eat anything now. "I'll be alright," she assured him. "Just a little indigestion."

"Fair enough," he replied. "Although it looks like all your ice cream melted."

"I think my eyes were bigger than my stomach, anyway," she said. She glanced around, stood and grabbed her jacket from the back of her chair, and slung her purse over her shoulder. She extended a hand. "I apologize for the quick exit, but I must be going." They shook hands and said their goodbyes. She couldn't wait to get home, put her feet up and relax with a nice heating pad.

Miriam was not surprised that she was soon hired on as Erwin's accountant. The moment they started talking, she knew she had the job. By the time Erwin had cleaned out his great uncle's mansion, she would often work side-by-side with him in his study. While this was an unconventional arrangement, she didn't mind the company, and it was convenient that she didn't need to set up meetings with him because she knew she would see him in person at least once a week. She got so caught up in some of the charity work, that she often lost track of time. Her newest project was researching local organizations to determine which one to present to him. He gave her some ideas regarding his interests and where he would like his funds to go, but her job was to find which groups were the most reputable and did the best work with his monetary gifts.

The top contenders were a food bank and a shelter for orphans. Both of these causes were near and dear to Miriam's heart, but she wasn't quite sure where they ranked for Erwin. He looked like a man who had never dealt with hunger or poverty in his entire life. Everything he had ever needed had been given to him. He was born into wealth, which meant he would never have to work a day in his life if he didn't want to. Yet, at the same time, he always seemed industrious and resourceful with his money. In general, he invested wisely and lived off the interest. His children and ex-wives would be able to live comfortably for years, even if he suddenly passed away.

She was a bit surprised to learn he had six ex-wives already, at barely 40. It seemed he went through them like water. There were a few pictures in strategic places, and each looked quite different from the others. A few photos were with a striking redhead, others with a thin, blue-eyed blonde. There were several with a fairly average-looking woman with short brown hair and two young boys. Miriam wondered how many children Erwin had accumulated over the years and how much contact he had with them. He never spoke of them. But in the end, none of it was any of her business. They had a primarily professional relationship, and she intended to keep it that way, although she did catch him looking at her occasionally. She knew she was attractive. Her former employer had done the same, looked but never touched, and it was an arrangement she was comfortable with.

She straightened her papers on the small desk sitting beside Erwin's much larger oak one and glanced up at him. He was wearing his glasses, pouring over the latest returns and financial statements, and barely noticed her leaving for the day. She gathered her folders, placing them carefully into her leather briefcase. As she stood, however, she doubled over in pain. It had been months since she'd had an episode in public, and it was so embarrassing to have this happen now, here, in front of her boss. Despite her best efforts, she let out a small yelp.

"Miriam?" he came rushing to her side, helping hold her upright. "What's wrong?"

She grimaced, eased herself back into the chair, and gazed helplessly at him. "I'm just not feeling well," she lied. Understatement of the year, she thought to herself.

"Is there anything I can get you?" he asked. "Maybe a glass of water?"

"Sure. That'd be great." Anything to get him to leave the room for a moment. She didn't want him to see her like this, weak and not in control of her own body.

He hurried out of the room. In the few minutes while he was gone, she practiced breathing exercises, hoping the pain would subside but knowing it most likely wouldn't. Not until she laid down for a few hours. Her doctor had finally diagnosed her with endometriosis, and although she didn't entirely understand what that meant, she did know that the pain she felt each month was far from ordinary. At the same time, it wasn't uncommon among young women like herself. What a curse God had given her. Maybe because she wasn't a believer, she thought. She didn't believe that, but it felt like she was being punished for something she didn't do, and she felt a little like Eve eating the apple because a snake whispered in her ear. This pain was indeed some sort of divine punishment.

Erwin finally returned with some ice water, his face wrinkled with worry. She struggled to smile at him, assure him everything was alright when it couldn't be further from the truth. She took a few small sips, and sudden nausea washed over her. She stood and began rushing toward the bathroom, but another wave of pain stabbed at her abdomen before she could get there. She crumpled to the floor in the hallway, trying to cling to the wall as she fell.

"Miriam!" Erwin chased after her, catching her before she fell to her knees. "What's wrong?" he asked. "What's happening?"

She didn't have the strength to answer him, just moaned in agony.

"I'm taking you to the hospital right now," he insisted.

"No, no, I'll be fine. Just give me a minute," she begged. "I just need to rest a little."

He clutched her aching body to his, but she barely noticed his arms wrapped around her. "Miriam, we need to get you to the doctor."

The next hour went by in a blur of agonizing pain. Erwin drove furiously to the ER while she tried to explain this pain was expected, for her at least. While she moaned and struggled through the wait at the hospital, he refused to believe her.

"What do you mean there's nothing they can do?" he said. "There must be something. You can't live like this, Miriam."
"It's only a few days a month," she repeated back to him, the same thing she had heard from doctors for years.

"A few days a month too many," he countered.

When they had been waiting for more than half an hour and several others had been taken before Miriam, Erwin marched up to the counter, demanding they give her a bed. "Can't you see she's in pain?" he asked the attendant at the counter. "Can you at least give her something to stop the pain?"

The receptionist looked back blankly. She was just trying to do her job. "Have you tried over-the-counter medications?"

Erwin nearly growled back at her. "You think we'd be here if those were working?"

"We are full up right now, but I'll get her a bed as soon as possible," she promised.

"Please do." His words were polite, but his tone remained gruff.

He returned to Miriam's side, angry that he could do nothing to help ease her suffering. Eventually, a nurse came out to walk her back to her room. Erwin followed, resting heavily on a bedside chair while the nurse took down Miriam's medical history.

Eventually, the nurse turned to him. "And you're the husband?" she asked.

"No, no," Erwin replied. "A friend. Well, I'm her employer. She collapsed at work."

"We've got things handled here if you want to step outside. We can give you a call later if you would like."

"I'm not going anywhere." He crossed his arms over his chest, pouting like a child.

"It's okay," Miriam interjected. "He can stay. I'd like the company."

The nurse decided not to pry. "I'm just going to take your vitals then, Miriam. The doctor will be in shortly."

Miriam's continuing pain made those few minutes of waiting for the doctor feel like an eternity. Erwin felt helpless, but at least he could be there for her. At one point, he reached over to hold her hand in his, squeezing her fingers slightly. He managed to say something reassuring but didn't believe it himself. 'Everything is going to be fine' sounded like a lie as soon as it left his lips.

"Thank you," she managed. "For staying with me."

"Of course," he replied. "I won't leave you."

Eventually, the doctor arrived. After learning of her endometriosis diagnosis, he poked and prodded her with gloved hands, asking her to rate her pain level. Erwin resisted the urge to yell at the man to stop. The doctor was causing her more pain, but he needed to know the severity of the pain and exactly where it hurt. He scheduled her for an MRI and ordered some intravenous pain medication.

Shortly after the doctor left the room, the nurse returned with the medication and added it directly to her IV line. Once the pain medication began to take effect, Miriam slipped into a light, uneasy sleep. Erwin stayed by her side, watching carefully over her.

Later, the nurse returned, waking her for the MRI. She explained that the MRI was an excellent way for them to get an image of the soft tissues of her abdomen, primarily her uterus, and any additional tissue that may have grown outside the uterus. They could then make plans for surgery to remove the tissue, if necessary. Miriam nodded, accepting her fate. She would be grateful for anything to improve her quality of life.

"So if they do the surgery," Erwin asked. "She won't have the pain anymore?"

"There is always the possibility that the tissue could grow back," the nurse admitted.

"What then? More surgery?"

"Honestly, the only way to ensure it won't grow back would be to remove the uterus altogether."

"You mean like a hysterectomy?" asked Miriam.

"Exactly. But I assure you, that would be the last resort," the nurse replied. "Especially because it would make you unable to have children."

Miriam fought the urge to laugh. She knew this was serious, but she had never really wanted children in the first place. "Anything to get rid of this blasted pain," she said. "Really and truly, that's all I want."

"Understandable," said the nurse. "But first thing's first. Let's get you an MRI."

Miriam had never had an MRI before and was daunted at the prospect. She had seen them in hospital dramas, the big cylindrical tubes that made patients nervous and claustrophobic. At least she didn't need to drink any type of contrast for this particular scan. She had heard those weren't exactly the most pleasant tasting. All she needed to do was lie still and try to relax. She stretched out on the cold table and waited while she was brought into the machine.

She couldn't see anything but the inside, the sides and cylindrical roof of the thing, just inches away from her face. It wasn't that bad, she reasoned, nothing worse than feeling like you'd been buried alive. Just when she thought she could doze off for a few minutes, the entire machine emitted a series of tapping and thunking noises. She imagined loved ones shoveling dirt on her coffin, each load falling heavy as they filled her grave. She opened her eyes momentarily and then shut them again immediately. She heard a voice from the observation booth, echoing in the room like the voice of God. "Just try to relax," said the voice. "This will all be over soon." Oh, I hope so, she thought to herself. I hope to feel like a human again soon, without pain.

After the MRI, they wheeled her into another room. It was a bit larger than the emergency room bay. It looked like she would be staying and getting officially admitted to the hospital. After another wonderful dose of pain medication, she woke to find Erwin at her side again.

"How are you feeling?" he asked, reaching for her hand.

"Better," she replied. "For now. Less nauseous for sure."

"How was the MRI?"

"A little scary, but it's over now."

"I guess they'll be scheduling you for surgery. They told me they won't be able to get you in until tomorrow morning."

"Alright."

"Do you want me to call anybody? Family?"

"No one that would care." She sighed heavily. She hadn't spoken to her parents since they gave her the boot at eighteen. She wasn't about to start talking to them now, and she had no siblings.

"Do you want me to stay?" he asked.

"Overnight? No, you don't need to."

"I know I don't *need* to, but I will if you want me to."

"No, you should go get some sleep. I'll be fine."

He stayed by her bedside until she managed to sleep again and quietly snuck out. She didn't even notice he had left until the nurse returned for vitals, and the room was empty. She appreciated that he had been there for her, though, and looked forward to the next time she would see him. No other employer would have stayed by her side like that.

Chapter 42

MIRIAM COHEN, 1976

The laparoscopic surgery was scheduled for the following morning. The doctor explained to Miriam that he would be going in through a small incision in her belly button and scraping out the extra tissue which had grown in and around her uterus. It was this extra tissue, he explained, that had been causing her painful cramping each time she got her period.

"Are you sure it won't just grow back?" she asked. "I would hate to go through all of this again."

"That is a possibility, but we will do our best to remove as much of the tissue as possible."

"The nurse had mentioned the possibility of a hysterectomy?" she offered.

The doctor shot daggers at the nurse, who looked like she was trying to hide behind the IV rig. "The nurse shouldn't be giving medical advice without my directive," he scolded. "A hysterectomy is an option, but that would be our last resort."

"If it meant I wouldn't have to deal with this ever again, why aren't we considering It?" asked Miriam.

"I don't think you understand the enormity of a hysterectomy. Removing everything, including your ovaries, would induce early menopause, which would cause hormonal fluctuations and all the things that come along with it, like hot flashes. It would also render you sterile, meaning you could never have children," the doctor said. "I wouldn't recommend it to a young woman like yourself."

"But it's my body," Miriam argued. "Isn't it my decision to make? I want a second opinion."

"Your surgery is already scheduled," the doctor insisted. "This is the course of action I suggest."

She could tell he was starting to get irritated with her, but she wanted to ensure she was making the right decision. "I told you, I want a second opinion."

The doctor stormed out of the room, leaving Miriam with the nurse, who shyly extricated herself from the medical equipment alongside the bed.

"I'm sorry," the nurse said. "It wasn't my place to say anything."

"No," argued Miriam. "I'm glad you did. Imagine how many surgeries I might need if I followed his advice. I don't want to be in and out of here several times. I want to be done with this."

"Honestly," the nurse added. "I'm not sure you'll be able to get a hysterectomy, unless you can get him to sign off on it."

"What do you mean?"

"He's the chief surgeon. That kinda thing would need his approval, even if you can get another doctor to sign off on it, and they usually don't."

"Well, why didn't you say that, to begin with?" Miriam struggled to sit up in bed. The heat rose to her cheeks. "Is this just a wild goose chase?"

The nurse nodded, gulping. "There are a few things that would need to happen for you to be able to have a hysterectomy. First, you are under 25, so it is typically not recommended unless medically necessary. You have no children, so it would be especially frowned upon. Then, there is the issue that a spouse would need to consent."

"But I'm not married and don't want children."

"That's not up to you."

"But why not?"

The nurse quickly gave up arguing and left the room. Miriam sat there in the cold silence, contemplating her fate. There had to be some way around this; she just hadn't figured it out yet.

Just then, Erwin ambled in, clutching a convenience store coffee. There were bags under his eyes, and he looked like he hadn't slept a wink. "Good morning, beautiful," he said.

"Beautiful?" she scoffed. "Hardly."

"What's the latest?" he asked.

"I think I'm at a standstill. I asked for a second opinion, and everybody stormed out."

"What do you mean?"

"I think I'm still scheduled for surgery, but I insisted on exploring my options, including a hysterectomy. Then the nurse shut me down, saying I'm too young and crazy for not wanting children. But, if I had a husband who could sign off on it, a man to make decisions about *my* body, they'd start cutting, no questions asked." She glanced at the look of concern on Erwin's face, his caring eyes, and became impulsive. "Want to marry me?"

"Wait, what?" He stumbled over the words, nearly spilling his coffee.

She leaned closer to him, reaching for his hand. "I mean it. If you married me, you could sign off on the hysterectomy."

Erwin carefully set his coffee down on the side table. "Marriage isn't something to joke about, Miriam. And you know my track record."

"I do. That's why I know you're not entirely against the idea."

"But it would be a sham. I know you don't feel that way about me." She noticed he said nothing about his feelings on the matter. Maybe he had taken a liking to her in the past few months, maybe more than just a liking.

She squeezed his hand. "Let's do it," she urged. "Marry me so I can get a hysterectomy." She fought the nervous laughter that threatened to escape her throat. She didn't think it was a joke; she just couldn't believe her life. It felt so strange and surreal, like none of this was actually happening.

"What about the surgery?" asked Erwin. "The lapro-whatsit?"

"Flag down a nurse," Miriam suggested.

Erwin found a nurse, and they explained the situation, at least as much as necessary, for her to know. Miriam insisted she did not want to go through with the surgery and wanted to be released from the hospital to get a second opinion before going forward. The nurse objected, reminding Miriam of the pain she would most likely endure if they didn't operate soon. At the same time, they couldn't hold her hostage if she didn't want to stay. Eventually, the nurse produced a form for Miriam to sign, acknowledging that she was leaving against the doctor's orders and taking full responsibility for any negative consequences. The hospital didn't want to get sued after all.

The nurse removed Miriam's IV, returned her clothes, and brought in a wheelchair. Erwin pulled the car up and then returned to wheel her out.

"How are you feeling?" he whispered in her ear, pushing her through the hallway and into the elevator.

"I'm still all doped up on morphine," she replied. "Ask me in a few hours, and I might have a different answer."

"I think I might have some Vicodin left over from when I strained my back last year," he offered. "If you need it, just tell me. We might need a few days to get everything in order."

"Unfortunately," she agreed. "Unless you want to fly me to Vegas."

"That's not a half-bad idea."

She glanced up and smiled at him. She loved this man already.

* * *

Whirlwind didn't even begin to describe their wedding. Erwin drove them immediately to the airport, where they booked the first available flight to Las Vegas. Miriam managed to nap most of the flight as she rode a wave of ebbing and flowing discomfort. Although Erwin had offered Vicodin, they hadn't stopped at the house to grab it. She took a few ibuprofen and washed them down with sparkling water, which served as a stopgap for the time being.

When they arrived, the strip was already lit with flashing neon lights, a bright vein of color in the middle of the desert. Erwin hailed a cab, and they went to the courthouse. There was a bit of a line, but they were well-staffed, and it moved quickly. When they reached the front of the line, they each provided their identification, and the clerk helped them fill out the marriage certificate. The clerk's eyes grew wide as Erwin answered questions regarding his previous marriages, but he kept his mouth shut.

"Would you like a civil ceremony or a wedding?" the clerk asked. "We have a directory of chapels to choose from if you like." He hefted a thick directory toward them, but Erwin waved it away.

"A civil ceremony will be fine," Miriam answered.

The clerk directed them to a courtroom full of eager couples, and they waited their turn. Although she wasn't feeling the greatest, Miriam couldn't help but smile at some of the couples waiting with them. There were several young couples, looking barely old enough to get legally hitched, and then there was one older couple, holding hands and smiling shyly at one another. She wondered if they were here to renew their vows or if they had found each other late in life.

Suddenly, she wished she had something more suitable to wear. This was unexpected because this was purely a business transaction as far as she was concerned. It didn't matter what she was wearing. A petite Asian woman was roaming the hallway, selling white roses to whoever would purchase one. Erwin opened his wallet to hand the woman a few crisp dollars and bought one for her.

"I know it isn't much," he muttered, then realized they didn't even have rings to exchange. "You wait here," he instructed and ran from the courthouse.

Miriam impatiently fidgeted, still trying to wrap her mind around all that was happening. It was so fast and sudden that she felt like she had whiplash. Did she want to go through with this? Did she have any choice?

Erwin returned what felt like moments later, with two tiny sterling silver bands. He had bought them from a convenience store down the street. Miriam suppressed a laugh as she examined them. She had worn better rings as a teenager earning waitress tips.

"I promise to buy you a better one when we get home," Erwin whispered.

"No, I like this one," she teased him. "No one will try to mug me for it."

"That's for sure."

Miriam watched as one of the waiting brides broke into tears, yelling and hitting her intended groom with small, angry fists. That marriage would go well, she thought. The girl pulled the veil from her head and threw it at her partner, shouting, "I can't believe you would do that! With my sister!"Miriam forced herself to look away. At least she found out before marrying him, she mused. The girl ran from the room, the boy following her with a slow, dejected stride. The veil fell to the floor, and Miriam waited a few minutes before walking over to pick it up.

Erwin glanced in her direction. "What are you doing?" he asked.

She ran her hands through the veil, straightening it. She pushed the comb into her hair and pulled the white tulle over her face. "I can't get married without a veil," she replied, returning to his side.

"Are you sure that's the one you want? It might be cursed or something."

"It's the one I've got. It'll do the job."

"I guess it's no worse than these rings." They giggled together like schoolchildren. This whole thing really felt a little ridiculous and made them excited.

Finally, it was their turn. The officiant called them forward by name, glancing over the paperwork to ensure everything was in order. He was an older man and looked a bit tired at this hour of the night.

"Did you bring any witnesses?" he asked them.

Erwin shook his head.

"Would anyone here like to stand in as witnesses?" he asked the room.

"We can do it," said a very-pregnant bride, raising her hand. She and her groom stepped forward to join their party. They shook hands, exchanging introductions until the officiant cleared his throat.

"Alright. Let's get this show on the road. I haven't got all day," he said. Then, motioning to those still waiting, "And neither does anyone else here." He cleared his throat again and started his oratory. He sounded a bit like a failed actor who put far too much emphasis on his words. At least he wasn't an Elvis impersonator, thought Miriam.

"Ladies and Gentlemen, welcome to the marriage of Erwin and Miriam. Erwin and Miriam have found that special someone to love and trust with heart, mind, and soul. They have found someone to support them and comfort them in times of trial. They have good reason to be happy together, and we rejoice with them in their union."

He glanced around at the couples gathered there as if he were admonishing them. "Marriage is an honorable estate, not to be entered lightly but thoughtfully and reverently. Marriage is a commitment to take another person as a friend, companion, and lover. The uniting of this couple is an occasion of great significance which we can all celebrate." He paused for a moment to catch his breath. Miriam wondered how many times a day (a night?) he had said these words. Did they still have any meaning for him, or was it just rote memorization at this point?

"Marriage is not a casual event, nor is it simply a private affair between two individuals. Marriage is to be entered into responsibly. It deserves and needs the support of a wider commitment to each other by offering Erwin and Miriam our continued support, love, and best wishes in their lives together, in their love together, which they publicly express in this ceremony." The officiant coughed loudly at this point. "Even though I know none of you are likely to see each other ever again, much less me." The pregnant bride and her groom tittered at this. The rest of the room remained silent.

"Do you have the rings?" he asked Erwin.

Miriam watched as Erwin pulled them from his back pocket. This was happening. Right here, right now, she was getting married.

The officiant continued. "The marriage ring seals the vows of marriage and represents a promise of eternal and everlasting love. As you place the ring on Miriam's finger, Erwin, I want you to repeat after me."

Erwin nodded. He reached for Miriam's hand, which shook slightly.

"I promise to you, Miriam, before those gathered here, to commit my love to you; to respect your individuality; to be with you through life's changes; and to nurture and strengthen the love between us as long as we both shall live," he repeated after the officiant.

The ring barely fit, but Erwin managed to wedge it onto her finger. Now it was her turn.

"I promise to you, Erwin, before those gathered here, to commit my love to you; to respect your individuality; to be with you through life's changes; and to nurture and strengthen the love between us as long as we both shall live." She could hear her voice quavering, but she managed to make her way through it. She slid the ring onto Erwin's hand and then held it. She felt like she was hanging on to him for dear life. Somehow, they'd get through this together, she just wasn't quite sure how they would manage.

The officiant addressed the audience again. "We who have come together today have heard the willingness of Erwin and Miriam to be joined in marriage. They have come of their own free will and, in our presence, have declared their love and commitment to each other. They have given and received a ring as a symbol of their promises. Therefore, by the power vested in me by the laws of the state of Nevada, I take great pride and pleasure as I declare them husband and wife. You may now kiss your bride."

Erwin turned to her, gently pushed the veil away from her face, and planted the softest kiss on her lips. She smiled back at him. This was real now. There was no turning back. She barely heard the officiant's final words over the frantic beating of her heart.

"Ladies and gentlemen, I now present to you Mr. and Mrs. Wilson."

Chapter 43

PRESENT DAY

"So you married a man to get a hysterectomy?" I asked Miriam.

"I know, it sounds crazy, doesn't it?"

"Yes, a little bit," I admitted.

She glanced at me over her coffee mug, which had been topped off at least twice. "It seemed to be my only real option, but it was ridiculous. Just an hour after we were wed, Erwin tried to take me to the Four Queens, but I was ready to return to the emergency room. We spent most of the night there, and I went straight into surgery the next day. This time it was the hysterectomy. I spent most of what would have been our honeymoon laid up in bed, recovering."

"I've spoken with at least one other of Mr. Wilson's ex-wives who married him out of necessity. She told me they eventually came to love each other more traditionally, as husband and wife. Was that the case for you as well?" I asked.

"We got along well enough," explained Miriam. "But we remained mostly business. I came to live with him, mostly out of convenience, but I was still his employee, and he was my boss. We kept it professional for the most part."

"And I also have this, of course." I pulled the Mr. Wilson's Wives business card from my pocket. "Which led me to you in the first place. What can you tell me about the organization?"

"I knew this question was coming," she said, chuckling. "Mr. Wilson's Wives was my brainchild, but he readily agreed. After we had been married for a time, I met another woman I thought he might be able to help. She was my friend but also my hairdresser. After her employer learned she had gotten herself pregnant out of wedlock, she was fired from her job, and the father of her child refused to take responsibility. In many cases, Erwin agreed to step up when other men wouldn't."

"That would explain why so many of his children aren't biologically his?" I asked.

"Exactly. Not every situation was an unfortunate or unplanned pregnancy, but many of them were. There was at least one instance when the woman decided to go through with getting an abortion, but we were there to support her through that as well."

"When you say "we" do you mean to imply that you played a part in all of these arrangements?"

"Actually, yes. I took care of the business side of things. Erwin provided the funds, and in many cases, the solid support a sham marriage can bring."

I must have made a face at this.

"I know, it's pretty crazy, isn't it?" she exclaimed.

I had to agree. "What boggles my mind, though, is how many women he married. After having spoken to some of his earlier wives, I know not all of them were part of Mr. Wilson's Wives organization, and it sounds like some of the later wives weren't directly involved in it either. Just how many women did he marry in this fashion?"

"Fifteen, sixteen, including myself. Daphne found him without the direct assistance of the organization. Basically, my role was to find and vet the girls through word-of-mouth or referrals, and I also managed the monetary side of things. It wasn't that different from how you would think of an arranged marriage or a marriage of convenience. Most marriages only lasted a year or two, long enough to legitimize them legally. Upon divorce, which the woman always initiated, I would arrange for them to receive alimony payments. This way, they could continue to be supported financially and were free to remarry more traditionally."

"And you were directly involved in all of this."

"I've dedicated my life to this."

"What happens now that Mr. Wilson has passed away?"

"We continue with funds from the estate. The organization has transitioned. Thankfully most women don't need the actual presence of a man to get them out of a bind anymore."

"Does the most recent wife know about this?"

"No, and she never will, as long as you keep mum. Erwin wanted to marry one last time for love and wanted to keep everything separate. I had established a separate office outside of his residence decades ago. Imagine how awkward it would be if I still lived there with each subsequent bride!"

"I can't. I can't even fathom any of this," I admitted. Then, reality hit me. "This would make such a wonderful story. It would fly off the shelves."

"I know, but I hope you understand why I ask you not to proceed with your project. Not only would this revelation mar the reputations of all the women involved, but it could also affect their illegitimate children."

I stared down at my teacup, imagining I could boil the tepid water with the heat of my frustration. "But it would make such a great story," I whispered, almost to myself.

She reached one hand over to place it on top of mine. "I know, honey. I hope you realize that just means you are incredibly good at what you do."

I looked up, scowling back at her. I was not convinced. Everything seemed to be falling apart around me. What had I spent my entire summer doing? Chasing my tail? What good did this do me?

"And I'm sure you'll find something equally compelling to write about, just not this," she added. With that, she gathered her things and strode quickly from the restaurant, leaving me to wallow in what felt like genuine defeat.

Eventually, I forced myself out of my chair and took the stairs back to my hotel suite. I needed time to process, to sort through everything in my head. I devised ways I could still go forward with my writing. What if I changed everyone's names? What if I edited specific details and tried writing in a more generalized way so people couldn't be easily identified? What if I wrote the story as a fiction novel "based on a true story"? That last idea felt the most ingenuine, like I would be lying, even to myself, about the source of my inspiration. Would Michael know what to do? Was I ready to share my devastation with him?

The only thing I could focus on was my sudden, urgent need to get home and be surrounded by my comfortable office, where the words would come more easily. I packed up my things, taking one last look at the suite, which had served me well for the past few days. I was eager to sleep in my own bed with my own pillow, though. Although it was small and a bit cramped, even smaller than this hotel suite, I felt homesick for my apartment.

I left Weston just before nightfall and drove through the night, leaving a summer's worth of work behind me. It would still be there in the morning, but I wouldn't be. I didn't even bother winding my way through the backroads but hopped directly on the highway. I couldn't wait to put as much space as possible between me and this place. I would deal with the wreckage in the morning.

* * *

After a surprisingly short nap, as soon as I got home, I brewed a fresh pot of coffee and glanced at my notes. I had written so many things down by hand but hadn't even managed to type much out. There were also the tape-recorded sessions from when I went interviewing with Luis. Despite everything, I hoped the little brat was doing well back home again. It was probably where he belonged, not gallivanting around with me, sneaking underage beers, and interviewing old ladies. Maybe he had just left out of sheer boredom, despite the few privileges I had given him. What had I been thinking, trying to use him for unpaid labor as some sort of assistant? I had been so unprofessional this whole time, not planning or outlining anything. How could I even begin to make sense of all this?

I wasn't sure where to start but eventually opted for transcribing the text of the tape-recorded interviews. That wouldn't require much thought, just careful typing. I thought back to the two women we had interviewed at Wide Awake Cafe, the friends who had both married Mr. Wilson, seemingly for his money, before Miriam had created the Mr. Wilson's Wives organization. It felt like ages ago that I had that conversation with Natalie. I started with a few notes before getting into the transcription. "Natalie Bernard and Stella DeVries had been best friends since the second grade..."

After a few minutes of transcribing, I was startled by a loud knock on the door. Who even knew I was back in my apartment? Was Bruno still stalking me? I stepped onto the front stoop to find Luis sheepishly grinning at me.

Chapter 44

"I oughta kill you for that stunt you pulled, little man!" I shouted at my brother.

He shrunk away but didn't say anything.

Despite myself, I wrapped him in the biggest bear hug, squeezing so hard I could hear the bones in his back crack.

"Jeeze, Liz," he complained. "Can't you just say hello like a normal person?"

I was still holding him in the hug, refusing to let go. "You scared me so much when you ran off like that. I thought I lost you."

"Lost me?" He finally struggled free from the hug.

"I thought someone kidnapped you or something. I didn't know where you went or why."

"It's not that big of a deal, really," he said, still grinning because he knew it was a big deal to me. "I just had to get back for my driver's test."

"And you couldn't have just told me that?!" Then, my brain started to process what he had just said. "Wait, your driver's test? Did you drive here?"

"Sure did." He motioned to a large black SUV parked in front.

"That's yours?! How did you manage that? Did Ma finally break down and buy one of her kids a car?"

"I paid for it," he boasted.

"With what money?" I asked.

"I've been working since I was fourteen, silly. What do you think I did with all that money?"

"You still couldn't have afforded this by yourself."

"Marcos helped out. He fixed it up real nice for me, didn't he?"

"Looks good," I agreed. Then I turned back to him. "I can't believe you're driving! Congrats!" I wrapped him in another hug.

"Enough with all the hugging!" He struggled out of my embrace. "Are you coming or what?"

"Coming where?" I asked.

"I'm on my way to Cece's quince. I have a few errands to run, but I thought I'd give you a lift."

I took a few steps backward. "I don't think I'm invited."

"Of course you are, silly. Why wouldn't you be invited?"

"Maria's still mad at me. The last conversation we had...she was still pretty upset about everything."

"Well, screw her. You're coming. Everyone's gonna be there. It wouldn't be a party without you."

I scoffed at that. "Besides, I can't come dressed like this." I was wearing an old, stained t-shirt and baggy lounge pants.

"Tell you what," he offered. I'll grab the cake and balloons, then return for you. Will that give you enough time to get ready?"

"It should. Why are you running all the errands? Shouldn't Maria be doing that?"

"She's getting Cece all done up for this, and she wants to take pictures of everything."

"Of course she does."

"I'll be back, just don't be too long. Everybody's gonna be looking at Cece, not you."

"I suppose that's true."

I ran back inside, shutting the door behind me. My transcription would have to wait for later. I had at least a half-hour to get ready, so I jumped in the shower. The warm water felt terrific running down my back. I wished I could stand there for a few more minutes, but there wasn't enough time for a long, leisurely wash. Not today, anyway. After drying my hair, I tugged on a little black dress and some short heels. As soon as I put on my lipstick, Luis was at the door.

The back of his SUV was filled to the brim with red and pink helium balloons. "Where's the cake?" I asked.

"Back seat," he replied as he slid behind the steering wheel. "Don't worry," he added. "I'll drive real slow. Not like I have much choice in this traffic."

I endured listening to Luis' music during the drive, which I would equate to mumble rap. It was an unwritten rule that the driver gets to choose the tunes. Eventually, though, my insecurities rose to the surface. I reached over to turn the volume down.

"Do you really think I'll be welcome?" I asked.

"Of course, you will," he replied. "It's a special occasion. How long do you think Maria can hold a grudge? Or any of the rest of them?"

"It's been over a year," I pointed out.

"Well, screw them."

"Luis! Language!" I admonished him playfully.

"Seriously, though. This is supposed to be Cece's day. You're coming for her, not for them, right?"

"I'm not sure they'll see it that way."

"It'll be fine," he said. "Besides, after an hour or so, they'll all be so tipsy they won't care."

A lot of drinking did happen at these family gatherings. I remembered the first quinceanera I'd attended for my cousin Stephanie. I'd had my first sangria at that party and had quickly regretted it when I felt nauseous afterward. It was delicious, but I couldn't handle the wine. Luis was probably right. What was I so worried about?

Luis parked outside the hall and grabbed the cake from the back. I followed behind with two fistfuls of balloons. We got to the front door and realized we could not open it without setting something down. I struggled to knock without letting go of any balloons. Maria opened the door and immediately scowled at me. So much for wishful thinking.

"What are you doing here?" she demanded.

"I'm here for the party. I brought balloons."

"That I paid for."

"I'm trying to help."

"Like hell you are." She snatched some of the balloons from me and tried to grab the other bunch from me as well. I held onto them tightly, refusing to let go.

"What are you doing?" I demanded.

"You weren't invited," she shouted in my face as she continued to snag balloons from my hand. A few of them broke loose in the tussle and got whipped up in the wind. I watched helplessly as they floated up into the sky.

"Maria, stop," shouted Luis from behind us.

"She's not supposed to be here," screamed Maria.

Once she had stolen all of the balloons from me, I stepped back and took a beat. "I'm not here for you," I said quietly. "I'm here for Cecelia."

"You're not here for anybody." Maria spat on the ground and hurried back into the hall, dragging the balloons with her.

After catching my breath, I opened the door for Luis. He whispered, "I'm sorry," as he followed Maria.

"Looks like I'm not welcome here," I muttered, feeling defeated.

"I'll let Cece know you're here. Just wait here. We'll get this sorted out," he said.

I sat on a bench just outside the door. I shouldn't have come. What made me think Maria would just drop everything and let me in? I hadn't expected such a hostile greeting, but it's not like I expected a big warm welcome, either. Luis' optimism had tricked me into thinking everything would be fine.

Just then, my phone rang. It was Michael. I let it go to voicemail. I could deal with him later. I could only handle one crisis at a time.

Eventually, Cece emerged from the front door, looking for the whole world like a fairytale princess. She wore a pink dress with gigantic skirts that made her look like a sparkling cupcake. Her hair was done up in a cascade of ringlets, and her lips were so red she looked like an absolute doll. Spying me, she rushed over and held her hands out to me.

"Auntie Lizzie! You made it!" She nearly jumped up and down with excitement.

"Of course I did, sweetheart. I wouldn't miss this for the world." I could feel myself tearing up, even though I had promised myself I wouldn't cry. "You look so beautiful, Cece."

She tried to pull me into an embrace, but I held her at arm's length. "You don't want to mess up your perfect makeup," I warned her.

"I can't believe my mom won't let you come inside."

"That's her decision," I said, trying to keep my voice calm. "I came here for you, not for her."

"Why can't you two just kiss and make up? Why is she so mad at you?" Cece looked up at me with wide, innocent eyes. If only she knew, if she could understand the full extent of it.

"I broke her trust," I replied. How could I explain it in a way she would understand? "Have you ever told a friend a secret they promised to keep?"

"Yeah, me and Grace tell each other everything!"

"What if they didn't keep the promise and told everybody the secret instead?"

"Why would someone do that?" she asked. "Did you tell my mom's secrets?"

"That's exactly what I did," I explained.

"Why would you do that?" she asked. "You promised not to tell."

"I did promise, but I told people anyway. I wrote a whole book about her and your grandma's secrets, too."

"That's a lot of secrets!"

"It is, and I told many people, complete strangers."

"But why?"

"I wasn't thinking about them. I was only thinking about myself," I said, realizing the truth of those words as I said them. "They were such good secrets, and I thought other people would be interested in hearing them."

"I would be so angry with Grace if she told all my secrets. I don't think I'd want to be her friend anymore."

"Exactly, and that's why your mom is so mad at me."

Cece nodded. "Why don't you just say you're sorry?" she asked.

"I think it's too late for that now. Her secrets are already out there. I can't take that back."

"It would be a start," she offered.

If only it were that simple, I thought. If only I could start again with a clean slate. If Maria understood how much I admired her, for her strength, for raising such a wonderful young girl on her own, maybe she would see that telling her story was my way of honoring her.

"Come on," said Cece. "You two need to work this out. I'm tired of you being mad at each other. I want my Auntie back."

I resisted, but she grabbed my hand and pulled me into the hall. As soon as I stepped in, I gasped in awe. The entire ballroom was festooned with pink and red streamers, several balloons flew above each table, and an extensive buffet stretched the room's length, covered in hot, delicious foods, enchiladas, tamales, and fajitas. Two large punch bowls, brimming with sangria and cherry limeade, stood at one end.

And Luis hadn't lied. Everyone was there. My aunts and uncles and cousins, and their children. So many children, running and playing and jumping around with frenetic energy. And my Ma, sitting at a table, sipping sangria, smiling like a queen presiding over the festivities. She looked so happy to be surrounded by her beautiful family.

I spied Maria standing before a ten-piece live band, giving them last-minute instructions before they would begin to play. Cecelia dragged me over to her just as the music began. Maria turned and wrinkled her nose in disgust as soon as she saw me.

"Ma, look who's here!" exclaimed Cece, scampering off to join her cousins, betraying her youth despite her grown-up attire.

"So you snuck in," said Maria. She scowled.

"Cece insisted," I replied. "Please, just give me a chance," I begged.

"You've had your chances," she replied. She started to walk away from me, bee-lining for the buffet. I followed. She poured herself a large glass of sangria.

"Can we just talk?" I asked.

She paused, poured a second glass, and handed it to me. "I guess we can talk," she replied. "But there's nothing to say."

I took a long swig from my sangria and followed her to a table, where we sat.

"I don't think I ever said I'm sorry," I started.

"No, you didn't. You never even told us about it until after it was out in the world for everyone to read."

"I'll admit, that was unfair," I said.

"Unfair?" she countered. "Unfair? It was more than unfair. It was hurtful." She paused for a moment, then continued, growing more heated as she spoke. "It was hurtful that you would write such things about your own family, that you would tell strangers our secrets, and that you would do all of this without asking permission or at least warning us about what you were doing. Do you know what it was like to get my hair done at the stylist and listen to those girls gossiping about me? Suddenly everyone knew things about me and my family, things that I hadn't told a soul but you!"

"Okay," I replied. "I get it."

"I don't think you do." She stared at me. This was the first in-person conversation we had managed to have in the past several months, and she was still seething with anger toward me. "Why did you do it?" she asked, eventually.

"Because I thought it was a good story," I replied.

"A good story? That's it? A good story?"

I took a moment to collect my thoughts. "No, I think it was more than that," I admitted. "I was just so in awe of you and Ma. You always seemed to have it together, have it figured out, even when the world was falling apart. And you did it all on your own, as strong independent women without needing a man for help."

"And you think we did that because we wanted to?" she asked.

I gulped.

"We did what we had to do to survive," she said. "We learned to be strong because we couldn't afford to be weak. There wasn't time for anything else. We didn't have any other option."

At that moment, I wished I could tell her about Mr. Wilson's Wives. I wished I could tell her about the women who had found another way out, albeit an incredibly unconventional way. I wanted to explain what I had been spending my entire summer on and why these women needed to have their stories told.

"But you survived," I managed. I couldn't begin to explain the rest. "I loved you both and still love you so much. I wanted to tell the world why. I'm sorry you didn't see it that way."

"It wasn't your story to tell," Maria replied, still staring me down. "It was mine, and maybe I wasn't ready to tell it yet." She took one last gulp of her sangria and walked away.

Cece ran up to the table then, smiling excitedly. "So you talked! Are you friends again?"

"Not quite," I replied. "But I think we'll get there, eventually."

"Well, good. I don't like when you're mad at each other." She ran off again. If only it were that simple, I thought.

Chapter 45

My phone rang again. Michael. I'd have to respond to him eventually. I stepped outside to give him a call back. He picked up immediately.

"Why haven't you been answering my calls?" he asked. "Are you avoiding me?"

"No, I'm at my niece's quinceanera," I replied.

"Oh, good! Are you finally getting back in good with your family?"

"It's a process, but I think so."

"What's the latest? I haven't gotten any updates from you in a while, and I still haven't gotten those chapters you promised me."

"About that..."

"Uh-oh," he said. "I sense some hesitation. We don't have any time for hesitation. The time for hesitation has gone and passed."

"I don't think I'll get those to you after all."

"You mean, you need another extension? It might take a bit of finagling, but I might be able to manage another week or two for you."

"No, I don't think I will do it at all."

"What do you mean?" he asked. "Are you saying what I think you're saying? You've put so much work into this. You can't back out now. What about that advance I got you? You do realize you've got to pay that back, right?"

My stomach sank. I had forgotten about that, but I'd have to work out the details later. "I can't do it," I said. "I just can't."

"So, nothing? You're just gonna drop everything and leave me in the lurch? You've always been very professional, Elizabeth. I can't believe you're going to do this to me now. I put my neck on the line for you, more than once."

"I know, and I appreciate it."

"Then, what? What's the problem? You've got cold feet?"

I was getting so sick of everyone being angry with me. I had to resist the urge to just hang up on him. I owed him some sort of explanation.

"It's just... It's not my story to tell. It's a great story, one of thc best I've ever heard, but it's not *my* story."

THE END

Acknowledgement

The author would like to thank the following individuals and organizations for their support and advice while creating this novel. None of this would have been possible without their help. The Great Beta Team for reading through the roughest of rough drafts, especially Nicolas Michael Ravnikar, Ashley LaBarber and Darlene Coleman for your insights into what could be changed and revised. The Kenosha Writers' Guild for their feedback on several individual scenes as I began line editing. Donovan Scherer at Studio Moonfall for all the encouragement and for connecting me with other indie authors. Several of these already-published authors offered sage advice, including TR Nickle and Jessie Rose (among others).

For all the education and encouragement, my creative writing teachers throughout the years (too many to name). For being a sounding board throughout the process, my husband Joel Bolyard. And to all my family and friends who have been so supportive over the last year, and throughout the years with all my writing projects. Thank you for all you do.

ABOUT THE AUTHOR

Kaitlyn Bolyard teaches writing and literature at DePaul University and Carthage College. She lives in Wisconsin with her chef husband, who keeps her well-fed. She writes mostly poetry because it can be finished in one sitting. This is her first novel.

Visit www.kaitlynbolyard.com for additional publications and author events.

Books by This Author

ECHOING BACK AT YOU: A DECADE OF SOCIAL MEDIA POETRY

Kaitlyn Bolyard uses social media statuses as the fodder for her poetry, often with strange and hilarious results. Some of her most recent poems have even taken on a more insightful tone, allowing readers to look into what is happening in the world and how it affects our day-to-day lives. For the past decade (2011-2021), she has been crafting these poems, posting them on social media, borrowing from friends' statuses, writing for friends, and sharing at open mics.

Now available on Amazon.

www.ingramcontent.com/pod-product-compliance
Lightning Source LLC
Chambersburg PA
CBHW070437300726
48975CB00007B/1958